SAM THE SUDDEN

BY

P.G. WODEHOUSE

Author of "Bill the Conqueror",
"Carry On, Jeeves!", etc.

To Edgar Wallace

SAM THE SUDDEN

CHAPTER I

SAM STARTS ON A JOURNEY

ALL day long, New York, stewing in the rays of a late
August sun, had been growing warmer and warmer; until
now, at three o'clock in the afternoon, its inhabitants, with
the exception of a little group gathered together on the
tenth floor of the Wilmot Building on Upper Broadway, had
divided themselves by a sort of natural cleavage into two
main bodies—the one crawling about and asking those they
met if this was hot enough for them, the other maintaining
that what they minded was not so much the heat as the
humidity.

The reason for the activity prevailing on the tenth floor
of the Wilmot was that a sporting event of the first magni-
tude was being pulled off there—Spike Murphy, of the John
B. Pynsent Export and Import Company, being in the act
of contesting the final of the Office Boys' High-Kicking
Championship against a willowy youth from the Consolidated
Eyebrow Tweezer and Nail File Corporation.

The affair was taking place on the premises of the former
firm, before a small but select audience consisting of a few
stenographers, chewing gum; some male wage slaves in shirt
sleeves; and Mr. John B. Pynsent's nephew, Samuel Shotter,
a young man of agreeable features, who was acting as referee.

In addition to being referee, Sam Shotter was also the
patron and promoter of the tourney; the man but for whose
2

vision and enterprise a wealth of young talent would have lain undeveloped, thereby jeopardising America's chances should an event of this kind ever be added to the programme of the Olympic Games. It was he who, wandering about the office in a restless search for methods of sweetening an uncongenial round of toil, had come upon Master Murphy practising kicks against the wall of a remote corridor, and had encouraged him to kick higher. It was he who had arranged matches with representatives of other firms throughout the building. And it was he who out of his own pocket had provided the purse which, as the lad's foot crashed against the plaster a full inch above his rival's best effort, he now handed to Spike, together with a few well-chosen words.

"Murphy," said Sam, "is the winner. After a contest conducted throughout in accordance with the best traditions of American high kicking, he has upheld the honour of the John B. Pynsent Ex and Imp and retained his title. In the absence of the boss, therefore, who has unfortunately been called away to Philadelphia and so is unable to preside at this meeting, I take much pleasure in presenting him with the guerdon of victory, this handsome dollar bill. Take it, Spike, and in after years, when you are a grey-haired alderman or something, look back to this moment and say to yourself— —"

Sam stopped, a little hurt. He thought he had been speaking rather well, yet already his audience was walking out on him. Spike Murphy, indeed, was running.

"Say to yourself——"

"When you are at leisure, Samuel," observed a voice behind him, "I should be glad of a word with you in my office."

Sam turned.

"Oh, hullo, uncle," he said.

He coughed; Mr. Pynsent coughed.

"I thought you had gone to Philadelphia," said Sam.

"Indeed?" said Mr. Pynsent.

He made no further remark, but proceeded sedately to his room, from which he emerged again a moment later with a patient look of inquiry on his face.

"Come here, Sam," he said. "Who," he asked, pointing, "is this?"

Sam peeped through the doorway and perceived, tilted back in a swivel chair, a long, lean man of repellent aspect. His large feet rested comfortably on the desk, his head hung sideways and his mouth was open. From this mouth, which was of generous proportions, there came a gurgling snore.

"Who," repeated Mr. Pynsent, "is this gentleman?"

Sam could not help admiring his uncle's unerring instinct—that amazing intuition which had led him straight to the realisation that if an uninvited stranger was slumbering in his pet chair, the responsibility must of necessity be his nephew Samuel's.

"Good Lord!" he exclaimed. "I didn't know he was there."

"A friend of yours?"

"It's Hash."

"I beg your pardon?"

"Hash Todhunter, you know, the cook of the *Araminta*. You remember I took a trip a year ago on a tramp steamer? This fellow was the cook. I met him on Broadway this afternoon and gave him lunch. I brought him back here because he wanted to see the place where I work."

"Work?" said Mr. Pynsent, puzzled.

"I had no notion he had strayed into your room."

Sam spoke apologetically, but he would have liked to point out that the blame for all these embarrassing occur-

4

rences was really Mr. Pynsent's. If a man creates the impression that he is going to Philadelphia and then does not go, he has only himself to thank for any complications that may ensue. However, this was a technicality with which he did not bother his uncle.

"Shall I wake him?"

"If you would be so good. And having done so, take him away and store him somewhere and then come back. I have much to say to you."

Shaken by a vigorous hand, the sleeper opened his eyes and permitted himself to be led, still in a trancelike condition, out of the room and down the passage to the cubbyhole where Sam performed his daily duties. Here, sinking into a chair, he fell asleep again; and Sam left him and went back to his uncle. Mr. Pynsent was staring thoughtfully out of the window as he entered.

"Sit down, Sam," he said.

Sam sat down.

"I'm sorry about all that, uncle."

"All what?"

"All that business that was going on when you came in."

"Ah, yes. What was it, by the way?"

"Spike Murphy was seeing if he could kick higher than a kid from a firm downstairs."

"And did he?"

"Yes."

"Good boy," said Mr. Pynsent approvingly. "You arranged the competition, no doubt?"

"Yes, as a matter of fact, I did."

"You would. You have been in my employment," proceeded Mr. Pynsent evenly, "three months. In that time you have succeeded in thoroughly demoralising the finest office force in New York."

"Oh, uncle!" said Sam reproachfully.

5

"Thoroughly," repeated Mr. Pynsent. "The office boys call you by your Christian name."

"They will do it," sighed Sam. "I clump their heads, but the habit persists."

"Last Wednesday I observed you kissing my stenographer."

"The poor little thing had toothache."

"Also, Mr. Ellaby informs me that your work is a disgrace to the firm." There was a pause. "The English public school is the curse of the age," said Mr. Pynsent dreamily.

To a stranger the remark might have sounded irrelevant, but Sam understood its import. He appreciated it for what it was—a nasty crack.

"Did they teach you anything at Wrykyn, Sam, except football?"

"Oh, yes."

"What?"

"Oh, lots of things."

"I have seen no evidence of it. Why your mother sent you to that place, instead of to some good business college, I cannot imagine."

"Well, you see, father had been there——"

Sam broke off. Mr. Pynsent, he was aware, had not been fond of the late Anthony Shotter—considering, and possibly correctly, that his dead sister had, in marrying that amiable but erratic person, been guilty of the crowning folly of a frivolous and fluffy-headed life.

"A strong recommendation," said Mr. Pynsent dryly.

Sam had nothing to say to this.

"You are very like your father in a great many ways," said Mr. Pynsent.

Sam let this one go by too. They were coming off the bat a bit fast this morning, but there was nothing to be done about it.

6

"And yet I am fond of you, Sam," resumed Mr. Pynsent after a brief pause.

This was more the stuff.

"And I am fond of you, uncle," said Sam in a hearty voice. "When I think of all you have done for me——"

"But," went on Mr. Pynsent, "I feel that I shall like you even better three thousand miles away from the offices of the Pynsent Export and Import Company. We are parting, Sam—and immediately."

"I'm sorry."

"I, on the other hand," said Mr. Pynsent, "am glad."

There was a silence. Sam, feeling that the interview, having reached this point, might be considered over, got up.

"Wait a moment," said his uncle. "I want to tell you what plans I have made for your future."

Sam was agreeably surprised. He had not supposed that his future would be of interest to Mr. Pynsent.

"Have you made plans?"

"Yes; everything is settled."

"This is fine, uncle," said Sam cordially. "I thought you were going to drive me out into the snow."

"Do you remember meeting an Englishman named Lord Tilbury at dinner at my house?"

Sam did indeed. His Lordship had got him wedged into a corner after the meal and had talked without a pause for more than half an hour.

"He is the proprietor of the Mammoth Publishing Company, a concern which produces a great many daily and weekly papers in London."

Sam was aware of this. Lord Tilbury's conversation had been almost entirely autobiographical.

"Well, he is returning to England on Saturday on the *Mauretania,* and you are going with him."

"Eh?"

7

"He has offered to employ you in his business."

"But I don't know anything about newspaper work."

"You don't know anything about anything," Mr. Pynsent pointed out gently. "It is the effect of your English public-school education. However, you certainly cannot be a greater failure with Lord Tilbury than you have been with me. That wastepaper basket over there has been in my office only four days, and already it knows more about the export and import business than you would learn if you stayed here fifty years."

Sam made plaintive noises. Fifty years, he considered, was an overstatement.

"I concealed nothing of this from Lord Tilbury, but nevertheless he insists on engaging you."

"Odd," said Sam. He could not help feeling a little flattered at this intense desire for his services on the part of a man who had met him only once. Lord Tilbury might be a bore, but there was no getting away from the fact that he had that gift without which no one can amass a large fortune—that strange, almost uncanny gift for spotting the good man when he saw him.

"Not at all odd," said Mr. Pynsent. "He and I are in the middle of a business deal. He is trying to persuade me to do something which at present I have not made up my mind to do. He thinks that by taking you off my hands he will put me under an obligation. So he will."

"Uncle," said Sam impressively, "I will make good."

"You'd better," returned Mr. Pynsent, unmelted. "It is your last chance. There is no earthly reason why I should go on supporting you for the rest of your life, and I do not intend to do it. If you make a mess of things at Tilbury House, don't think that you can come running back to me. There will be no fatted calf. Remember that."

"I will, uncle, I will. But don't worry. Something tells

8

me I am going to be good. I shall like going to England."

"I am glad to hear that. Well, that is all. Good afternoon."

"You know, it's rather strange that you should be sending me over there," said Sam meditatively.

"I don't think so. I am glad to have the chance."

"What I mean is—do you believe in palmists?"

"I do not. Good-bye."

"Because a palmist told me——"

"The door," said Mr. Pynsent, "is one of those which close automatically when the handle is released."

Having tested this statement and proved it correct, Sam went back to his own quarters, where he found Mr. Clarence (Hash) Todhunter, the popular and energetic chef of the tramp steamer *Araminta*, awake and smoking a short pipe.

"Who was the old boy?" inquired Mr. Todhunter.

"That was my uncle, the head of the firm."

"Did I go to sleep in his room?"

· "You did."

"I'm sorry about that, Sam," said Hash, with manly regret. "I had a late night last night."

He yawned spaciously. Hash Todhunter was a lean, stringy man in the early thirties, with a high forehead and a ruminative eye. Irritated messmates who had played poker with him had sometimes compared this eye to that of a perishing fish; but to the critic whose judgment was not biased and inflamed by recent pecuniary losses it would have been more suggestive of a parrot which has looked on life and found it full of disillusionment. There was a strong pessimistic streak in Hash, and in his cups he was accustomed to hint darkly that if every one had their rights he would have been in the direct line of succession to an earldom. It was a long and involved story, casting great discredit

on all the parties concerned; but as he never told it twice
in the same way, little credence was accorded to it by a dis-
criminating fo'c'sle. For the rest, he cooked the best dry
hash on the Western Ocean, but was not proud.

"Hash," said Sam, "I'm going over to England."

"Me too. We sail Monday."

"Do you, by Jove!" said Sam thoughtfully. "I'm supposed to be going on the *Mauretania* on Saturday, but I've
half a mind to come with you instead. I don't like the idea
of six days *tête-à-tête* with Lord Tilbury."

"Who's he?"

"The proprietor of the Mammoth Publishing Company,
where I am going to work."

"Have you got the push here then?"

It piqued Sam a little that this untutored man should so
readily have divined the facts. He also considered that
Hash had failed in tact. He might at least have pretended
that he supposed it to be a case of handing in a resignation.

"Yes, you might perhaps put it that way."

"Not because of me sittin' in his chair?"

"No. There are, apparently, a number of reasons. Hash,
it's a curious thing, my uncle taking it into his head to shoot
me over to England. The other day a palmist told me that
I was shortly going to take a long journey, at the end of which
I should meet a fair girl. . . . Hash!"

"Ur?"

"I want to show you something."

He fumbled in his pocket and produced a note-case. Having done this, he paused. Then, seeming to overcome a
momentary hesitation, he opened the case and from it, with
the delicacy of an Indian priest at a shrine handling a precious relic, extracted a folded piece of paper.

A casual observer, deceived by a certain cheery irrespon-
sibility that marked his behaviour, might have set Sam Shotter

down as one of those essentially material young men in whose armour romance does not easily find a chink. He would have erred in this assumption. For all that he weighed a hundred and seventy pounds of bone and sinew and had when amused —which was often—a laugh like that of the hyena in its native jungle, there was sentiment in Sam. Otherwise this paper would scarcely have been in his possession.

"But before showing it to you," he said, eyeing Hash intently, "I would like to ask you a question. Do you see anything funny, anything laughable, anything at all ludicrous, in a fellow going for a fishing trip to Canada and being stuck in a hut miles from anywhere with nothing to read and nothing to listen to except the wild duck calling to its mate and the nifties of a French-Canadian guide who couldn't speak more than three words of English——"

"No," said Hash.

"I haven't finished. Do you—to proceed—see anything absurd in the fact that such a fellow, in such a situation, finding the photograph of a beautiful girl tacked up on the wall of the hut by some previous visitor, and having nothing else to look at for five weeks, should have fallen in love with this photograph? Think before you answer."

"No," said Hash, after consideration. He was not a man who readily detected the humorous aspect of anything.

"That's good," said Sam. "And lucky for you. Because had you let one snicker out of yourself—just one—I would have smitten you rather forcibly on the beezer. Well, I did."

"Did what?"

"Found this picture tacked up on the wall and fell in love with it. Look!"

He unfolded the paper reverently. It now revealed itself as a portion of a page torn from one of those illustrated journals which brighten the middle of the Englishman's week. Its sojourn on the wall of the fishing hut had not improved it.

It was faded and yellow, and over one corner a dark stain had spread itself, seeming to indicate that some occupant of the hut had at one time or another done a piece of careless carving. Nevertheless, he gazed at it as a young knight might have gazed upon the Holy Grail.

"Well?"

Hash surveyed the paper closely.

"That's mutton gravy," he said, pointing at the stain and forming a professional man's swift diagnosis. "Beef wouldn't be so dark."

Sam regarded his friend with a glance of concentrated loathing which would have embarrassed a more sensitive man.

"I show you this lovely face, all aglow with youth and the joy of life," he cried, "and all that seems to interest you is that some foul vandal, whose neck I should like to wring, has splashed his beastly dinner over it. Heavens, man, look at that girl! Have you ever seen such a girl?"

"She's not bad."

"Not bad! Can't you see she's simply marvellous?"

The photograph did, indeed, to a great extent justify Sam's enthusiasm. It represented a girl in hunting costume, standing beside her horse. She was a trim, boyish-looking girl of about eighteen, slightly above the medium height; and she gazed out of the picture with clear, grave, steady eyes. At the corner of her mouth there was a little thoughtful droop. It was a pretty mouth; but Sam, who had made a study of the picture and considered himself the world's leading authority upon it, was of opinion that it would look even prettier when smiling.

Under the photograph, in leaded capitals, ran the words:

A FAIR DAUGHTER OF NIMROD.

Beneath this poetical caption, it is to be presumed, there had originally been more definite information as to

12

the subject's identity, but the coarse hand which had wrenched the page from its setting had unfortunately happened to tear off the remainder of the letterpress.

"Simply marvellous," said Sam emotionally. "What's that thing of Tennyson's about a little English rosebud, she?"

"Tennyson? There was a feller when I was on the *Sea Bird*, called Pennyman——"

"Oh, shut up! Isn't she a wonder, Hash! And what is more—fair, wouldn't you say?"

Hash scratched his chin. He was a man who liked to think things over.

"Or dark," he said.

"Idiot! Don't tell me those eyes aren't blue."

"Might be," admitted Hash grudgingly.

"And that hair would be golden, or possibly a very light brown."

"How'm I to know?"

"Hash," said Sam, "the very first thing I do when I get to England is to find out who that girl is."

"Easy enough." Hash pointed the stem of his pipe at the caption. "Daughter of Nimrod. All you got to do is get a telephone directory and look him up. It'll give the address as well."

"How do you think of these things?" said Sam admiringly. "The only trouble is, suppose old man Nimrod lives in the country. He sounds like a hunting man."

"Ah!" said Hash. "There's that, o' course."

"No, my best scheme will be to find out what paper this is torn out of, and then search back through the files for the picture."

"Maybe," said Hash. He had plainly lost interest in the subject.

Sam was gazing dreamily at the picture.

"Do you see that little dimple just by the chin, Hash?

My goodness, I'd give something to see that girl smile!"
He replaced the paper in his note-case and sighed. "Love
is a wonderful thing, Hash."

Mr. Todhunter's ample mouth curled sardonically.

"When you've seen as much of life as I have," he replied, "you'd rather have a cup of tea."

CHAPTER II
KAY OF VALLEY FIELDS

THE nameless individual who had torn from its setting the
photograph which had so excited the admiration of Sam
Shotter had, as has been already indicated, torn untidily.
Had he exercised a little more care, that love-lorn young
man would have seen beneath the picture the following:

MISS KAY DERRICK, DAUGHTER OF COL. EUSTACE DERRICK,
OF MIDWAYS HALL, WILTS.

And if he had happened to be in Piccadilly Circus on
a certain afternoon some three weeks after his conversation
with Hash Todhunter, he might have observed Miss Derrick
in person. For she was standing on the island there waiting for a Number Three omnibus.

His first impression, had he so beheld her, would certainly have been that the photograph, attractive though it
was, did not do her justice. Four years had passed since
it had been taken, and between the ages of eighteen and
twenty-two many girls gain appreciably in looks. Kay Derrick was one of them. He would then have observed that
his views on her appearance had been sound. Her eyes,
as he had predicted, were blue—a very dark, warm blue
like the sky on a summer night—and her hair, such of it
as was visible beneath a becoming little hat, was of a soft

14

golden brown. The third thing he would have noticed about her was that she looked tired. And, indeed, she was. It was her daily task to present herself at the house of a certain Mrs. Winnington-Bates, in Thurloe Square, South Kensington, to read to that lady and to attend to her voluminous correspondence. And nobody who knew Mrs. Winnington-Bates at all intimately would have disputed the right of any girl who did this to look as tired as she pleased.

The omnibus arrived and Kay climbed the steps to the roof. The conductor presented himself, punch in hand.

"Fez, pliz."

"Valley Fields," said Kay.

"Q," said the conductor.

He displayed no excitement as he handed her the ticket, none of that anxious concern exhibited by those who met the young man with the banner marked Excelsior; for the days are long past when it was considered rather a dashing adventure to journey to Valley Fields. Two hundred years ago, when highwaymen roved West Kensington and snipe were shot in Regent Street, this pleasant suburb in the Postal Division S.E. 21 was a remote spot to which jaded bucks and beaux would ride when they wanted to get really close to Nature. But now that vast lake of brick and asphalt which is London has flooded its banks and engulfed it. The Valley Fields of to-day is a mass of houses, and you may reach it not only by omnibus but by train, and even by tram.

It was a place very familiar to Kay now, so that at times she seemed to have been there all her life; and yet actually only a few months had elapsed since she had been washed up on its shores like a piece of flotsam; or, to put the facts with less imagery, since Mr. Wrenn, of San Rafael, Burberry Road, had come forward on the death of her

15

parents and offered her a home there. This Mr. Wrenn being the bad Uncle Matthew who in the dim past—somewhere around the year 1905—splashed a hideous blot on the Derrick escutcheon by eloping with Kay's Aunt Enid.

Kay had been a child of two at the time, and it was not till she was eight that she heard the story, her informant being young Willoughby Braddock, the stout boy who, with the aid of a trustee, owned the great house and estates adjoining Midways. It was a romantic story—of a young man who had come down to do Midways for the Stately-Homes-of-England series appearing in the then newly established Pyke's *Home Companion;* who in the process of doing it had made the acquaintance of the sister of its owner; and who only a few weeks later had induced her to run away and marry him, thereby—according to the view-point of the family—ruining her chances in this world and her prospects in the next.

For twenty years Matthew Wrenn had been the family outcast, and now time had accomplished one more of its celebrated revenges. The death of Colonel Derrick, which had followed that of his wife by a few months, had revealed the fact that in addition to Norman blood he had also had the simple faith which the poet ranks so much more highly—it taking the form of trusting prospectuses which should not have deceived a child and endeavouring to make up losses caused by the diminishing value of land with a series of speculations, each of them more futile and disastrous than the last. His capital had gone to the four winds, Midways had gone to the mortgagees, and Kay, apprised of these facts by a sympathetic family lawyer, had gone to Mr. Matthew Wrenn, now for many years the editor of that same Pyke's *Home Companion* of which he had once been the mere representative.

The omnibus stopped at the corner of Burberry Road,

and Kay, alighting, walked toward San Rafael. Burberry Road is not one of the more fashionable and wealthy districts of Valley Fields, and most of the houses in it are semi-detached. San Rafael belonged to this class, being joined, like a stucco Siamese Twin, in indissoluble union to its next-door neighbour, Mon Repos. It had in front of it a strip of gravel, two apologetic-looking flower beds with evergreens in them, a fence, and in the fence a gate, modelled on the five-barred gates of the country.

Out of this gate, as Kay drew near, there came an elderly gentleman, tall, with grey hair and a scholarly stoop.

"Why, hullo, darling," said Kay. "Where are you off to?"

She kissed her uncle affectionately, for she had grown very fond of him in the months of their companionship.

"Just popping round to have a chat with Cornelius," said Mr. Wrenn. "I thought I might get a game of chess."

In actual years Matthew Wrenn was on the right side of fifty; but as editors of papers like Pyke's *Home Companion* are apt to do, he looked older than he really was. He was a man of mild and dreamy aspect, and it being difficult to imagine him in any dashing rôle, Kay rather supposed that the energy and fire which had produced the famous elopement must have come from the lady's side.

"Well, don't be late for dinner," she said. "Is Willoughby in?"

"I left him in the garden." Mr. Wrenn hesitated. "That's a curious young man, Kay."

"It's an awful shame that he should be inflicted on you, darling," said Kay. "His housekeeper shooed him out of his house, you know. She wanted to give it a thorough cleaning. And he hates staying at clubs and hotels, and I've known him all my life, and he asked me if we could put him up, and—well, there you are. But cheer up, it's only for to-night."

"My dear, you know I'm only too glad to put up any

friend of yours. But he's such a peculiar young fellow. I have been trying to talk to him for an hour, and all he does is to look at me like a goldfish."

"Like a goldfish?"

"Yes, with his eyes staring and his lips moving without any sound coming from them."

Kay laughed.

"It's his speech. I forgot to tell you. The poor lamb has got to make a speech to-night at the annual dinner of the Old Boys of his school. He's never made one before, and it's weighing on his mind terribly."

Mr. Wrenn looked relieved.

"Oh, I didn't know. Honestly, my dear, I thought that he must be mentally deficient." He looked at his watch. "Well, if you think you can entertain him, I will be going along."

Mr. Wrenn went on his way; and Kay, passing through the five-barred gate, followed the little gravel path which skirted the house and came into the garden.

Like all the gardens in the neighbourhood, it was a credit to its owner—on the small side, but very green and neat and soothing. The fact that, though so widely built over, Valley Fields has not altogether lost its ancient air of rusticity is due entirely to the zeal and devotion of its amateur horticulturists. More seeds are sold each spring in Valley Fields, more lawn mowers pushed, more garden rollers borrowed, more snails destroyed, more green fly squirted with patent mixtures, than in any other suburb on the Surrey side of the river. Brixton may have its Bon Marché and Sydenham its Crystal Palace; but when it comes to pansies, roses, tulips, hollyhocks and nasturtiums, Valley Fields points with pride.

In addition to its other attractive features, the garden of San Rafael contained at this moment a pinkish, stoutish, solemn young man in a brown suit, who was striding up and down the lawn with a glassy stare in his eyes.

"Hullo, Willoughby," said Kay.

The young man came out of his trance with a strong physical convulsion.

"Oh, hullo, Kay."

He followed her across the lawn to the tea table which stood in the shade of a fine tree. For there are trees in this favoured spot as well as flowers.

"Tea, Willoughby?" said Kay, sinking gratefully into a deck chair. "Or have you had yours?"

"Yes, I had some. . . . I think——" Mr. Braddock weighed the question thoughtfully. "Yes. . . . Yes, I've had some."

Kay filled her cup and sipped luxuriously.

"Golly, I'm tired!" she said.

"Had a bad day?"

"Much the same as usual."

"Mrs. B. not too cordial?"

"Not very. And, unfortunately, the son and heir cordiality itself."

Mr. Braddock nodded.

"A bit of a trial, that lad."

"A bit."

"Wants kicking."

"Very badly."

Kay gave a little wriggle of distaste. Technically, her duties at Thurloe Square consisted of reading and writing Mrs. Winnington-Bates' letters; but what she was engaged for principally, she sometimes thought, was to act as a sort of spiritual punching bag for her employer. To-day that lady had been exceptionally trying. Her son, on the other hand, who had recently returned to his home after an unsuccessful attempt to learn poultry farming in Sussex, and was lounging about it with little to occupy him, had shown himself, in his few moments of opportunity, more than usually gallant. What life needed to make it a trifle easier, Kay felt, was for Mrs. Bates to admire her a little more and for Claude Bates to admire her a little less.

"I remember him at school," said Mr. Braddock. "A worm."

"Was he at school with you?"

"Yes. Younger than me. A beastly little kid who stuffed himself with food and frousted over fires and shirked games. I remember Sam Shotter licking him once for stealing jam sandwiches at the school shop. By the way, Sam's coming over here. I had a letter from him."

"Is he? And who is he? You've never mentioned his name before."

"Haven't I told you about old Sam Shotter?" asked Mr. Braddock, surprised.

"Never. But he sounds wonderfully attractive. Anyone who licked Claude Bates must have a lot of good in him."

"He was at school with me."

"What a lot of people seem to have been at school with you!"

"Well, there were about six hundred fellows at Wrykyn, you know. Sam and I shared a study. Now there is a chap I envy. He's knocked about all over the world, having all sorts of fun. America one day, Australia the next, Africa the day after."

"Quick mover," said Kay.

"The last I heard from him he was in his uncle's office in New York, but in this letter he says he's coming over to work at Tilbury House."

"Tilbury House? Really? I wonder if uncle will meet him."

"Don't you think it would be a sound move if I gave

him a dinner or something where he could meet a few of the lads? You and your uncle, of course—and if I could get hold of old Tilbury."

"Do you know Lord Tilbury?"

"Oh, yes; I play bridge with him sometimes at the club. And he took my shooting last year."

"When does Mr. Shotter arrive?"

"I don't know. He says it's uncertain. You see, he's coming over on a tramp steamer."

"A tramp steamer? Why?"

"Well, it's the sort of thing he does! Sort of thing I'd like to do too."

"You?" said Kay, amazed. Willoughby Braddock had always seemed to her a man to whose well-being the refinements—and even the luxuries—of civilisation were essential. One of her earliest recollections was of sitting in a tree and hurling juvenile insults at him, it having come to her ears through reliable channels that he habitually wore bed socks. "What nonsense, Willoughby! You would hate roughing it."

"I wouldn't," said Mr. Braddock stoutly. "I'd love a bit of adventure."

"Well, why don't you have it? You've got plenty of money. You could be a pirate of the Spanish Main if you wanted."

Mr. Braddock shook his head wisfully.

"I can't get away from Mrs. Lippett."

Willoughby Braddock was one of those unfortunate bachelors who are doomed to live under the thrall of either a housekeeper or a valet. His particular cross in life was his housekeeper, his servitude being rendered all the more unescapable by the fact that Mrs. Lippett had been his nurse in the days of his childhood. There are men who can defy a woman. There are men who can cope with a faithful old retainer. But if there are men who can tackle a faithful old female retainer who has frequently smacked them with the back of a hair-brush, Willoughby Braddock was not one of them.

"She would have a fit or go into a decline or something if I tried to break loose."

"Poor old Willoughby! Life can be very hard, can't it? By the way, I met my uncle outside. He was complaining that you were not very chummy."

"No, was he?"

"He said you just sat there looking at him like a goldfish."

"Oh, I say!" said Mr. Braddock remorsefully. "I'm awfully sorry. I mean, after he's been so decent, putting me up and everything. I hope you explained to him that I was rightfully worried about this speech."

"Yes, I did. But I don't see why you should be. It's perfectly simple making a speech. Especially at an Old Boys' dinner, where they won't expect anything very much. If I were you, I should just get up and tell them one or two funny stories and sit down again."

"I've got one story," said Mr. Braddock more hopefully. "It's about an Irishman."

"Pat or Mike?"

"I thought of calling him Pat. He's in New York and he goes down to the dock and he sees a diver coming up out of the water—in a diving suit, you know—and he thinks the fellow—the diver, you understand—has walked across the Atlantic and wishes he had thought of doing the same himself so as to have saved the fare, don't you know."

"I see. One of those weak-minded Irishmen."

"Do you think it will amuse them?" asked Mr. Braddock, anxiously.

"I should think they would roll off their seats."

"No, really?" He broke off and stretched out a hand

22

in alarm. "I say, you weren't thinking of having one of those rock cakes, were you?"

"I was. But I won't if you don't want me to. Aren't they good?"

"Good? My dear old soul," said Mr. Braddock earnestly, "they are Clara's worst effort—absolutely her very worst. I had to eat one because she came and stood over me and watched me do it. It beats me why you don't sack that girl. She's a rotten cook."

"Sack Claire?" Kay laughed. "You might just as well try to sack her mother."

"I suppose you're right."

"You can't sack a Lippett."

"No, I see what you mean. I wish she wasn't so dashed familiar with a fellow, though."

"Well, she has known you almost as long as I have. Mrs. Lippett has always been a sort of mother to you, so I suppose Claire regards herself as a sort of sister."

"Yes, I suppose it can't be helped," said Mr. Braddock bravely. He glanced at his watch. "Ought to be going and dressing. I'll find you out here before I leave?"

"Oh, yes."

"Well, I'll be pushing along. I say, you do think that story about the Irishman is all right?"

"Best thing I ever heard," said Kay loyally.

For some minutes after he had left her she sat back in her chair with her eyes closed, relaxing in the evening stillness of this pleasant garden.

"Finished with the tea, Miss Kay?"

Kay opened her eyes. A solid little figure in a print dress was standing at her side. A jaunty maid's cap surmounted this person's tow-coloured hair. She had a perky nose and a wide, friendly mouth, and she beamed upon Kay devotedly.

"Brought you these," she said, dropping a rug, two

cushions, and a footstool, beneath the burden of which she had been staggering across the lawn like a small pack mule. "Make you nice and comfortable, and then you can get a nice nap. I can see you're all tired out."

"That's awfully good of you, Claire. But you shouldn't have bothered."

Claire Lippett, daughter of Willoughby Braddock's autocratic housekeeper, and cook and maid-of-all-work at San Rafael, was a survivor of the Midways epoch. She had entered the Derrick household at the age of twelve, her duties at that time being vague and leaving her plenty of leisure for surreptitious bird's-nesting with Kay, then thirteen. On her eighteenth birthday she had been promoted to the post of Kay's personal maid, and from that moment may be said formally to have taken charge. The Lippett motto was Fidelity, and not even the famous financial crash had been able to dislodge this worthy daughter of the clan. Resolutely following Kay into exile, she had become, as stated, Mr. Wrenn's cook. And, as Mr. Braddock had justly remarked, a very bad cook too.

"You oughtn't to go getting yourself all tired, Miss Kay. You ought to be sitting at your ease."

"Well, so I am," said Kay.

There were times when, like Mr. Braddock, she found the Lippett protectiveness a little cloying. She was a high-spirited girl and wanted to face the world with a defiant "Who cares?" And it was not easy to do this with Claire coddling her all the time as if she were a fragile and sensitive plant. Resistance, however, was useless. Nobody had ever yet succeeded in curbing the motherly spirit of the Lippetts, and probably nobody ever would.

"Meantersay," explained Claire, adjusting the footstool, "you ought not to be soiling your hands with work, that's what I mean. It's a shame you should be having to——"

24

She stopped abruptly. She had picked up the tea tray and made a wounding discovery.

"You haven't touched my rock cakes," she said in a voice in which reproach and disappointment were nicely blended. "And I made them for you special."

"I didn't want to spoil my dinner," said Kay hastily. Claire was a temperamental girl, quick to resent slurs on her handiwork. "I'm sure you've got something nice."

Claire considered the point.

"Well, yes and no," she said. "If you're thinking of the pudding, I'm afraid that's off. The kitten fell into the custard."

"No!"

"She did. And when I'd fished her out there wasn't hardly any left. Seemed to have soaked it into her like as if she was a sponge. Still, there 'ud be enough for you if Mr. Wrenn didn't want any."

"No, it doesn't matter, thanks," said Kay earnestly.

"Well, I'm trying a new soup, which'll sort of make up for it. It's one I read in a book. It's called pottage ar lar princess. You're sure you won't have one of these rock cakes, Miss Kay? Put strength into you."

"No, thanks, really."

"Right-ho; just as you say."

Miss Lippett crossed the lawn and disappeared, and a soothing peace fell upon the garden. A few minutes later, however, just as Kay's head was beginning to nod, from an upper window there suddenly blared forth on the still air a loud and raucous voice, suggestive of costermongers advertising their Brussels sprouts or those who call the cattle home across the Sands of Dee.

"I am reminded by a remark of our worthy president," roared the voice, "of a little story which may be new to some of you present here to-night. It seems that a certain

25

Irishman had gone down to New York—I mean, he was in New York and had gone down to the docks—and while there—while there————"

The voice trailed off. Apparently the lungs were willing but the memory was weak. Presently it broke out in another place.

"For the school, gentlemen, our dear old school, occupies a place in our hearts—a place in our hearts—in the hearts of all of us—in all our hearts—in our hearts, gentlemen—which nothing else can fill. It forms, if I may put it that way, Mr. President and gentlemen—forms—forms—forms a link that links the generations. Whether we are fifty years old or forty or thirty or twenty, we are none the less all of us contemporaries. And why? Because, gentlemen, we are all—er—linked by that link."

"Jolly good!" murmured Kay, impressed.

"That is why, Mr. President and gentlemen, though I am glad, delighted, pleased, happy and—er—overjoyed to see so many of you responding to the annual call of our dear old school, I am not surprised."

From the kitchen door, a small knife in one hand and a half-peeled onion in the other, there emerged the stocky figure of Claire Lippett. She gazed up at the window wrathfully.

"Hi!"

"No, not surprised."

"Hi!"

"And talking of being surprised, I am reminded of a little story which may be new to some of you present here to-night. It seems that a certain Irishman————"

From the days when their ancestresses had helped the menfolk of the tribe to make marauding Danes wish that they had stayed in Denmark, the female members of Claire Lippett's family had always been women of action. Having said "Hi!" twice, their twentieth-century descendant seemed to consider that she had done all that could reasonably be expected of her in the way of words. With a graceful swing of her right arm, she sent the onion shooting upward. And such was the never-failing efficiency of this masterly girl that it whizzed in through the open window, from which, after a brief interval, there appeared, leaning out, the dress-shirted and white-tied upper portion of Mr. Willoughby Braddock. He was rubbing his ear.

"Be quiet, can't you?" said Miss Lippett.

Mr. Braddock gazed austerely into the depths. Except that the positions of the characters were inverted and the tone of the dialogue somewhat different, it might have been the big scene out of *Romeo and Juliet*.

"What did you say?"

"I said be quiet. Miss Kay wants to get a bit of sleep. How can she get a bit of sleep with that row going on?"

"Clara!" said Mr. Braddock portentously.

"Claire," corrected the girl coldly, insisting on a point for which she had had to fight all her life.

Mr. Braddock gulped.

"I shall—er—I shall speak to your mother," he said.

It was a futile threat, and Claire signified as much by jerking her shoulder in a scornful and derogatory manner before stumping back to the house with all the honours of war. She knew—and Mr. Braddock knew that she knew—that complaints respecting her favourite daughter would be coldly received by Mrs. Lippett.

Mr. Braddock withdrew from the window, and presently appeared in the garden, beautifully arrayed.

"Why, Willoughby," said Kay admiringly, "you look wonderful!"

The kindly compliment did much to soothe Mr. Braddock's wounded feelings.

27

"No, really?" he said; and felt, as he had so often felt before, that Kay was a girl in a million, and that if only the very idea of matrimony did not scare a fellow so confoundedly, a fellow might very well take a chance and see what would happen if he asked her to marry him.

"And the speech sounded fine."

"Really? You know, I got a sudden fear that my voice might not carry."

"It carries," Kay assured him.

The clouds which her compliments had chased from Mr. Braddock's brow gathered again.

"I say, Kay, you know, you really ought to do something about that girl Clara. She's impossible. I mean, throwing onions at a fellow."

"You mustn't mind. Don't worry about her; it'll make you forget your speech. How long are you supposed to talk?"

"About ten minutes, I imagine. You know, this is going to just about kill me."

"What you must do is drink lots and lots of champagne."

"But it makes me spotty."

"Well, be spotty. I shan't mind."

Mr. Braddock considered.

"I will," he said. "It's a very good idea. Well, I suppose I ought to be going."

"You've got your key? That's right. You won't be back till pretty late, of course. I'll go and tell Claire not to bolt the door."

When Kay reached the kitchen she found that her faithful follower had stepped out of the pages of *Romeo and Juliet* into those of *Macbeth*. She was bending over a cauldron, dropping things into it. The kitten, now comparatively dry and decustarded, eyed her with bright interest from a shelf on the dresser.

"This is the new soup, Miss Kay," she announced with modest pride.

"It smells fine," said Kay, wincing slightly as a painful aroma of burning smote her nostrils. "I say, Claire, I wish you wouldn't throw onions at Mr. Braddock."

"I went up and got it back," Claire reassured her. "It's in the soup now."

"You'll be in the soup if you do that sort of thing. What," asked Kay virtuously, "will the neighbours say?"

"There aren't any neighbours," Claire pointed out. A wistful look came into her perky face. "I wish some one would hurry up and move into Mon Ree-poss," she said. "I don't like not having next-doors. Gets lonely for a girl all day with no one to talk to."

"Well, when you talk to Mr. Braddock, don't do it at the top of your voice. Please understand I don't like it."

"Now," said Claire simply, "you're cross with me." And without further preamble she burst into a passionate flood of tears.

It was this sensitiveness of hers that made it so difficult for the young chatelaine of San Rafael to deal with the domestic staff. Kay was a warm-hearted girl, and a warm-hearted girl can never be completely at her ease when she is making cooks cry. It took ten minutes of sedulous petting to restore the emotional Miss Lippett to her usual cheerfulness.

"I'll never raise my voice so much as above a whisper to the man," she announced remorsefully at the end of that period. "All the same——"

Kay had no desire to reopen the Braddock argument.

"That's all right, Claire. What I really came to say was—don't put the chain up on the front door to-night, because Mr. Braddock is sure to be late. But he will come in quite quietly and won't disturb you."

"He'd better not," said Miss Lippett grimly. "I've got a revolver."

"A revolver!"

"Ah!" Claire bent darkly over her cauldron. "You never know when there won't be burglars in these low parts. The girl at Pontresina down the road was telling me they'd had a couple of milk cans sneaked off their doorstep only yesterday. And I'll tell you another thing, Miss Kay. It's my belief there's been people breaking into Mon Ree-poss."

"What would they do that for? It's empty."

"It wasn't empty last night. I was looking out of the window with one of my noo-ralgic headaches—must have been between two and three in the morning—and there was mysterious lights going up and down the staircase."

"You imagined it."

"Begging your pardon, Miss Kay, I did not imagine it. There they were, as plain as plain. Might have been one of these electric torches the criminal classes use. If you want to know what I think, Miss Kay, that Mon Ree-poss is what I call a house of mystery, and I shan't be sorry when somebody respectable comes and takes it. The way it is now, we're just as likely as not to wake up and find ourselves all murdered in our beds."

"You mustn't be so nervous."

"Nervous?" replied Claire indignantly. "Nervous? Take more than a burglar to make me nervous. All I'm saying is, I'm prepared."

"Well, don't go shooting Mr. Braddock."

"That," said Miss Lippett, declining to commit herself, "is as may be."

CHAPTER III

SAILORS DON'T CARE

SOME five hours after Willoughby Braddock's departure from San Rafael, a young man came up Villiers Street, and turning into the Strand, began to stroll slowly eastward. The Strand, it being the hour when the theatres had begun to empty themselves, was a roaring torrent of humanity and vehicles; and he looked upon the bustling scene with the affectionate eye of one who finds the turmoil of London novel and attractive. He was a nice-looking young man, but what was most immediately noticeable about him was his extraordinary shabbiness. Both his shoes were split across the toe; his hands were in the pockets of a stained and weather-beaten pair of blue trousers; and he gazed about him from under the brim of a soft hat which could have been worn without exciting comment by any scarecrow.

So striking was his appearance that two exquisites, emerging from the Savoy Hotel and pausing on the pavement to wait for a vacant taxi, eyed him with pained disapproval as he approached, and then, starting, stared in amazement.

"Good Lord!" said the first exquisite.

"Good heavens!" said the second.

"See who that is?"

"S. P. Shotter! Used to be in the School House."

"Captain of football my last year."

"But, I say, it can't be! Dressed like that, I mean."

"It is."

"Good heavens!"

"Good Lord!"

These two were men who had, in the matter of costume,

31

a high· standard. Themselves snappy and conscientious
dressers, they judged their fellows hardly. Yet even an in-
dulgent critic would have found it difficult not to shake his
head over the spectacle presented by Sam Shotter as he
walked the Strand that night.

The fact is it is not easy for a young man of adventurous
and inquisitive disposition to remain dapper throughout a
voyage on a tramp steamer. The *Araminta,* which had
arrived at Millwall Dock that afternoon, had taken fourteen
days to cross the Atlantic, and during those fourteen days
Sam had entered rather fully into the many-sided life of
the ship. He had spent much time in an oily engine-room;
he had helped the bos'n with a job of painting; he had
accompanied the chief engineer on his rambles through the
coal bunkers; and on more than one occasion had endeared
himself to languid firemen by taking their shovels and doing a little amateur stoking. One cannot do these things
and be foppish.

Nevertheless, it would have surprised him greatly had
he known that his appearance was being adversely criticised,
for he was in that happy frame of mind when men forget
they have an appearance. He had dined well, having as
his guest his old friend Hash Todhunter. He had seen a
motion picture of squashy sex appeal. And now, having
put Hash on an east-bound tram, he was filled with that
pleasant sense of well-being and content which comes on
those rare occasions when the world is just about right.
So far from being abashed by the shabbiness of his exterior, Sam found himself experiencing, as he strolled along
the Strand, a gratifying illusion of having bought the place.
He felt like the young squire returned from his travels and
revisiting the old village.

Nor, though he was by nature a gregarious young man
and fond of human society, did the fact that he was alone

depress him. Much as he liked Hash Todhunter, he had not been sorry to part from him. Usually an entertaining companion, Hash had been a little tedious to-night, owing to a tendency to confine the conversation to the subject of a dog belonging to a publican friend of his which was running in a whippet race at Hackney Marshes next morning. Hash had, it seemed, betted his entire savings on this animal, and not content with this, had pestered Sam to lend him all his remaining cash to add to the investment. And though Sam had found no difficulty in remaining firm, it is always a bore to have to keep saying no.

The two exquisites looked at each other apprehensively.

"Shift ho, before he touches us, what?" said the first.

"Shift absolutely ho," agreed the second.

It was too late. The companion of their boyhood had come up, and after starting to pass had paused, peering at them from under that dreadful hat, which seemed to cut them like a knife, in the manner of one trying to identify half-remembered faces.

"Bates and Tresidder!" he exclaimed at length. "By Jove!"

"Hullo," said the first exquisite.

"Hullo," said the second.

"Well, well!" said Sam.

There followed one of those awkward silences which so often occur at these meetings of old schoolmates. The two exquisites were wondering dismally when the inevitable touch would come, and Sam had just recollected that these were two blighters whom, when *in statu pupillari*, he had particularly disliked. Nevertheless, etiquette demanded that a certain modicum of conversation be made.

"What have you been doing with yourselves?" asked Sam. "You look very festive."

"Been dining," said the first exquisite.

"Old Wrykynian dinner," said the second.

"Oh, yes, of course. It always was at this time of year, wasn't it? Lots of the lads there, I suppose?"

"Oh, yes."

"Good dinner?"

"Goodish," said the first exquisite.

"Not baddish," said the second.

"Rotten speeches, though."

"Awful!"

"Can't think where they dig these blokes up."

"No."

"That man Braddock."

"Frightful."

"Don't tell me the old Bradder actually made a speech!" said Sam, pleased. "Was he very bad?"

"Worst of the lot."

"Absolutely!"

"That story about the Irishman."

"Foul!"

"And all that rot about the dear old school."

"Ghastly!"

"If you ask me," said the first exquisite severely, "my opinion is that he was as tight as an owl."

"Stewed to the eyebrows," said the second.

"I watched him during dinner and he was mopping up the stuff like a vacuum cleaner."

There was a silence.

"Well," said the first exquisite uncomfortably, "we must be pushing on."

"Dashing off," said the second exquisite.

"Got to go to supper at the Angry Cheese."

"The where?" asked Sam.

"Angry Cheese. New night club in Panton Street. See you some time, what?"

"Oh, yes," said Sam.

Another silence was about to congeal, when a taxi crawled up and the two exquisites leaped joyfully in.

"Awful, a fellow going right under like that," said the first.

"Ghastly," said the second.

"Lucky we got away."

"Yes."

"He was shaping for a touch," said the first exquisite.

"Trembling on his lips," said the second.

Sam walked on. Although the Messrs. Bates and Tresidder had never been favourites of his, they belonged to what Mr. Braddock would have called – and, indeed, had called no fewer than eleven times in his speech that night—the dear old school; and the meeting with them had left him pleasantly stimulated. The feeling of being a *seigneur* revisiting his estates after long absence grew as he threaded his way through the crowd. He eyed the passers-by in a jolly, Laughing Cavalier sort of way, wishing he knew them well enough to slap them on the back. And when he reached the corner of Wellington Street and came upon a dishevelled vocalist singing mournfully in the gutter, he could not but feel it a personal affront that this sort of thing should be going on in his domain. He was conscious of a sensation of being individually responsible for this poor fellow's reduced condition, and the situation seemed to him to call for largess.

On setting out that night Sam had divided his money into two portions. His baggage, together with his letter of credit, had preceded him across the ocean on the *Mauretania;* and as it might be a day or so before he could establish connection with it, he had prudently placed the bulk of his ready money in his note-case, earmarking it for the purchase of new clothes and other necessaries on the

morrow so that he might be enabled to pay his first visit
to Tilbury House in becoming state. The remainder, suf-
ficient for the evening's festivities, he had put in his trousers
pockets.

It was into his right trousers pocket therefore that he
now groped. His fingers closed on a half-crown. He
promptly dropped it. He was feeling *seigneurial,* but not
so *seigneurial* as that. Something more in the nature of a
couple of coppers was what he was looking for, and it surprised him to find that except for the half-crown the pocket
appeared to be empty. He explored the other pocket.
That was empty too.

The explanation was, of course, that the life of pleasure
comes high. You cannot go stuffing yourself and a vora-
cious sea cook at restaurants, taking buses and Under-
ground trains all over the place, and finally winding up at
a cinema palace, without cutting into your capital. Sam
was reluctantly forced to the conclusion that the half-crown
was his only remaining spare coin. He was, accordingly,
about to abandon the idea of largess and move on, when
the vocalist, having worked his way through You're the
Sort of a Girl That Men Forget, began to sing that other
popular ballad entitled Sailors Don't Care. And it was no
doubt the desire to refute the slur implied in these words
on the great brotherhood of which he was an amateur
member that decided Sam to be lavish.

The half-crown changed hands.

Sam resumed his walk. At a quarter-past eleven at
night there is little to amuse and interest the stroller east
of Wellington Street, so he now crossed the road and turned
westward. And he had not been walking more than a few
paces when he found himself looking into the brightly
lighted window of a small restaurant that appeared to
specialise in shellfish. The slab beyond the glass was paved

with the most insinuating oysters. Overcome with emotion, Sam stopped in his tracks.

There is something about the oyster, nestling in its shell, which in the hours that come when the theatres are closed and London is beginning to give itself up to nocturnal revelry stirs right-thinking men like a bugle. There swept over Sam a sudden gnawing desire for nourishment. Oysters with brown bread and a little stout were, he perceived, just what this delightful evening demanded by way of a fitting climax. He pulled out his note-case. Even if it meant an inferior suit next morning, one of those Treasury notes which lay there must be broken into here and now.

It seemed to Sam, looking back later at this moment, that at the very first touch the note-case had struck him as being remarkably thin. It appeared to have lost its old jolly plumpness, as if some wasting fever had struck it. Indeed, it gave the impression, when he opened it, of being absolutely empty.

It was not absolutely empty. It is true that none of the Treasury notes remained, but there was something inside—a dirty piece of paper on which were words written in pencil. He read them by the light that poured from the restaurant window:

"DEAR SAM,—You will doubtless be surprised, Sam, to learn that I have borowed your money. Dear Sam, I will send it back to-morrow A.M. prompt. Nothing can beat that wipet, Sam, so I have borowed your money.

"Trusting this finds you in the pink,

"Yrs. Obedtly,

"C. TODHUNTER."

Sam stood staring at this polished communication with sagging jaw. For an instant it had a certain obscurity, the word "wipet" puzzling him particularly.

Then, unlike the missing money, it all came back to him. The rush of traffic was diminishing now, and the roar of a few minutes back had become a mere rumble. It was almost as if London, sympathising with his sorrow, had delicately hushed its giant voice. To such an extent, in fact, was its voice hushed that that of the Wellington Street vocalist was once more plainly audible, and there was in what he was singing a poignant truth which had not impressed itself upon Sam when he had first heard it.

"Sailors don't care," chanted the vocalist. "Sailors don't care. It's something to do with the salt in the blood. Sailors don't care."

CHAPTER IV

SCENE OUTSIDE FASHIONABLE NIGHT-CLUB

THE mental condition of a man who at half-past eleven at night suddenly finds himself penniless and without shelter in the heart of the great city must necessarily be for a while somewhat confused. Sam's first coherent thought was to go back and try to recover that half-crown from the wandering minstrel. After a very brief reflection, however, he dismissed this scheme as too visionary for practical consideration. His acquaintance with the other had been slight, but he had seen enough of him to gather that he was not one of those rare spiritual fellows who give half-crowns back. The minstrel was infirm and old, but many years would have to elapse before he became senile enough for that. No, some solution on quite different lines was required; and, thinking deeply, Sam began to move slowly in the direction of Charing Cross.

He was as yet far from being hopeless. Indeed, his mood at this point might have been called optimistic; for he realised that if this disaster had been decreed by Fate from the beginning of time—and he supposed it had been, though that palmist had made no mention of it—it could hardly have happened at a more convenient spot. The Old Wrykynian dinner had only just broken up, which meant that this portion of London must be full of men who had been at school with him and would doubtless be delighted to help him out with a temporary loan. At any moment now he might run into some kindly old schoolfellow.

And almost immediately he did. Or, rather, the old schoolfellow ran into him. He had reached the Vaudeville Theatre and had paused, debating within himself the advisability of crossing the street and seeing how the hunting was on the other side, when a solid body rammed him in the back.

"Oh, sorry! Frightfully sorry! I say, awfully sorry!"

It was a voice which had been absent from Sam's life for some years, but he recognised it almost before he had recovered his balance. He wheeled joyfully round on the stout and red-faced young man who was with some difficulty retrieving his hat from the gutter.

"Excuse me," he said, "but you are extraordinarily like a man I used to know named J. W. Braddock."

"I am J. W. Braddock."

"Ah," said Sam, "that accounts for the resemblance."

He contemplated his erstwhile study companion with affection. He would have been glad at any time to meet the old Bradder, but he was particularly glad to meet him now. As Mr. Braddock himself might have put it, he was glad, delighted, pleased, happy and overjoyed. Willoughby Braddock, bearing out the words of the two exquisites, was obviously in a somewhat vinous condition, but Sam was no Puritan and was not offended by this. The thing about Mr. Braddock that impressed itself upon him to the exclusion of all else was the fact that he looked remarkably rich. He had that air, than which there is none more delightful, of being the sort of man who would lend a fellow a fiver without a moment's hesitation.

Willoughby Braddock had secured his hat, and he now replaced it in a sketchy fashion on his head. His face was flushed, and his eyes, always slightly prominent, seemed to protrude like those of a snail—and an extremely inebriated snail at that.

"Imarraspeesh," he said.

"I beg your pardon?" said Sam.

"I made a speesh."

"Yes, so I heard."

"You heard my speesh?"

"I heard that you had made one."

"How did you hear my speesh?" said Mr. Braddock, plainly mystified. "You weren't at the dinner."

"No, but——"

"You couldn't have been at the dinner," proceeded Mr. Braddock, reasoning closely, "because evening dress was obliggery and you aren't obliggery. I'll tell you what —between you and me, I don't know who the deuce you are."

"You don't know me?"

"No, I don't know you."

"Pull yourself together, Bradder. I'm Sam Shotter."

"Sham Sotter?"

"If you prefer it that way, certainly. I've always pro-nounced it Sam Shotter myself."

"Sam Shotter?"

"That's right."

Mr. Braddock eyed him narrowly.

"Look here," he said, "I'll tell you something—something that'll interest you—something that'll interest you very much. You're Sam Shotter."

"That's it."

"We were at school together."

"We were."

"The dear old school."

"Exactly."

Intense delight manifested itself in Mr. Braddock's face. He seized Sam's hand and wrung it warmly.

"How are you, my dear old chap, how are you?" he cried. "Old Sham Spotter, by gad! By Jove! By George! My goodness! Fancy that! Well, good-bye."

And with a beaming smile he suddenly swooped across the road and was lost to sight.

The stoutest heart may have its black moments. Depression claimed Sam for its own. There is no agony like that of the man who has intended to borrow money and finds that he has postponed the request till too late. With bowed shoulders he made his way eastward. He turned up Charing Cross Road, and thence by way of Green Street into Leicester Square. He moved listlessly along the lower end of the square, and presently, glancing up, perceived graven upon the wall the words, "Panton Street."

He halted. The name seemed somehow familiar. Then he remembered. The Angry Cheese, that haunt of wealth and fashion to which those fellows, Bates and Tresidder, had been going, was in Panton Street.

Hope revived in Sam. An instant before, the iron had seemed to have entered his soul, but now he squared his shoulders and quickened his steps. Good old Bates! Splendid old Tresidder! They were the men to help him out of this mess.

He saw clearly now how mistaken can be the callow judgments which we form when young. As an immature lad at school he had looked upon Bates and Tresidder with a jaundiced eye. He had summed them up in his

41

mind, after the hasty fashion of youth, as ticks and blisters. Aye, and even when he had encountered them half an hour ago after the lapse of years, their true nobility had not been made plain to him. It was only now, as he padded along Panton Street like a leopard on the trail, that he realised what excellent fellows they were and how fond he was of them. They were great chaps—corkers, both of them. And when he remembered that with a boy's blindness to his sterling qualities he had once given Bates six of the juiciest with a walking stick, he burned with remorse and shame.

It was not difficult to find the Angry Cheese. About this newest of London's night clubs there was nothing coy or reticent. Its doorway stood open to the street, and cabs were drawing up in a constant stream and discharging fair women and well-tailored men. Furthermore, to render identification easy for the very dullest, there stood on the pavement outside a vast commissionaire, brilliantly attired in the full-dress uniform of a Czecho-Slovakian field-marshal and wearing on his head a peaked cap circled by a red band, which bore in large letters of gold the words "Angry Cheese."

"Good evening," said Sam, curvetting buoyantly up to this spectacular person. "I want to speak to Mr. Bates."

The field-marshal eyed him distantly. The man, one would have said, was not in sympathy with him. Sam could not imagine why. With the prospect of a loan in sight, he himself was liking everybody.

"Misteroo?"

"Mr. Bates."

"Mr. Yates?"

"Mr. Bates. Mr. Bates. You know Mr. Bates?" said Sam. And such was the stimulating rhythm of the melody into which the unseen orchestra had just burst that he very nearly added, "He's a bear, he's a bear, he's a bear."

"Bates?"

"Or Tresidder."

"Make up your mind," said the field-marshal petulantly.

At this moment, on the opposite side of the street, there appeared the figure of Mr. Willoughby Braddock, walking with extraordinary swiftness. His eyes were staring straight in front of him. He had lost his hat.

"Bradder!" cried Sam.

Mr. Bradder looked over his shoulder, waved his hand, smiled a smile of piercing sweetness and passed rapidly into the night.

Sam was in a state of indecision similar to that of the dog in the celebrated substance-and-shadow fable. Should he pursue this will-o'-the-wisp, or should he stick to the sound Conservative policy of touching the man on the spot? What would Napoleon have done?

He decided to remain.

"Fellow who was at school with me," he remarked explanatorily.

"Ho!" said the field-marshal, looking like a stuffed sergeant-major.

"And now," said Sam, "can I see Mr. Bates?"

"You cannot."

"But he's in there."

"And you're out 'ere," said the field-marshal.

He moved away to assist a young lady of gay exterior to alight from a taxicab. And as he did so someone spoke from the steps:

"Ah, there you are!"

Sam looked up relieved. Dear old Bates was standing in the lighted doorway.

Of the four persons who made up the little group collected about the threshold of the Angry Cheese, three now spoke simultaneously.

43

Dear old Bates said: "This is topping! Thought you weren't coming."

The lady said: "Awfully sorry I'm late, old cork."

Sam said: "Oh, Bates!"

He was standing some little space removed from the main body when he spoke, and the words did not register. The lady passed on into the building. Bates was preparing to follow her when Sam spoke again. And this time nobody within any reasonable radius could have failed to hear him.

"Hi, Bates!"

"Hey!" said the field-marshal, massaging his ear with a look of reproach and dislike.

Bates turned, and as he saw Sam, there spread itself over his face the startled look of one who, wandering gaily along some primrose path, sees gaping before him a frightful chasm or a fearful serpent or some menacing lion in the undergrowth. In this crisis, Claude Bates did not hesitate. With a single backward spring—which, if he could have remembered it and reproduced it later on the dancing floor, would have made him the admired of all—he disappeared, leaving Sam staring blankly after him.

A large fat hand, placed in no cordial spirit on his shoulder, awoke Sam from his reverie. The field-marshal was gazing at him with a loathing which he now made no attempt to conceal.

"You 'op it," said the field-marshal. "We don't want none of your sort 'ere."

"But I was at school with him," stammered Sam. The thing had been so sudden that even now he could not completely realise that what practically amounted to his own flesh and blood had thrown him down cold.

"At school with 'im too, was you?" said the field-marshal. "The only school you was ever at was Borstal. You

4 44

'op it, and quick. That's what you do before I call a policeman."

Inside the night club, Claude Bates, restoring his nervous system with a whisky and soda, was relating to his
friend Tresidder the tale of his narrow escape.

"Absolutely lurking on the steps!" said Bates.

"Ghastly!" said Tresidder.

CHAPTER V
PAINFUL AFFAIR AT A COFFEE-STALL

LONDON was very quiet. A stillness had fallen upon it,
broken only by the rattle of an occasional cab and the footsteps of some home-seeking wayfarer. The lamplight shone
on glistening streets, on pensive policemen, on smoothly
prowling cats, and on a young man in a shocking suit of
clothes whose faith in human nature was at zero.

Sam had now no definite objective. He was merely
walking aimlessly with the idea of killing time. He wandered
on, and presently found that he had passed out of the haunts
of fashion into a meaner neighbourhood. The buildings had
become dingier, the aspect of the perambulating cats more
sinister and blackguardly. He had in fact reached the district which, in spite of the efforts of its inhabitants to get
it called Lower Belgravia, is still known as Pimlico. And
it was near the beginning of Lupus Street that he was
roused from his meditations by the sight of a coffee-stall.

It brought him up standing. Once more he had suddenly become aware of that gnawing hunger which had afflicted him outside the oyster restaurant. Why he should
be hungry, seeing that not so many hours ago he had consumed an ample dinner, he could not have said. A psycho-
logist, had one been present, would have told him that the

45

pangs of starvation from which he supposed himself to suffer were purely a figment of the mind, and that it was merely his subconscious self reacting to the suggestion of food. Sam, however, had positive inside information to the contrary; and he halted before the coffee-stall, staring wolfishly.

There was not a large attendance of patrons. Three only were present. One was a man in a sort of uniform who seemed to have been cleaning streets, the two others had the appearance of being gentlemen of leisure. They were leaning restfully on the counter, eating hard-boiled eggs.

Sam eyed them resentfully. It was just this selfish sort of epicureanism, he felt, that was the canker which destroyed empires. And when the man in uniform, wearying of eggs, actually went on to supplement them with a slice of seedcake, it was as if he were watching the orgies that preceded the fall of Babylon. With gleaming eyes he drew a step closer, and was thus enabled to overhear the conversation of these sybarites.

Like all patrons of coffee-stalls, they were talking about the Royal family, and for a brief space it seemed that a perfect harmony was to prevail. Then the man in uniform committed himself to the statement that the Duke of York wore a moustache, and the gentlemen of leisure united to form a solid opposition.

"'E ain't got no moustache," said one.

"Cert'n'ly 'e ain't got no moustache," said the other.

"Wot," inquired the first gentleman of leisure, "made you get that silly idea into your 'ead that 'e's got a moustache?"

"'E's got a smorl clipped moustache," said the man in uniform stoutly.

"A smorl clipped moustache?"

"A smorl clipped moustache."

"You say he's got a smorl clipped moustache?"

46

"Ah! A smorl clipped moustache."

"Well, then," said the leader of the opposition, with the air of a cross-examining counsel who has dexterously trapped a reluctant witness into a damaging admission, "that's where you make your ruddy error. Because 'e ain't got no smorl clipped moustache."

It seemed to Sam that a little adroit diplomacy at this point would be in his best interests. He had not the pleasure of the duke's acquaintance and so was not really entitled to speak as an expert, but he decided to support the man in uniform. The good graces of a fellow of his careless opulence were worth seeking. In a soaring moment of optimism it seemed to him that a hard-boiled egg and a cup of coffee were the smallest reward a loyal supporter might expect. He advanced into the light of the naphtha flare and spoke with decision.

"This gentleman is right," he said. "The Duke of York has a small clipped moustache."

The interruption appeared to come on the three debaters like a bombshell. It had on them an effect much the same as an uninvited opinion from a young and newly joined member would have on a group of bishops and generals in the smoking-room of the Athenæum Club. For an instant there was a shocked silence; then the man in uniform spoke.

"Wot do you want, stickin' your ugly fat 'ead in?" he demanded coldly.

Shakespeare, who knew too much ever to be surprised at man's ingratitude, would probably have accepted this latest evidence of it with stoicism. It absolutely stunned Sam. A little peevishness from the two gentlemen of leisure he had expected, but that his sympathy and support should be received in this fashion by the man in uniform was simply disintegrating. It seemed to be his fate to-night to lack appeal for men in uniform.

"Yus," agreed the leader of the opposition, "'oo arsked
you to shove in?"

"Comin' stickin' 'is 'ead in!" sniffed the man in uniform.

All three members of the supper party eyed him with
manifest disfavour. The proprietor of the stall, a silent hairy
man, said nothing: but he, too, cast a chilly glance of
hauteur in Sam's direction. There was a sense of strain.

"I only said——" Sam began.

"And 'oo arsked you to?" retorted the man in uniform.

The situation was becoming difficult. At this tense
moment, however, there was a rattling and a grinding of
brakes, and a taxicab drew up at the kerb, and out of its
interior shot Mr. Willoughby Braddock.

"Getta cuppa coffee," observed Mr. Braddock explanatorily to the universe.

CHAPTER VI

A FRIEND IN NEED

OF certain supreme moments in life it is not easy to
write. The workaday teller of tales, whose gifts, if any, lie
rather in the direction of recording events than of analys-
ing emotion, finds himself baffled by them. To say that
Sam Shotter was relieved by this sudden reappearance of
his old friend would obviously be inadequate. Yet it is
hard to find words that will effectually meet the case. Perhaps it is simplest to say that his feelings at this juncture
were to all intents and purposes those of the garrison
besieged by savages in the final reel of a motion-picture
super-super-film when the operator flashes on the screen
the sub-title, "Hurrah! Here come the United States
Marines!"

And blended with this heart-shaking thankfulness, came

instantaneously the thought that he must not let the poor fish get away again.

"Here, I say!" said Mr. Braddock, becoming aware of a clutching hand upon his coat sleeve.

"It's all right, Bradder, old man," said Sam. "It's only me."

"Who?"

"Me."

"Who are you?"

"Sam Shotter."

"Sam Shotter?"

"Sam Shotter."

"Sam Shotter who used to be at school with me?"

"The very same."

"Are you Sam Shotter?"

"I am."

"Why, so you are!" said Mr. Braddock, completely convinced. He displayed the utmost delight at this reunion. "Mosestraornary coincidence," he said as he kneaded Sam lovingly about the shoulder. "I was talking to a fellow in the Strand about you only an hour ago."

"Were you, Bradder, old man?"

"Yes; nasty ugly-looking fellow. I bumped into him, and he turned round and the very first thing he said was, 'Do you know Sam Shotter?' He told me all sorts of interesting things about you too—all sorts of interesting things. I've forgotten what they were, but you see what I mean."

"I follow you perfectly, Bradder. What's become of your hat?"

A look of relieved happiness came into Willoughby Braddock's face.

"Have you got my hat? Where is it?"

"I haven't got your hat."

"You said you had my hat."

49

"No, I didn't."

"Oh!" said Mr. Braddock, disappointed. "Well, then, come and have a cuppa coffee."

It was with the feelings of a voyager who after much buffeting comes safely at last to journey's end that Sam ranged himself alongside the counter which for so long had been but a promised land seen from some distant Mount Pisgah. The two gentlemen of leisure had melted away into the night, but the uniformed man remained, eating seed-cake with a touch of bravado.

"This gentleman a friend of yours, Sam?" asked Mr. Braddock, having ordered coffee and eggs.

"I should say not," said Sam with aversion. "Why, he thinks the Duke of York has a small clipped moustache!"

"No!" said Mr. Braddock, shocked.

"He does."

"Man must be a thorough ass."

"Dropped on his head when a baby, probably."

"Better have nothing to do with him," said Mr. Braddock in a confidential bellow.

The meal proceeded on its delightful course. Sam had always been fond of Willoughby Braddock, and the spacious manner in which he now ordered further hard-boiled eggs showed him that his youthful affection had not been misplaced. A gentle glow began to steal over him. The coffee was the kind of which, after a preliminary mouthful, you drink a little more just to see if it is really as bad as it seemed at first, but it was warm and comforting. It was not long before the world appeared very good to Sam. He expanded genially. He listened with courteous attention to Mr. Braddock's lengthy description of his speech at the Old Wrykynian dinner, and even melted sufficiently to extend an olive branch to the man in uniform.

"Looks like rain," he said affably.

"Who does?" asked Mr. Braddock, puzzled.

"I was addressing the gentleman behind you," said Sam.

Mr. Braddock looked cautiously over his shoulder.

"But are we speaking to him?" he asked gravely. "I thought——"

"Oh, yes," said Sam tolerantly. "I fancy he's quite a good fellow really. Wants knowing, that's all."

"What makes you think he looks like rain?" asked Mr. Braddock, interested.

The chauffeur of the taxicab now added himself to their little group. He said that he did not know about Mr. Braddock's plans, but that he himself was desirous of getting to bed. Mr. Braddock patted him on the shoulder with radiant bonhomie.

"This," he explained to Sam, "is a most delightful chap. I've forgotten his name."

The cabman said his name was Evans.

"Evans! Of course. I knew it was something beginning with a G. This is my friend Evans, Sam. I forget where we met, but he's taking me home."

"Where do you live, Bradder?"

"Where do I live, Evans?"

"Down at Valley Fields, you told me," said the cabman.

"Where are you living, Sam?"

"Nowhere."

"How do you mean—nowhere?"

"I have no home," said Sam with simple pathos.

"I'd like to dig you one," said the man in uniforn.

"No home?" cried Mr. Braddock, deeply moved. "Nowhere to sleep to-night, do you mean? I say, look here, you must absolutely come back with me. Evans, old chap, do you think there would be room for one more in that cab of yours? Because I particularly want this gentleman

51

to come back with me. My dear old Sam, I won't listen
to any argument."

"You won't have to."

"You can sleep on the sofa in the drawing-room. You
ready, Evans, old man? Splendid! Then let's go."

From Lupus Street, Pimlico, to Burberry Road, Valley
Fields, is a distance of several miles, but to Sam the drive
seemed a short one. This illusion was not due so much
to the gripping nature of Mr. Braddock's conversation,
though that rippled on continuously, as to the fact that,
being a trifle weary after his experiences of the night, he
dozed off shortly after they had crossed the river. He
awoke to find that the cab had come to a standstill outside a wooden gate which led by a short gravel path to a
stucco-covered house. A street lamp, shining feebly, was
strong enough to light up the name San Rafael. Mr. Braddock paid the cabman and ushered Sam through the gate.
He produced a key after a little searching, and having
mounted the steps opened the door. Sam found himself
in a small hall, dimly lighted by a turned-down jet of gas.

"Go right in," said Mr. Braddock. "I'll be back in a
moment. Got to see a man."

"Got to what?" said Sam, surprised.

"Got to see a man for a minute. Fellow named Evans,
who was at school with me. Most important."

And with that curious snipelike abruptness which char-
acterised his movements to-night, Willoughby Braddock
slammed the front door violently and disappeared.

Sam's feelings, as the result of his host's impulsive
departure, were somewhat mixed. To the credit side of the
ledger he could place the fact that he was safely under
the shelter of a roof, which he had not expected to be an
hour ago; but he wished that, before leaving, his friend
had given him a clue as to where was situated this draw-

ing-room with its sofa whereon he was to spend the remainder of the night.

However, a brief exploration would no doubt reveal the hidden chamber. It might even be that room whose door faced him across the hall.

He was turning the handle with the view of testing this theory, when a voice behind him, speaking softly but with a startling abruptness, said, "Hands up!"

At the foot of the stairs, her wide mouth set in a determined line, her tow-coloured hair adorned with gleaming curling pins, there was standing a young woman in a pink dressing gown and slippers. In her right hand, pointed at his head, she held a revolver.

CHAPTER VII

SAM AT SAN RAFAEL

It is not given to every girl who makes prophecies to find those prophecies fulfilled within a few short hours of their utterance; and the emotions of Claire Lippett, as she confronted Sam in the hall of San Rafael, were akin to those of one who sees the long shot romp in ahead of the field or who unexpectedly solves the cross-word puzzle. Only that evening she had predicted that burglars would invade the house, and here one was, as large as life. Mixed, therefore, with her disapproval of this midnight marauder, was a feeling almost of gratitude to him for being there. Of fear she felt no trace. She presented the pistol with a firm hand.

One calls it a pistol for the sake of technical accuracy. To Sam's startled sense it appeared like a young cannon, and so deeply did he feel regarding it that he made it the subject of his opening remark—which, by all the laws of etiquette, should have been a graceful apology for and explanation of his intrusion.

"Steady with the howitzer!" he urged.

"What say?" said Claire coldly.

"The lethal weapon—be careful with it. It's pointing at me."

"I know it's pointing at you."

"Oh, well, so long as it only points," said Sam.

He felt a good deal reassured by the level firmness of her tone. This was plainly not one of those neurotic, fluttering females whose fingers cannot safely be permitted within a foot of pistol trigger.

There was a pause. Claire, still keeping the weapon poised, turned the gas up. Upon which, Sam, rightly feeling that the ball of conversation should be set rolling by himself, spoke again.

"You are doubtless surprised," he said, plagiarising the literary style of Mr. Todhunter, "to see me here."

"No, I'm not."

"You're not?"

"No. You keep those hands of yours up."

Sam sighed.

"You wouldn't speak to me in that harsh tone," he said, "if you knew all I had been through. It is not too much to say that I have been persecuted this night."

"Well, you shouldn't come breaking into people's houses," said Claire primly.

"You are labouring under a natural error," said Sam. "I did not break into this charming little house. My presence, Mrs. Braddock, strange as it may seem, is easily explained."

"Who are you calling Mrs. Braddock?"

"Aren't you Mrs. Braddock?"

"No."

54

"You aren't married to Mr. Braddock?"

"No, I'm not."

Sam was a broad-minded young man.

"Ah, well," he said, "in the sight of God, no doubt——"

"I'm the cook."

"Oh," said Sam, relieved, "that explains it."

"Explains what?"

"Well, you know, it seemed a trifle odd for a moment that you should be popping about here at this time of night with your hair in curlers and your little white ankles peeping out from under a dressing gown."

"Coo!" said Claire in a modest flutter. She performed a swift adjustment of the garment's folds.

"But if you're Mr. Braddock's cook——"

"Who said I was Mr. Braddock's cook?"

"You did."

"I didn't any such thing. I'm Mr. Wrenn's cook."

"Mr. who?"

"Mr. Wrenn."

This was a complication which Sam had not anticipated.

"Let us get this thing straight," he said. "Am I to understand that this house does not belong to Mr. Braddock?"

"Yes, you are. It belongs to Mr. Wrenn."

"But Mr. Braddock had a latch-key."

"He's staying here."

"Ah!"

"What do you mean—ah?"

"I intended to convey that things are not so bad as I thought they were. I was afraid for a moment that I had got into the wrong house. But it's all right. You see, I met Mr. Braddock a short while ago and he brought me back here to spend the night."

"Oh?" said Claire. "Did he? Ho! Oh, indeed?"

Sam looked at her anxiously. He did not like her manner.

"You believe me, don't you?"

"No, I don't."

"But surely——"

"If Mr. Braddock brought you here, where is he?"

"He went away. He was, I regret to say, quite considerably squiffled. Immediately after letting me in he dashed off, banging the door behind him."

"Likely!"

"But listen, my dear little girl——"

"Less of it!" said Claire austerely. "It's a bit thick if a girl can't catch a burglar without having him start to flirt with her."

"You wrong me!" said Sam. "You wrong me! I was only saying——"

"Well, don't."

"But this is absurd. Good heavens, use your intelligence! If my story wasn't true, how could I know anything about Mr. Braddock?"

"You could easily have asked around. What I say is if you were all right and you really knew Mr. Braddock you wouldn't be going about in a suit of clothes like that. You look like a tramp."

"Well, I've just come off a tramp steamer. You mustn't go judging people by appearances. I should have thought they would have taught you that at school."

"Never you mind what they taught me at school."

"You have got me all wrong. I'm a millionaire—or rather, my uncle is."

"Mine's the Shah of Persia."

"And a few weeks ago he sent me over to England, the idea being that I was to sail on the *Mauretania*. But that would have involved sharing a suite with a certain Lord

Tilbury and the scheme didn't appeal to me. So I missed the ship and came over on a cargo boat instead."

He paused. He had an uncomfortable feeling that the story sounded thin. He passed it in a swift review before his mind. Yes, thin.

And it was quite plain from her expression that the resolute young lady before him shared this opinion.

She wrinkled her small nose sceptically, and, having finished wrinkling it, sniffed.

"I don't believe a word of it," she said.

"I was afraid you wouldn't," said Sam. "True though it is, it has a phony ring. Really to digest that story, you have to know Lord Tilbury. If you had the doubtful pleasure of the acquaintance of that king of bores, you would see that I acted in the only possible way. However, if it's too much for you, let it go, and we will approach the matter from a new angle. The whole trouble seems to be my clothes, so I will make you a sporting offer. Overlook them for the moment, give me your womanly trust and allow me to sleep on the drawing-room sofa for the rest of the night, and not only will blessings reward you but I will promise you—right here and now—that in a day or two I will call at this house and let you see me in the niftiest rig-out that ever man wore. Imagine it! A brand-new suit, custom-made, silk serge linings, hand-sewed, scallops on the pocket flaps—and me inside! Is it a bet?"

"No, it isn't."

"Think well! When you first see that suit you will say to yourself that the coat doesn't seem to sit exactly right. You will be correct. The coat will not sit exactly right. And why? Because there will be in the side-pocket a large box of the very finest mixed chocolates, a present for a good girl. Come now! The use of the drawing-room for the few remaining hours of the night. It is not much to ask."

Claire shook her head inflexibly.

"I'm not going to risk it," she said. "By rights I ought march you out into the street and hand you over to the policeman."

"And have him see you in curling pins? No, no!"

"What's wrong with my curling pins?" demanded Claire fiercely.

"Nothing, nothing," said Sam hastily. "I admire them. It only .occurred to me as a passing thought——"

"The reason I don't do it is because I'm tender-hearted and don't want to be too hard on a feller."

"It is a spirit I appreciate," said Sam. "And would that there had been more of it abroad in London this night."

"So out you go, and don't let me hear no more of you. Just buzz off, that's all I ask. And be quick about it, because I need my sleep."

"I was wrong about those chocolates," said Sam. "Silly mistake to make. What will really be in that side-pocket will be a lovely diamond brooch."

"And a motor car and a ruby ring and a new dress and a house in the country, I suppose. Outside!"

Sam accepted defeat. The manly spirit of the Shotters was considerable, but it could be broken.

"Oh, all right, I'll go. One of these days, when my limousine splashes you with mud, you will be sorry for this."

"And don't bang the door behind you," ordered the ruthless girl.

CHAPTER VIII
SAM AT MON REPOS

STANDING on the steps and gazing out into the blackness, Sam now perceived that in the interval between his entrance into San Rafael and his exit therefrom, the night,

in addition to being black, had become wet. A fine rain
had begun to fall, complicating the situation to no small
extent.

For some minutes he remained where he was, hoping
for Mr. Braddock's return. But the moments passed and
no sound of footsteps, however distant, broke the stillness;
so, after going through a brief commination service in which
the names of Hash Todhunter, Claude Bates and Willoughby
Braddock were prominently featured, he decided to make
a move. And it was as he came down from the steps on
to the little strip of gravel that he saw a board leaning
drunkenly toward him a few paces to his left, and read on
that board the words "To Let, Furnished."

This opened up an entirely new train of thought. It
revealed to him what he had not previously suspected, that
the house outside which he stood was not one house but
two houses. It suggested, moreover, that the one to which
the board alluded was unoccupied, and the effect of this
was extraordinarily stimulating.

He hurried along the gravel; and rounding the angle
of the building, saw dimly through the darkness a structure
attached to its side which looked like a conservatory. He
bolted in; and with a pleasant feeling of having circum-
vented Fate, sat down on a wooden shelf intended as a
resting place for potted geraniums.

But Fate is not so easily outmanœuvred. Fate, for its
own inscrutable reasons, had decided that Sam was to be
thoroughly persecuted to-night, and it took up the attack
again without delay. There was a sharp cracking sound
and the wooden shelf collapsed in ruin Sam had many
excellent qualities, but he did not in the least resemble a
potted geranium, and he went through the woodwork as if
it had been paper. And Fate, which observes no rules of
the ring and has no hesitation about hitting a man when

he is down, immediately proceeded to pour water down his neck through a hole in the broken roof.

Sam rose painfully. He saw now that he had been mistaken in supposing that this conservatory was a home from home. He turned up his coat collar and strode wrathfully out into the darkness. He went round to the back of the house with the object of ascertaining if there was an outside coal cellar where a man might achieve dryness, if not positive comfort. And it was as he stumbled along that he saw the open window.

It was a sight which in the blackness of the night he might well have missed; but suffering had sharpened his senses, and he saw it plainly—an open window only a few feet above the ground. Until this moment the idea of actually breaking into the house had not occurred to him; but now, regardless of all the laws which discourage such behaviour, he put his hand on the sill and scrambled through. The rain, as if furious at the escape of its prey, came lashing down like a shower bath.

Sam moved carefully on. Groping his way, he found himself at the foot of a flight of stairs. He climbed these cautiously and became aware of doors to left and right.

The room to the right was empty, but the other one contained a bed. It was a bed, however, that had been reduced to such a mere scenario that he decided to leave it and try his luck downstairs. The board outside had said "To Let, Furnished," which suggested the possibility of a drawing-room sofa. He left the room and started to walk down the stairs.

At first, as he began the descent, the regions below had been in complete darkness. But now a little beam of light suddenly pierced the gloom—a light that might have been that of an electric torch. It was wavering uncertainly, as if whoever was behind it was in the grip of a strong emotion of some kind.

Sam also was in the grip of a strong emotion. He stopped and held his breath. For the space of some seconds there was silence. Then he breathed again.

Perfect control of the breathing apparatus is hard to acquire. Singers spend years learning it. Sam's skill in that direction was rudimentary. It had been his intention to let his present supply of breath gently out and then, very cautiously, to take another supply gently in. Instead of which he gave vent to a sound so loud and mournful that it made his flesh creep. It was half a snort and half a groan, and it echoed through the empty house like a voice from the tomb.

This, he felt, was the end. Further concealment was obviously out of the question. Dully resentful of the curse that seemed to be on him to-night, he stood waiting for the inevitable challenge from below.

No challenge came. Instead there was a sharp clatter of feet, followed by a distant scrabbling sound. The man behind the torch had made a rapid exit through the open window.

For a moment Sam stood perplexed. Then the reasonable explanation came to him. It was no caretaker who had stood there, but an intruder with as little right to be on the premises as he himself. And having reached this conclusion, he gave no further thought to the matter. He was feeling extraordinarily sleepy now and speculations as to the identity of burglars had no interest for him. His mind was occupied entirely by the question of whether or not there was a sofa in the drawing-room.

There was, and a reasonably comfortable sofa too. Sam had reached the stage where he could have slept on spikes, and this sofa seemed to him as inviting as the last word in beds, with all the latest modern springs and box mattresses. He lay down, and sleep poured over him like a healing wave.

CHAPTER IX
BREAKFAST FOR ONE

IT was broad daylight when he woke. Splashes of sunlight were on the floor, and outside a cart clattered cheerfully. Rising stiffly, he was aware of a crick in the neck and of that unpleasant sensation of semi-suffocation which comes to those who spend the night in a disused room with the windows closed. More even than a bath and a shave, he desired fresh air. He made his way down the passage to the window by which he had entered. Outside, glimpses of a garden were visible. He climbed through and drew a deep breath.

The rain of the night had left the world sweet and clean. The ragged grass was all jewelled in the sunshine, and birds were singing in the trees. Sam stood drinking in the freshness of it all, feeling better every instant.

Finally, having performed a few of those bending and stretching exercises which form such an admirable corrective to the effects of a disturbed night, he strolled down the garden path, wishing he could somehow and at no very distant date connect with a little breakfast.

"For goodness sake!" said a voice.

He looked up. Over the fence which divided the garden from the one next door a familiar face was peering. It was his hostess of last night. But, whereas then she had been curling-pinned and dressing-gowned, she was now neatly clad in print and wore on her head a becoming cap. Her face, moreover, which had been hard and hostile, was softened by a friendly grin.

62

"Good morning," said Sam.

"How did you get there?"

"When you turned me out into the night," said Sam reproachfully, "I took refuge next door."

"I say, I'm sorry about that," said the girl remorsefully. "But how was I to know that you were telling the truth?" She giggled happily. "Mr. Braddock came back half an hour after you had left. He made such a rare old row that I came down again——"

"And shot him, I hope. No? A mistake, I think."

"Well, then he asked where you were. He said your name was Evans."

"He was a little confused. My name is Shotter. I warned you that he was not quite himself. What became of him then?"

"He went up to bed. I've just taken him up a tray, but all he did was to look at it and moan and shut his eyes again. I say, have you had any breakfast?"

"Don't torture me."

"Well, hop over the fence then. I'll get you some in two ticks."

Sam hopped. The sun seemed very bright now, and the birds were singing with a singular sweetness.

"Would it also run to a shave and a bath?" he asked, as they walked toward the house.

"You'll find Mr. Wrenn's shaving things in the bathroom."

"Is this heaven?" said Sam. "Shall I also find Mr. Wrenn by any chance?"

"Oh, no; him and Miss Kay have been gone half an hour."

"Excellent! Where is this bathroom?"

"Up those stairs, first door to the left. When you come down, go into that room there and I'll bring the tray in. It's the drawing-room, but the dining-room table isn't cleared yet."

"I shall enjoy seeing your drawing-room, of which I have heard so much."

"Do you like eggs?"

"I do—and plenty of them. Also bacon—a good deal of bacon. Oh, and by the way——" added Sam, leaning over the banisters.

"Yes?"

"—— toast—lots and lots of toast."

"I'll get you all you can eat."

"You will? Tell me," said Sam, "it has been puzzling me greatly. How do you manage to get that dress on over your wings?"

CHAPTER X

SAM FINDS A PHOTOGRAPH

SAM, when he came downstairs some twenty minutes later, was definitely in what Mr. Hash Todhunter would have described as the pink. The night had been bad, but joy had certainly come in the morning. The sight of the breakfast tray on a small table by the window set the seal on his mood of well-being; and for a long, luxurious space he had eyes for nothing else. It was only after he had consumed the eggs, the bacon, the toast, the coffee and the marmalade that he yielded to what is usually the first impulse of a man who finds himself in a strange room and began to explore.

It was some half minute later that Claire Lippett, clearing the dining-room table, was startled to the extent of dropping a butter dish by a loud shout or cry that seemed to proceed from the room where she had left her guest.

Hurrying thither, she found him behaving in a strange

64

manner. He was pointing at a photograph on the mantelpiece and gesticulating wildly.

"Who's that?" he cried as she entered. He seemed to
have difficulty with his vocal cords.

"Eh?"

"Who the devil's that?"

"Language!"

"Who is it? That girl—who is she? What's her name?"

"You needn't shout," said Claire, annoyed.

The photograph which had so excited this young man
was the large one that stood in the centre of the mantelpiece. It represented a girl in hunting costume, standing
beside her horse, and it was Claire's favourite. A dashing
and vigorous duster, with an impressive record of smashed
china and broken glass to her name, she always handled
this particular work of art with a gentle tenderness.

"That?" she said. "Why, that's Miss Kay, of course."

She came forward and flicked a speck of dust off the
glass.

"Taken at Midways, that was," she said, "two or three
years ago, before the old colonel lost his money. I was
Miss Kay's maid then—personal maid," she added with
pride. She regarded the photograph wistfully, for it stood
to her for all the pomps and glories of a vanished yesterday, for the brave days when there had been horses and
hunting costumes and old red chimneys against a blue sky
and rabbits in the park and sunlight on the lake and all
the rest of the things that made up Midways and prosperity.
"I remember the day that photograph was took. It was
printed in the papers, that photograph was."

Sam continued to be feverish.

"Miss Kay? Who's Miss Kay?"

"Miss Kay Derrick, Mr. Wrenn's niece."

"The man who lives here, do you mean?"

"Yes. He gave Miss Kay a home when everything went smash. That's how I come to be here. I could have stopped at Midways if I'd of liked," she said. "The new people who took the place would have kept me on if I'd of wanted. But I said 'No,' I said. 'I'm going with Miss Kay,' I said. 'I'm not going to desert her in her mis-for-chewn,' I said."

Sam started violently.

"You don't mean—you can't mean—you don't mean she lives here?"

"Of course she does."

"Not actually lives here—not in this very house?"

"Certainly."

"My gosh!"

Sam quivered from head to foot. A stupendous idea had come to him.

"My gosh!" he cried again with bulging eyes. Then, with no more words—for it was a time not for words but for action—he bounded from the room.

To leap out of the front door and clatter down the steps to the board which stood against the fence was with Sam the work of a moment. Beneath the large letters of the To Let, Furnished, he now perceived other smaller letters informing all who might be interested that applications for the tenancy of that desirable semi-detached residence, Mon Repos, should be made to Messrs. Matters & Cornelius, House Agents, of Ogilvy Street, Valley Fields, S.E. He galloped up the steps again and beat wildly upon the door.

"Now what?" inquired Claire.

"Where is Ogilvy Street?"

"Up the road, first turning to the left."

"Thanks."

"You're welcome."

Out on the gravel he paused, pondered and returned.

66

"Back again?" said Claire.

"Did you say left or right?"

"Left."

"Thanks."

"Don't mention it," said Claire.

This time Sam performed the descent of the steps in a single leap. But reaching the gate, he was struck by a thought.

"Fond of exercise, aren't you?" said Claire patiently.

"Suddenly occurred to me," explained Sam, "that I'd got no money."

"What do you want me to do about it?"

"These house-agent people would expect a bit of money down in advance, wouldn't they?"

"Sounds possible. Are you going to take a house?"

"I'm going to take Mon Repos," said Sam. "And I must have money. Where's Mr. Braddock?"

"In bed."

"Where's his room?"

"Top floor back."

"Thanks."

"Dee-lighted," said Claire.

Her statement that the guest of the house was in bed proved accurate. Sam, entering the apartment indicated, found his old school friend lying on his back with open mouth and matted hair. He was snoring rhythmically. On a chair at his side stood a tray containing a teapot, toast and a cold poached egg of such raffish and leering aspect that Sam, moving swiftly to the dressing table, averted his eyes as he passed.

The dressing table presented an altogether more pleasing picture. Heaped beside Mr. Braddock's collar box and hair-brushes was a small mountain of notes and silver—a fascinating spectacle with the morning sunshine playing on them. With twitching fingers, Sam scooped them up; and finding pencil and paper, paused for a moment, seeking for words.

It is foolish to attempt to improve on the style of a master. Hash Todhunter had shown himself in a class of his own at this kind of literary composition, and Sam was content to take him as a model. He wrote:

"DEAR BRADDER: You will doubtless be surprised to learn that I have borrowed your money. I will return it in God's good time. Meanwhile, as Sir Philip Sidney said to the wounded soldier, my need is greater than yours.

"Trusting this finds you in the pink,
"Yrs. Obedtly,
"S. SHOTTER."

Then, having propped the note against the collar box, he left the room.

A sense of something omitted, some little kindly act forgotten, arrested him at the head of the stairs. He returned; and taking the poached egg, placed it gently on the pillow beside his friend's head. This done, he went downstairs again, and so out on the broad trail that led to the premises of Messrs. Matters & Cornelius, House Agents, of Ogilvy Street.

CHAPTER XI
SAM BECOMES A HOUSEHOLDER

WHAT Mr. Matters would have thought of Sam as he charged breezily into the office a few minutes later we shall never know, for Mr. Matters died in the year 1910. Mr. Cornelius thought him perfectly foul. After one swift, appraising stare through his gold-rimmed spectacles, he went so far as to share this opinion with his visitor.

"I never give to beggars," he said. He was a venerable old man with a white beard and bushy eyebrows, and he spoke with something of the intonation of a druid priest chanting at the altar previous to sticking the knife into the human sacrifice. "I do not believe in indiscriminate charity."

"I will fill in your confession book some other time," said Sam. "For the moment, let us speak of houses. I want to take Mon Repos in Burberry Road."

The druid was about to recite that ancient rune which consists of the solemn invocation to a policeman, when he observed with considerable surprise that his young visitor was spraying currency in great quantities over the table. He gulped. It was unusual for clients at his office to conduct business transactions in a manner more suitable to the Bagdad of the *Arabian Nights* than to a respectable modern suburb. He could hardly have been more surprised if camels laden with jewels and spices had paraded down Ogilvy Street.

"What is all this?" he asked, blinking.

"Money," said Sam.

"Where did you get it?"

He eyed Sam askance. And Sam, who, as the heady result of a bath, shave, breakfast and the possession of cash, had once more forgotten that there was anything noticeable about his appearance, gathered that here was another of the long line of critics who had failed to recognise his true worth at first sight.

"Do not judge me by the outer crust," he said. "I am shabby because I have been through much. When I stepped aboard the boat at New York I was as natty a looking young fellow as you could wish to see. People nudged one another as I passed along the pier and said, 'Who is he?'"

"You come from America?"

"From America."

"Ah!" said Mr. Cornelius, as if that explained every-thing.

"My uncle," said Sam, sensing the change in the atmo-sphere and pursuing his advantage, "is Mr. John B. Pynsent, the well-to-do millionaire, of whom you have doubtless heard. . . . You haven't? One of our greatest captains of industry. He made a vast fortune in fur."

"In fur? Really?"

"Got the concession for providing the snakes at the Bronx Zoo with earmuffs, and from that moment never looked back."

"You surprise me," said Mr. Cornelius. "Most inter-esting."

"A romance of commerce," agreed Sam. "And now, returning to this matter of the house——"

"Ah, yes," said Mr. Cornelius. His voice, as he eyed the money on the table, was soft and gentle. He still looked like a druid priest, but a druid priest on his afternoon off. "For how long a period did you wish to rent Mon Repos, Mr.—er——"

"Shotter is the name. . . . Indefinitely."

"Shall we say three months' rent in advance?"

"Let us say just those very words."

"And as to references——"

Sam was on the point of giving Mr. Wrenn's name, un-til he recollected that he had not yet met that gentleman. Using his shaving brush and razor and eating food from his larder seemed to bring them very close together. He reflected.

"Lord Tilbury," he said. "That's the baby."

"Lord Tilbury, of the Mammoth Publishing Company?" said Mr. Cornelius, plainly awed. "Do you know him?"

"Know him? We're more like brothers than anything. There's precious little Lord Tilbury ever does without consulting me. It might be a good idea to call him up on the phone now. I ought to let him know that I've arrived."

Mr. Cornelius turned to the telephone, succeeded after an interval in getting the number, and after speaking with various unseen underlings, tottered reverently as he found himself talking to the great man in person. He handed the instrument to Sam.

"His Lordship would like to speak to you, Mr. Shotter."

"I knew it, I knew it," said Sam. "Hello! Lord Tilbury? This is Sam. How are you? I've just arrived. I came over in a tramp steamer, and I've been having all sorts of adventures. Give you a good laugh. I'm down at Valley Fields at the moment, taking a house. I've given your name as a reference. You don't mind? Splendid! Lunch? Delighted. I'll be along as soon as I can. Got to get a new suit first. I slept in my clothes last night. . . . Well, good-bye. It's all right about the references," he said, turning to Mr. Cornelius. "Carry on."

"I will draw up the lease immediately, Mr. Shotter. If you will tell me where I am to send it——"

"Send it?" said Sam, surprised. "Why, to Mon Repos, of course."

"But——"

"Can't I move in at once?"

"I suppose so, if you wish it. But I fancy the house is hardly ready for immediate tenancy. You will need linen."

"That's all right. A couple of hours shopping will fix that."

Mr. Cornelius smiled indulgently. He was thoroughly pro-Sam by now.

"True American hustle," he observed, waggling his white beard. "Well, I see no objection, if you make a point of it. I will find the key for you. Tell me, Mr. Shotter," he asked as he rummaged about in drawers, "what has caused

this great desire on your part to settle in Valley Fields?
Of course, as a patriotic inhabitant, I ought not to be
surprised. I have lived in Valley Fields all my life, and
would not live anywhere else if you offered me a million
pounds."

"I won't."

"I was born in Valley Fields, Mr. Shotter, and I love
the place, and I am not ashamed to say so.

"'Breathes there the man with soul so dead,'" inquired
Mr. Cornelius, "'Who never to himself hath said, This is
my own, my native land! Whose heart hath ne'er within
him burn'd as home his footsteps he hath turn'd from
wandering on a foreign strand?'"

"Ah!" said Sam. "That's what we'd all like to know,
wouldn't we?"

"'If such there breathe,'" proceeded Mr. Cornelius,
"'go, mark him well! For him no minstrel raptures swell.
High though his titles, proud his name, boundless his wealth
as wish can claim, despite those titles, power and pelf, the
wretch, concentreed all in self——'"

"I have a luncheon engagement at 1.30," said Sam.

"'——Living, shall forfeit fair renown, and, doubly dying,
shall go down to the vile dust from whence he sprung,
unwept, unhonour'd and unsung.'

"Those words, Mr. Shotter——"

"A little thing of your own?"

"Those words, Mr. Shotter, will appear on the title page
of the history of Valley Fields, which I am compiling—a
history dealing not only with its historical associations, which
are numerous, but also with those aspects of its life which
my occupation as house agent has given me peculiar op-
portunities of examining. I get some queer clients, Mr.
Shotter."

Sam was on the point of saying that the clients got a

queer house agent, thus making the thing symmetrical, but he refrained from doing so.

"It may interest you to know that a very well-known criminal, a man who might be described as a second Charles Peace, once resided in the very house which you are renting."

"I shall raise the tone."

"Like Charles Peace, he was a most respectable man to all outward appearances. His name was Finglass. Nobody seems to have had any suspicion of his real character until the police, acting on information received, endeavoured to arrest him for the perpetration of a great bank robbery."

"Catch him?" said Sam, only faintly interested.

"No; he escaped and fled the country. But I was asking you what made you settle on Valley Fields as a place of residence. You would seem to have made up your mind very quickly."

"Well, the fact is, I happened to catch sight of my next-door neighbours, and it struck me that they would be pleasant people to live near."

Mr. Cornelius nodded.

"Mr. Wrenn is greatly respected by all who know him."

"I liked his razor," said Sam.

"If you are going to Tilbury House it is possible that you may meet him. He is the editor of Pyke's *Home Companion.*"

"Is that so?" said Sam. "Pyke's *Home Companion,* eh?"

"I take it in regularly."

"And Mr. Wrenn's niece? A charming girl, I thought."

"I scarcely know her," said Mr. Cornelius indifferently. "Young women do not interest me."

The proverb about casting pearls before swine occurred to Sam.

"I must be going," he said coldly. "Speed up that

lease, will you? And if anyone else blows in and wants to take the house, bat them over the head with the office ruler."

"Mr. Wrenn and I frequently play a game of chess together," said Mr. Cornelius.

Sam was not interested in his senile diversions.

"Good morning," he said stiffly, and passed out into Ogilvy Street.

CHAPTER XII
SAM IS MUCH TOO SUDDEN
§ 1

THE clocks of London were striking twelve when Sam, entering the Strand, turned to the left and made his way toward Fleet Street to keep his tryst with Lord Tilbury at the offices of the Mammoth Publishing Company.

In the interval which had elapsed since his parting from Mr. Cornelius a striking change had taken place in his appearance, for he had paid a visit to that fascinating shop near Covent Garden which displays on its door the legend, "Cohen Bros., Ready-Made Clothiers," and is the Mecca of all who prefer to pluck their garments ripe off the bough instead of waiting for them to grow. The kindly brethren had fitted him out with a tweed suit of bold pattern, a shirt of quality, underclothing, socks, a collar, sock suspenders, a handkerchief, a tie pin and a hat with the same swift and unemotional efficiency with which, had he desired it, they would have provided the full costume of an Arctic explorer, a duke about to visit Buckingham Palace, or a big-game hunter bound for Eastern Africa. Nor had they failed him in the matter of new shoes and a wanghee. It was, in short, an edition-de-luxe of S. Pynsent Shotter, richly bound and profusely illustrated, that now presented itself to the notice of the public.

The tonic effect of new clothes is recognised by all students of human nature. Sam walked with a springy jauntiness, and his gay bearing, combined with the brightness of his exterior, drew many eyes upon him.

Two of these eyes belonged to a lean and stringy man of mournful countenance who was moving in the opposite direction, away from London's newspaper land. For a moment they rested upon Sam in a stare that had something of dislike in it, as if their owner resented the intrusion upon his notice of so much cheerfulness. Then they suddenly widened into a stare of horror, and the man stopped, spellbound. A hurrying pedestrian, bumping into him from behind, propelled him forward, and Sam, coming up at four miles an hour, bumped into him in front. The result of the collision was a complicated embrace, from which Sam was extricating himself with apologies when he perceived that this person with whom he had become entangled was no stranger, but an old friend.

"Hash!" he cried.

There was nothing in Mr. Todhunter's aspect to indicate pleasure at the encounter. He breathed heavily and spoke no word.

"Hash, you old devil!" said Sam joyfully.

Mr. Todhunter licked his lips uncomfortably. He cast a swift glance over his shoulder, as if debating the practicability of a dive into the traffic. He endeavoured, without success, to loosen the grip of Sam's hand on his coat sleeve.

"What are you wriggling for?" asked Sam, becoming aware of this.

"I'm not wriggling," said Hash. He spoke huskily and in a tone that seemed timidly ingratiating. If the voice of Mr. Cornelius had resembled a druid priest's, Clarence Todhunter's might have been likened to that of the victim on

the altar. "I'm not wriggling, Sam. What would I want
to wriggle for?"

"Where did you spring from, Hash?"

Mr. Todhunter coughed.

"I was just coming from leaving a note for you, Sam, at
that place, Tilbury House, where you told me you'd be."

"You're a great letter-writer, aren't you?"

The allusion was not lost upon Mr. Todhunter. He
gulped and his breathing became almost stertorous.

"I want to explain about that, Sam," he said. "Explain, if I may use the term, fully. Sam," said Mr. Todhunter thickly, "what I say and what I always have said
is, when there's been a little misunderstanding between
pals—pals, if I may use the expression, what have stood
together side by side through thick and through thin—pals
what have shared and shared alike——" He broke off. He
was not a man of acute sensibility, but he could see that
the phrase, in the circumstances, was an unhappy one.
"What I say is, Sam, when it's like that—well, there's nothing like letting bygones be bygones and, so to speak,
burying the dead past. As a man of the world, you bein'
one and me bein' another——"

"I take it," said Sam, "from a certain something in
your manner, that that moth-eaten whippet of yours did
not win his race."

"Sam," said Mr. Todhunter, "I will not conceal it from
you. I will be frank, open and above board. That whippet
did not win."

"Your money then—and mine—is now going to support
some bookie in the style to which he has been accustomed?"

"It's gorn, Sam," admitted Mr. Todhunter in a deathbed
voice. "Yes, Sam, it's gorn."

"Then come and have a drink," said Sam cordially.

"A drink?"

"Or two."

He led the way to a hostelry that lurked coyly among shops and office buildings. Hash followed, marvelling. The first stunned horror had passed, and his mind, such as it was, was wrestling with the insoluble problem of why Sam, with the facts of the whippet disaster plainly before him, was so astoundingly amiable.

The hour being early even for a perpetually thirsty community like that of Fleet Street, the saloon bar into which they made their way was free from the crowds which would have interfered with a quiet chat between old friends. Two men who looked like printers were drinking beer in a corner, while at the counter a haughty barmaid was mixing a cocktail for a solitary reveller in a velours hat. This individual had just made a remark about the weather in a rich and attractive voice, and his intonation was so unmistakably American that Sam glanced at him as he passed; and, glancing, half stopped, arrested by something strangely familiar about the man's face.

It was not a face which anyone would be likely to forget if they had seen it often; and the fact that it brought no memories back to him inclined Sam to think that he could never have met this rather striking-looking person, but must have seen him somewhere on the street or in an hotel lobby. He was a handsome, open-faced man of middle age.

"I've seen that fellow before somewhere," he said, as he sat with Hash at a table by the window.

" 'Ave you?" said Hash, and there was such a manifest lack of interest in his tone that Sam, surprised at his curtness, awoke to the realisation that he had not yet ordered refreshment. He repaired the omission and Hash's drawn face relaxed.

"Hash," said Sam, "I owe you a lot."

"Me?" said Hash blankly.

"Yes. You remember that photograph I showed you?"

"The girl—Nimrod?"

"Yes. Hash, I've found her, and purely owing to you. If you hadn't taken that money it would never have happened."

Mr. Todhunter, though he was far from understanding, endeavoured to assume a simper of modest altruism. He listened attentively while Sam related the events of the night.

"And I've taken the house next door," concluded Sam, "and I move in to-day. So, if you want a shore job, the post of cook in the Shotter household is open. How about it?"

A sort of spasm passed across Hash's wooden features.

"You want me to come and cook?"

"I've got to get a cook somewhere. Can you leave the · ship?"

"Can I leave the ship? Mister, you watch and see how quick I can leave that ruddy ocean-going steam kettle! I've been wanting a shore job ever since I was cloth-head enough to go to sea."

"You surprise me," said Sam. "I have always looked on you as one of those tough old salts who can't be happy away from deep waters. I thought you sang chanteys in your sleep. Well, that's splendid. You had better go straight down to the house and start getting things fixed up. Here's the key. Write the address down—Mon Repos, Burberry Road, Valley Fields."

A sharp crash rang through the room. The man at the bar, who had finished his cocktail and was drinking a whisky and soda, had dropped his glass.

"'Ere!" exclaimed the barmaid, startled, a large hand on the left side of her silken bosom.

The man paid no attention to her cry. He was staring with marked agitation at Sam and his companion.

"How do I get there?" asked Hash.

"By train or bus—there's any number of ways."

"And I can go straight into the house?"

"Yes; I've taken it from this morning."

Sam hurried out. Hash, pausing to write down the address, became aware that he was being spoken to.

"Say, pardon me," said the fine-looking man, who was clutching at his sleeve. "Might I have a word with you, brother?"

"Well?" said Hash suspiciously. The last time an American had addressed him as brother it had cost him eleven dollars and seventy-five cents.

"Did I understand your pal who's gone out to say that he had rented a house named Mon Repos down in Valley Fields?"

"Yes, you did. What of it?"

The man did not reply. Consternation was writ upon his face, and he passed a hand feebly across his broad forehead. The silence was broken by the cold voice of the barmaid.

"That'll be threepence I'll kindly ask you for, for that glass," said the barmaid. "And if," she added with asperity, "you 'ad to pay for the shock you give me, it 'ud cost you a tenner."

"Girlie," replied the man sadly, watching Hash as he shambled through the doorway, "you aren't the only one that's had a shock."

§ 2

While Sam was walking down Fleet Street on his way to Tilbury House, thrilled with the joy of existence and swishing the air jovially with his newly purchased wanghee, in Tilbury House itself the proprietor of the Mammoth Publishing Company was pacing the floor of his private office, his thumbs in the armholes of his waistcoat, his eyes staring bleakly before him.

Lord Tilbury was a short, stout, commanding-looking man, and practically everything he did had in it something of the Napoleonic quality. His demeanour now suggested Napoleon in captivity, striding the deck of the *Bellerophon* with vultures gnawing at his breast.

So striking was his attitude that his sister, Mrs. Frances Hammond, who had called to see him, as was her habit when business took her into the neigbourhood of Tilbury House, paused aghast in the doorway, while the obsequious boy in buttons who was ushering her in frankly lost his nerve and bolted.

"Good gracious, Georgie!" she cried. "What's the matter?"

His Lordship came to a standstill and something faintly resembling relief appeared in his square-cut face. Ever since the days when he had been plain George Pyke, starting in business with a small capital and a large ambition, his sister Frances had always been a rock of support. It might be that her advice would help him to cope with the problem which was vexing him now.

"Sit down, Francie," he said. "Thank goodness you've come. Just the person I want to talk to."

"What's wrong?"

"I'm telling you. You remember that when I was in America I met a man named Pynsent?"

"Yes."

"This man Pynsent was the owner of an island off the coast of Maine."

"Yes, I know. And you——"

"An island," continued Lord Tilbury, "densely covered with trees. He used it merely as a place of retirement, for the purpose of shooting and fishing; but when he invited me there to spend a week-end I saw its commercial possibilities in an instant."

"Yes, you told me. You————"

"I said to myself," proceeded Lord Tilbury, one of whose less engaging peculiarities it was that he never permitted the fact that his audience was familiar with a story to keep him from telling it again, "I said to myself, 'This island, properly developed, could supply all the paper the Mammoth needs and save me thousands a year!' It was my intention to buy the place and start paper mills."

"Yes, and————"

"Paper mills," said Lord Tilbury firmly. "I made an offer to Pynsent. He shilly-shallied. I increased my offer. Still he would give me no definite answer. Sometimes he seemed willing to sell, and then he would change his mind. And then, when I was compelled to leave and return to England, an idea struck me. He had been talking about his nephew and how he was anxious for him to settle down and do something————"

"So you offered to take him over here and employ him in the Mammoth," said Mrs. Hammond with a touch of impatience. She loved and revered her brother, but she could not conceal it from herself that he sometimes tended to be prolix. "You thought it would put him under an obligation."

"Exactly. I imagined I was being shrewd. I supposed that I was introducing into the affair just that little human touch which sometimes makes all the difference. Well, it will be a bitter warning to me never again to be too clever. Half the business deals in this world are ruined by one side or the other trying to be too clever."

"But, George, what has happened? What is wrong?"

Lord Tilbury resumed his patrol of the carpet.

"I'm telling you. It was all arranged that he should

sail back with me on the *Mauretania,* but when the vessel
left he was nowhere to be found. And then, about the
second day out, I received a wireless message saying, 'Sorry
not to be with you. Coming *Araminta.* Love to all.' I
could not make head or tail of it."

"No," said Mrs. Hammond thoughtfully; "it is very
puzzling. I think it may possibly have meant———"

"I know what it meant—now. The solution," said Lord
Tilbury bitterly, "was vouchsafed to me only an hour ago
by the boy himself."

"Has he arrived then?"

"Yes, he has arrived. And he travelled on a tramp
steamer."

"A tramp steamer! But why?"

"Why? Why? How should I know why? Last night,
he informed me, he slept in his clothes."

"Slept in his clothes? Why?"

"How should I know why? Who am I to analyse the
motives of a boy who appears to be a perfect imbecile?"

"But have you seen him?"

"No. He rang up on the telephone from the office of
a house agent in Valley Fields. He has taken a house there
and wished to give my name as a reference."

"Valley Fields? Why Valley Fields?"

"Don't keep on saying why," cried Lord Tilbury tem-
pestuously. "Haven't I told you a dozen times that I don't
know why—that I haven't the least idea why?"

"He does seem an eccentric boy."

"Eccentric? I feel as if I had allowed myself to be saddled
with the guardianship of a dancing dervish. And when
I think that if this young idiot gets into any sort of trouble
while he is under my charge, Pynsent is sure to hold me
responsible, I could kick myself for ever having been fool
enough to bring him over here."

"You mustn't blame yourself, Georgie."

"It isn't a question of blaming myself. It's a question of Pynsent blaming me and getting annoyed and breaking off the deal about the island."

And Lord Tilbury, having removed his thumbs from the armholes of his waistcoat in order the more freely to fling them heavenward, uttered a complicated sound which might be rendered phonetically by the word "Cor!", tenser and more dignified than the "Coo!" of the lower-class Londoner, but expressing much the same meaning.

In the hushed silence which followed, the buzzer on the desk sounded.

"Yes? Eh? Oh, send him up." Lord Tilbury laid down the instrument and turned to his sister grimly. "Shotter is downstairs," he said. "Now you will be able to see him for yourself."

Mrs. Hammond's first impression when she saw Sam for herself was that she had been abruptly confronted with something in between a cyclone and a large Newfoundland puppy dressed in bright tweeds. Sam's mood of elation had grown steadily all the way down Fleet Street, and he burst into the presence of his future employer as if he had just been let off a chain.

"Well, how are you?" he cried, seizing Lord Tilbury's hand in a grip that drew from him a sharp yelp of protest.

Then, perceiving for the first time the presence of a fair stranger, he moderated his exuberance somewhat and stared politely.

"My sister, Mrs. Hammond," said Lord Tilbury, straightening his fingers.

Sam bowed. Mrs. Hammond bowed.

"Perhaps I had better leave you," said Mrs. Hammond. "You will want to talk together."

"Oh, don't go," said Sam hospitably.

"I have business in Lombard Street," said Mrs. Hammond, discouraging with a cold look what seemed to her, rightly or wrongly, a disposition on the part of this young man to do the honours and behave generally as if he were trying to suggest that Tilbury House was his personal property but that any relative of Lord Tilbury was welcome there. "I have to visit my bank."

"I shall have to visit mine pretty soon," said Sam, "or the wolf will be scratching at the door."

"If you are short of funds——" began Lord Tilbury.

"Oh, I'm all right for the present, thanks. I pinched close on fifty pounds from a man this morning."

"You did what?" said Lord Tilbury blankly.

"Pinched fifty pounds. Surprising he should have had so much on him. But lucky—for me."

"Did he make any objection to your remarkable behaviour?"

"He was asleep at the time, and I didn't wake him. I just left a poached egg on his pillow and came away."

Lord Tilbury swallowed convulsively and his eye sought that of Mrs. Hammond in a tortured glare.

"A poached egg?" he whispered.

"So that he would find it there when he woke," explained Sam.

Mrs. Hammond had abandoned her intention of withdrawing and leaving the two men together for a cosy chat. Georgie, it seemed to her from his expression, needed a woman's loving support. Sam appeared to have affected him like some unpleasant drug, causing starting of the eyes and twitching of the muscles.

"It is a pity you missed the *Mauretania*, Mr. Shotter," she said. "My brother had hoped that you would travel with him so that you could have a good talk about what you were to do when you joined his staff."

"Great pity," said Sam, omitting to point out that it was for that very reason that he had allowed the *Mauretania* to depart without him. "However, it's all right. I have found my niche."

"You have done what?"

"I have selected my life work." He pulled out of his pocket a crumpled paper. "I would like to attach myself to Pyke's *Home Companion*. I bought a copy on my way here, and it is the goods. You aren't reading the serial by any chance, are you—"Hearts Aflame," by Cordelia Blair? A winner. I only had time to glance at the current instalment, but it was enough to make me decide to dig up the back numbers at the earliest possible moment. In case you haven't read it, it is Leslie Mordyke's wedding day, and a veiled woman with a foreign accent has just risen in the body of the church and forbidden the banns. And," said Sam warmly, "I don't blame her. It appears that years ago——"

Lord Tilbury was making motions of distress, and Mrs. Hammond bent solicitously, like one at a sick bed, to catch his fevered whisper.

"My brother," she announced, "wishes——"

"—was hoping," corrected Lord Tilbury.

"—was hoping," said Mrs. Hammond, accepting the emendation, "that you would join the staff of the *Daily Record* so that you might be under his personal eye."

Sam caught Lord Tilbury's personal eye, decided that he had no wish to be under it and shook his head.

"The *Home Companion,*" said Lord Tilbury, coming to life, "is a very minor unit of my group of papers."

"Though it has a large circulation," said Mrs. Hammond loyally.

"A very large circulation, of course," said Lord Tilbury; "but it offers little scope for a young man in your

position anxious to start on a journalistic career. It is not
—how shall I put it?—it is not a vital paper, not a paper
that really matters."

"In comparison with my brother's other papers," said
Mrs. Hammond.

"In comparison with my other papers, of course."

"I think you are wrong," said Sam. "I cannot imagine
a nobler life-work for any man than to help produce Pyke's
Home Companion. Talk about spreading sweetness and light,
why, Pyke's *Home Companion* is the paper that wrote the
words and music. Listen to this: 'A. M. B. (Brixton). You
ask me for a simple and inexpensive method of curing corns.
Get an ordinary swede, or turnip, cut and dig out a hole
in the top, fill the hole with common salt and allow to stand
till dissolved. Soften the corn morning and night with this
liquid.'"

"Starting on the reportorial staff of the *Daily Record,*"
said Lord Tilbury, "you would be in a position——"

"Just try to realise what that means," proceeded Sam.
"What it amounts to is that the writer of that paragraph
has with a stroke of the pen made the world a better place.
He has brightened a home. Possibly he has averted serious
trouble between man and wife. A. M. B. gets the ordinary
swede, digs out the top, pushes in the salt, and a week
later she has ceased to bully her husband and beat the
baby and is a ray of sunshine about the house—and all
through Pyke's *Home Companion.*"

"What my brother means——" said Mrs. Hammond.

"Similarly," said Sam, "with G. D. H. (Tulse Hill), who
wants to know how to improve the flavour of prunes. You
or I would say that the flavour of prunes was past pray-
ing for, that the only thing to do when cornered by a
prune was to set your teeth and get it over with. Not so
Pyke's——"

"He means——"

"—*Home Companion*. 'A little vinegar added to stewed prunes,' says the writer, 'greatly improves the flavour. And although it may seem strange, it causes less sugar to be used.' What happens? What is the result? G. D. H.'s husband comes back tired and hungry after a day's work. 'Prunes for dinner again, I suppose?' he says moodily. 'Yes, dear,' replies G. D. H., 'but of a greatly improved flavour.' Well, he doesn't believe her, of course. He sits down sullenly. Then, as he deposits the first stone on his plate, a delighted smile comes into his face. 'By Jove!' he cries. 'The flavour is greatly improved. They still taste like brown paper soaked in machine oil, but a much superior grade of brown paper. How did you manage it?' 'It was not I, dearest,' says G. D. H., 'but Pyke's *Home Companion*. Acting on their advice, I added a little vinegar, with the result that not only is the flavour greatly improved but, strange though it may seem, I used less sugar.' 'Heaven bless Pyke's *Home Companion!*' cries the husband. With your permission then," said Sam, "I will go straight to Mr. Wrenn and inform him that I have come to fight the good fight under his banner. 'Mr. Wrenn,' I shall say——"

Lord Tilbury was perplexed.

"Do you know Wrenn? How do you know Wrenn?"

"I have not yet had the pleasure of meeting him, but we are next-door neighbours. I have taken the house adjoining his. Mon Repos, Burberry Road, is the address. You can see for yourself how convenient this will be. Not only shall we toil all day in the office to make Pyke's *Home Companion* more and more of a force among the *intelligentsia* of Great Britain, but in the evenings, as we till our radishes, I shall look over the fence and say, 'Wrenn,' and Wrenn will say, 'Yes, Shotter?' And I shall say, 'Wrenn, how would it be to run a series on the eradication of pimples in canaries?' 'Shotter,' he will reply, dropping his spade in his enthusiasm, 'this is genius. 'Twas a lucky day, boy, for the old *Home Companion* when you came to us.' But I am wasting time. I should be about my business. Good-bye, Mrs. Hammond. Good-bye, Lord Tilbury. Don't trouble to come with me. I will find my way."

He left the room with the purposeful step of the man of affairs, and Lord Tilbury uttered a sound which was almost a groan.

"Insane!" he ejaculated. "Perfectly insane!"

Mrs. Hammond, womanlike, was not satisfied with simple explanation.

"There is something behind this, George!"

"And I can't do a thing," moaned His Lordship, chafing, as your strong man will, against the bonds of fate. "I simply must humour this boy, or the first thing I know he will be running off on some idiotic prank and Pynsent will be sending me cables asking why he has left me."

"There is something behind this," repeated Mrs. Hammond weightily. "It stands to reason. Even a boy like this young Shotter would not take a house next door to Mr. Wrenn the moment he landed unless he had some motive. George, there is a girl at the bottom of this."

Lord Tilbury underwent a sort of minor convulsion. His eyes bulged and he grasped the arms of his chair.

"Good God, Francie! Don't say that! Pynsent took me aside before I left and warned me most emphatically to be careful how I allowed this boy to come in contact with——er——members of the opposite sex."

"Girls," said Mrs. Hammond.

"Yes, girls," said Lord Tilbury, as if pleasantly surprised at this neat way of putting it. "He said he had had trouble a year or so ago——"

"Mr. Wrenn must have a daughter," said Mrs. Hammond, pursuing her train of thought. "Has Mr. Wrenn a daughter?"

"How the devil should I know?" demanded His Lordship, not unnaturally irritated. "I don't keep in touch with the home life of every man in this building."

"Ring him up and ask him."

"I won't. I don't want my staff to think I've gone off my head. Besides, you may be quite wrong."

"I shall be extremely surprised if I am," said Mrs. Hammond.

Lord Tilbury sat gazing at her pallidly. He knew that Francie had a sixth sense in these matters.

§ 3

At about the moment when Sam entered the luxuriously furnished office of the Mammoth Publishing Company's proprietor and chief, in a smaller and less ornate room in the same building Mr. Matthew Wrenn, all unconscious of the good fortune about to descend upon him in the shape of the addition to his staff of a live and go-ahead young assistant, was seated at his desk, busily engaged in promoting the best interests of that widely read weekly, Pyke's *Home Companion*. He was, in fact, correcting the proofs of an article—ably written, but too long to quote here— entitled What a Young Girl Can Do in Her Spare Time; Number 3, Bee Keeping.

He was interrupted in this task by the opening of the door, and looking up, was surprised to see his niece, Kay Derrick.

"Why, Kay!" said Mr. Wrenn. She had never visited him at his office so early as this, for Mrs. Winnington-Bates expected her serfs to remain on duty till at least four o'clock. In her blue eyes, moreover, there was a strange glitter that made him subtly uneasy. "Why, Kay, what are you doing here?"

Kay sat down on the desk. Having ruffled his grizzled hair with an affectionate hand, she remained for a while in silent meditation.

"I hate young men!" she observed at length. "Why isn't everyone nice and old—I mean elderly, but frightfully well preserved, like you, darling?"

"Is anything the matter?" asked Mr. Wrenn anxiously.

"Nothing much. I've left Mrs. Bates."

"I'm very glad to hear it, my dear. There is no earthly reason why you should have to waste your time slaving———"

"You're worse than Claire," said Kay, her eyes ceasing to glitter. "You both conspire to coddle me. I'm young and strong, and I ought to be earning my living. But," she went on, tapping his head with her finger to emphasise her words, "I will not continue in a job which involves being kissed by worms like Claude Bates. No, no, no, sir!"

Mr. Wrenn raised a shocked and wrathful face.

"He kissed you?"

"Yes. You had an article in the *Home Companion* last week, uncle, saying what a holy and beautiful thing the first kiss is. Well, Claude Bates' wasn't. He hadn't shaved and he was wearing a dressing gown. Also, he was pallid and greenish, and looked as if he had been out all night. Anything less beautiful and holy I never saw."

"He kissed you! What did you do?"

"I hit him very hard with a book which I was taking to read to Mrs. Bates. It was the Rev. Aubrey Jerningham's *Is There a Hell?* and I'll bet Claude thought there was. Until then I had always rather disliked Mrs. Bates' taste in literature, which shows how foolish I was. If she had preferred magazines, where would I have been? There were about six hundred pages of Aubrey Jerningham, bound in stiff cloth, and he blacked Claude's eye like a scholar and a gentleman. And at that moment in came Mrs. Bates."

"Yes?" said Mr. Wrenn, enthralled.

"Well, a boy's best friend is his mother. Have you ever seen one of those cowboy films where there is trouble in the bar-room? It was like that. Mrs. Bates started to dismiss me, but I got in first with my resignation, shooting from the hip, as it were. And then I came away, and here I am."

"The fellow should be horsewhipped," said Mr. Wrenn breathing heavily.

"He isn't worth bothering about," said Kay.

The riot of emotion into which she had been plunged by the addresses of the unshaven Bates had puzzled her. But now she understood. It was galling to suppose so monstrous a thing, but the explanation was, she felt, that there had been condescension in his embrace. If she had been Miss Derrick of Midways, he would not have summoned up the nerve to kiss her in a million years; but his mother's secretary and companion had no terrors for him. And at the thought a deep thrill of gratitude to the Rev. Aubrey Jerningham passed through Kay. How many a time, wearied by his duties about the parish, must that excellent clergyman have been tempted to scamp his work and shirk the labour of adding that extra couple of thousand words which just make all the difference to literature when considered in the light of a missile.

But he had been strong. He had completed his full six hundred pages and seen to it that his binding had been heavy and hard and sharp about the edges. For a moment, as she sat there, the Rev. Aubrey Jerningham seemed to Kay the one bright spot in a black world.

She was still meditating upon him when there was a hearty smack on the door and Sam came in.

"Good morning, good morning," he said cheerily.

And then he saw Kay, and on the instant his eyes widened into a goggling stare, his mouth fell open, his fingers clutched wildly at nothing, and he stood there, gaping.

Kay met his stare with a defiant eye. In her present mood she disliked all young men, and there seemed nothing about this one to entitle him to exemption from her loathing. Rather, indeed, the reverse, for his appearance jarred upon her fastidious taste.

If the Cohen Bros., of Covent Garden, have a fault, it is that they sometimes allow their clients to select clothes that are a shade too prismatic for anyone who is not at the same time purchasing a banjo and a straw hat with a crimson ribbon. Fittings take place in a dimly lit interior, with the result that suits destined to make phlegmatic horses shy in the open street seem in the shop to possess merely a rather pleasing vivacity. One of these Sam had bought, and it had been a blunder on his part. If he had intended to sing comic songs from a punt at Henley Regatta, he would have been suitably, even admirably, attired. But as a private gentleman he was a little on the bright side. He looked, in fact, like a bookmaker who won billiard tournaments, and Kay gazed at him with repulsion.

He, on the other hand, gazed at her with a stunned admiration. That photograph should have prepared him for something notable in the way of feminine beauty; but it seemed to him, as he raked her with eyes like small dinner plates, that it had been a libel, an outrage, a gross caricature. This girl before him was marvellous. Helen of Troy could have been nothing to her. He loved her shining eyes, unaware that they shone with loathing. He worshipped her rose-flushed cheeks, not knowing that they were flushed because he had been staring at her for thirty-three seconds without blinking and she was growing restive beneath his gaze.

Mr. Wrenn was the first to speak.

"Did you want anything?" he asked.

"What?" said Sam.

"Is there anything I can do for you?"

"Eh?"

Mr. Wrenn approached the matter from a fresh angle.

"This is the office of Pyke's *Home Companion*. I am Mr. Wrenn, the editor. Did you wish to see me?"

"Who?" said Sam.

At this point Kay turned to the window, and the withdrawal of her eyes had the effect of releasing Sam from his trance. He became aware that a grey-haired man, whom he dimly remembered having seen on his entry into the room some hours before, was addressing him.

"I beg your pardon?"

"You wished to see me?"

"Yes," said Sam; "yes, yes."

"What about?" asked Mr. Wrenn patiently.

The directness and simplicity of the question seemed to clear Sam's head. He recalled now what it was that had brought him here.

"I've come over from America to join the staff of Pyke's *Home Companion*."

"What!"

"Lord Tilbury wants me to."

"Lord Tilbury?"

"Yes; I've just been seeing him."

"But he has said nothing to me about this, Mr.———"

"———Shotter. No, we only arranged it a moment ago."

Mr. Wrenn was a courteous man, and though he was under the impression that the visitor was raving, he did not show it.

93

"Perhaps I had better see Lord Tilbury," he suggested rising. "By the way, my niece, Miss Derrick. Kay, my dear, Mr. Shotter."

The departure of the third party and the sudden institution of the intimacies of *tête-à-tête* had the usual effect of producing a momentary silence. Then Kay moved away from the window and came to the desk.

"Did you say you had come from America?" she asked, fiddling with Mr. Wrenn's editorial pencil. She had no desire to know, but she supposed she must engage this person in conversation.

"From America, yes. Yes, from America."

"Is this your first visit to England?" asked Kay, stifling a yawn.

"Oh, no. I was at school in England."

"Really? Where?"

"At Wrykyn."

Kay's attitude of stiff aloofness relaxed. She became interested.

"Good gracious! Of course!" She looked upon him quite benevolently. "A friend of yours was talking to me about you only yesterday—Willoughby Braddock."

"Do you know the Bradder?" gasped Sam, astounded.

"I've known him all my life."

A most extraordinary sensation flooded over Sam. It was hard to analyse, but its effects were thoroughly definite. At the discovery that this wonderful girl knew the old Bradder and that they could pave the way to a beautiful friendship by talking about the old Bradder, the office of Pyke's *Home Companion* became all at once flooded with brilliant sunshine. Birds twittered from the ceiling, and blended with their notes was the soft music of violins and harps.

"You really know the Bradder?"

"We were children together."

94

"What a splendid chap!"

"Yes, he's a dear."

"What a corker!"

"Yes!"

"What an egg!"

"Yes. Tell me, Mr. Shotter," said Kay, wearying of this eulogy, "do you remember a boy at your school named Bates?"

Sam's face darkened. Time had softened the anguish of that moment outside the Angry Cheese, but the sting still remained.

"Yes, I do."

"Willoughby Braddock told me that you once beat Bates with a walking stick."

"Yes."

"A large walking-stick?"

"Yes."

"Did you beat him hard?"

"Yes, as hard as ever I could lay it in."

A little sigh of gratification escaped Kay.

"Ah!" she said.

In the course of the foregoing conversation the two had been diminishing inch by inch the gap which had separated them at its outset, so that they had come to be standing only a short distance apart; and now, as she heard those beautiful words, Kay looked up into Sam's face with a cordial, congratulatory friendliness which caused him to quiver like a smitten blanc-mange. Then, while he was still reeling, she smiled. And it is at this point that the task of setting down the sequence of events becomes difficult for the historian.

For, briefly, what happened next was that Sam, groping forward in a bemused fashion and gathering her clumsily into his arms, kissed Kay.

§ 4

It might, of course, be possible to lay no stress upon this occurrence—to ignore it and pass on. In kissing, as kissing, there is nothing fundamentally reprehensible. The early Christians used to do it all the time to everyone they met. But the historian is too conscious of the raised eyebrows of his audience to attempt this attitude. Some explanation, he realises, some argument to show why Sam is not to be condemned out of hand, is imperative.

In these circumstances the embarrassing nature of the historian's position is readily intelligible. Only a short while back he was inviting the customers to shudder with loathing at the spectacle of Claude Bates kissing this girl, and now, all in a flash, he finds himself faced with the task of endeavouring to palliate the behaviour of Sam Shotter in doing the very same thing.

Well, he must do the best he can. Let us marshal the facts.

In the first place, there stood on Mr. Wrenn's desk, as on every other editorial desk in Tilbury House, a large framed card bearing the words, Do it Now! Who shall say whether this may not subconsciously have influenced the young man?

In the second place, when you have been carrying about a girl's photograph in your breast pocket for four months and brooding over it several times a day with a beating heart, it is difficult for you to regard that girl, when you eventually meet her, as a perfect stranger.

And in the third place—and here we approach the very root of the matter—there was the smile.

Girls as pretty as Kay Derrick, especially if their faces are by nature a little grave, should be extremely careful how and when they smile. There was that about Kay's

face when in repose which, even when she was merely
wondering what trimming to put on a hat, gave strangers
the impression that here was a pure white soul musing
wistfully on life's sadness. The consequence was that when
she smiled it was as if the sun had suddenly shone out
through clouds. Her smile seemed to make the world on
the instant a sweeter and a better place. Policemen, when
she flashed it on them after being told the way somewhere,'
became of a sudden gayer, happier policemen and sang as
they directed the traffic. Beggars, receiving it as a supplement to a small donation, perked up like magic and started
to bite the ears of the passers-by with an abandon that
made all the difference. And when they saw that smile
even babies in their perambulators stopped looking like
peevish poached eggs and became almost human.

And it was this smile that she had bestowed upon Sam.
And Sam, it will be remembered, had been waiting months
and months for it.

We have made out, we fancy, a pretty good case for
Samuel Shotter; and it was a pity that some kindly person
was not present in Mr. Wrenn's office at that moment to
place these arguments before Kay. For not one of them
occurred to her independently. She could see no excuse
whatever for Sam's conduct. She had wrenched herself
from his grasp and moved to the other side of the desk,
and across this she now regarded him with a blazing eye.
Her fists were clenched and she was breathing quickly.
She had the air of a girl who would have given a year's
pocket money for a copy of the Rev. Aubrey Jerningham's
Is There a Hell?

Gone was that delightful spirit of comradeship which,
when he had been telling of his boyish dealings with Claude,
had made him seem almost a kindred soul. Gone was
that soft sensation of gratitude which had come to her on

97

his assurance that he had not risked spoiling that repulsive youth by sparing the rod. All she felt now was that her first impressions of this young man had been right, and that she had been mauled and insulted by a black-hearted bounder whose very clothes should have warned her of his innate despicableness. It seems almost incredible that anyone should think such a thing of anybody, but it is a fact that in that instant Kay Derrick looked upon Sam as something even lower in the graduated scale of human sub-species than Claude Winnington-Bates.

As for Sam, he was still under the ether.

Nothing is more difficult for both parties concerned than to know what to say immediately after an occurrence like this. An agitated silence was brooding over the room, when the necessity for speech was removed by the re-entry of Mr. Wrenn.

Mr. Wrenn was not an observant man. Nor was he sensitive to atmosphere. He saw nothing unusual in his niece's aspect, nothing out of the way in Sam's. The fact that the air inside the office of Pyke's *Home Companion* was quivering with charged emotion escaped his notice altogether.

He addressed Sam genially.

"It is quite all right, Mr. Shotter. Lord Tilbury wishes you to start work on the *Companion* at once."

Sam turned to him with the vague stare of the newly awakened sleep-walker.

"It will be nice having you in the office," added Mr. Wrenn amiably. "I have been short-handed. By the way, Lord Tilbury asked me to send you along to him at once. He is just going out to lunch."

"Lunch?" said Sam.

"He said you were lunching with him."

"Oh, yes," said Sam dully.

98

Mr. Wrenn watched him shamble out of the room with a benevolent eye.

"We'll go and have a bite to eat too, my dear," he said, removing the alpaca coat which it was his custom to wear in the office. "Haven't had lunch with you since I don't know when." He reached for the hook which held his other coat. "I shall like having this young Shotter in the office," he said. "He seems a nice young fellow."

"He is the most utterly loathsome creature I have ever met," said Kay.

Mr. Wrenn, startled, dropped his hat.

"Eh? What do you mean?"

"Just what I say. He's horrible."

"But, my dear girl, you only met him five minutes ago."

"I know."

Mr. Wrenn stooped for his hat and smoothed it with some agitation.

"This is rather awkward," he said.

"What is?"

"Your feeling like that about young Shotter."

"I don't see why. I don't suppose I shall ever meet him again."

"But you will. I don't see how it can be prevented. Lord Tilbury tells me that this young man has taken a lease of Mon Repos."

"Mon Repos!" Kay clutched at the desk. "You don't mean Mon Repos next door to us?"

"Yes; and it is so difficult to avoid one's next-door neighbours."

Kay's teeth met with a little click.

"It can be done," she said.

CHAPTER XIII

INTRODUCING A SYNDICATE

ACROSS the way from Tilbury House, next door to the massive annex containing the offices of *Tiny Folk, Sabbath Jottings, British Girlhood,* the *Boys' Adventure Weekly* and others of the more recently established of the Mammoth Publishing Company's periodicals, there stands a ramshackle four-storeyed building of an almost majestic dinginess which Lord Tilbury, but for certain regulations having to do with ancient lights, would have swallowed up years ago, as he has swallowed the rest of the street.

The first three floors of this building are occupied by firms of the pathetic type which cannot conceivably be supposed to do any business, and yet hang on with dull persistency for decade after decade. Their windows are dirty and forlorn and most of the lettering outside had been worn away, so that on the second floor it would appear that trade is being carried on by the Ja— & Sum—r Rub— Co., while just above, Messrs. Smith, R-bi-s-n & G——, that mystic firm, are dealing in something curtly described as c——. It is not until we reach the fourth and final floor that we find the modern note struck.

Here the writing is not only clear and golden but, when read, stimulating to the imagination. It runs:

THE TILBURY DETECTIVE AGENCY, LTD.

J. SHERINGHAM ADAIR, Mgr.

Large and Efficient Staff

and conjures up visions of a suite of rooms filled with hawk-faced men examining bloodstains through microscopes or poring tensely over the papers connected with the singular affair of the theft of the maharajah's ruby.

On the morning, however, on which Sam Shotter paid his visit to Tilbury House, only one man was sitting in the office of the detective agency. He was a small and weedy individual clad in a suit brighter even than the one which Sam had purchased from the Brothers Cohen. And when it is stated in addition that he wore a waxed moustache and that his handkerchief, which was of coloured silk, filled the air with a noisome perfume, further evidence is scarcely required to convince the reader that he is being introduced to a most undesirable character. Nevertheless, the final damning fact may as well be revealed. It is this—the man was not looking out of window.

Tilbury Street is very narrow and the fourth-floor windows of this ramshackle building are immediately opposite those of the fourth floor of Tilbury House. Alexander Twist therefore was in a position, if he pleased, to gaze straight into the private sanctum of the proprietor of the Mammoth Publishing Company and obtain the spiritual uplift which could hardly fail to result from the spectacle of that great man at work. Alone of London's millions of inhabitants, he had it in his power to watch Lord Tilbury pacing up and down, writing at his desk or speaking into the dictaphone who knows what terrific thoughts.

Yet he preferred to sit at a table playing solitaire—and, one is prepared to bet, cheating. One need not, one fancies, say more.

So absorbed was Mr. Twist in his foolish game that the fact that someone was knocking on the door did not at first penetrate his senses. It was only when the person outside, growing impatient, rapped the panel with some hard object which might have been the handle of a lady's parasol, that he raised his head with a start. He swept the cards into a drawer, gave his coat a settling tug and rose alertly. The knock sounded like business, and Mr. Twist, who was not only J. Sheringham Adair, Mgr., but the large and efficient staff as well, was not the man to be caught unprepared.

"Come in," he shouted.

With a quick flick of his hand he scattered a top dressing of important-looking papers about and was bending over these with a thoughtful frown when the door opened.

At the sight of his visitor he relaxed the preoccupied austerity of his demeanour. The new-comer was a girl in the middle twenties, of bold but at the moment rather sullen good looks. She had the bright hazel eyes which seldom go with a meek and contrite heart. Her colouring was vivid, and in the light from the window her hair gleamed with a sheen that was slightly metallic.

"Why, hello, Dolly," said Mr. Twist.

"Hello," said the girl moodily.

"Haven't seen you for a year, Dolly. Never knew you were this side at all. Take a seat."

The visitor took a seat.

"For the love of pop, Chimp," she said, eyeing him with a languid curiosity, "where did you get the fungus?"

Mr. Twist moved in candid circles, and the soubriquet Chimp—short for Chimpanzee, by which he was known not only to his intimates but to police officials in America who would have liked to become more intimate than they were —had been bestowed upon him at an early stage of his career in recognition of a certain simian trend which critics affected to see in the arrangement of his features.

"Looks good, don't you think?" he said, stroking his moustache fondly. It and money were the only things he loved.

"Anything you say. And I suppose, when you know

you may be in the coop any moment, you like to have all
the hair you can while you can."

Mr. Twist felt a little wounded. He did not like badinage about his moustache. He did not like tactless allu-
sions to the coop. And he was puzzled by the unwonted
brusqueness of the girl's manner. The Dora Gunn he had
known had been a cheery soul, quite unlike this tight-lipped,
sombre-eyed person now before him.

The girl was looking about her. She seemed perplexed.

"What's all this?" she asked, pointing her parasol at
the writing on the window.

Mr. Twist smiled indulgently, and with a certain pride.
He was, he flattered himself, a man of ideas, and this of
presenting himself to the world as a private investigator he
considered one of his happiest.

"Just camouflage," he said. "Darned useful to have a
label. Keeps people from asking questions."

"It won't keep me from asking questions. That's what
I've come for. Say, can you tell the truth without straining
a muscle?"

"You know me, Dolly."

"Yes, that's why I asked. Well, I've come to get you
to tell me something. Nobody listening?"

"Not a soul."

"How about the office boy?"

"I haven't got an office boy. Who do you think I am
—Pierpont Morgan?"

Thus reassured, the girl produced a delicate handkerchief, formerly the property of Harrod's Stores and parted
from unwittingly by that establishment.

"Chimp," she said, brushing away a tear, "I'm sim'ly
miserable."

Chimp Twist was not the man to stand idly by while
beauty in distress wept before him. He slid up and was

placing an arm about her shoulder, when she jerked away.

"You can tie a can to that stuff," she said with womanly dignity. "I'd like you to know I'm married."

"Married?"

"Sure. Day before yesterday—to Soapy Molloy."

"Soapy!" Mr. Twist started. "What in the world did you want to marry that slab of Gorgonzola for?"

"I'll ask you kindly, if you wouldn't mind," said the girl in a cold voice, "not to go alluding to my husband as slabs of Gorgonzola."

"He is a slab of Gorgonzola."

"He is not. Well, anyway, I'm hoping he's not. It's what I come here to find out."

Mr. Twist's mind had returned to the perplexing matter of the marriage.

"I don't get this," he said. "I saw Soapy a couple of weeks back and he didn't say he'd even met you."

"He hadn't then. We only run into each other ten days ago. I was walking up the Haymarket and I catch sight of a feller behind me out of the corner of my eye, so I faint on him, see?"

"You're still in that line, eh?"

"Well, it's what I do best, isn't it?"

Chimp nodded. Dora Molloy—Fainting Dolly to her friends—was unquestionably an artist in her particular branch of industry. It was her practice to swoon in the arms of rich-looking strangers in the public streets and pick their pockets as they bent to render her assistance. It takes all sorts to do the world's work.

"Well then I seen it was Soapy, and so we go to lunch and have a nice chat. I always was strong for that boy, and we were both feeling kind of lonesome over here in London, so we fix it up. And now I'm sim'ly miserable."

104

"What," inquired Mr. Twist, "is biting you?"

"Well, I'll tell you. This is what's happened: Last night this bird Soapy goes out after supper and doesn't blow in again till four in the morning. Four in the morning, I'll trouble you, and us only married two days. Well, if he thinks a young bride's going to stand for that sort of conduct right plumb spang in the middle of what you might call the honeymoon, he's got a second guess due him."

"What did you do?" asked Mr. Twist sympathetically, but with a touch of that rather unctuous complacency which bachelors display at moments like this.

"I did plenty. And he tried to alibi himself by pulling a story. That story the grand jury is now going to investigate and investigate good. . . . Chimp, did you ever hear of a man named Finglass?"

There was that in Mr. Twist's manner that seemed to suggest that he was a reluctant witness, but he answered after a brief hesitation.

"Sure!"

"Oh, you did, eh? Well, who was he then?"

"He was big," said Chimp, and there was a note of reverence in his voice. "One of the very biggest, old Finky was."

"How was he big? What did he ever do?"

"Well, it was before your time and it happened over here, so I guess you may not have heard of it; but he took a couple of million dollars from the New Asiatic Bank."

Mrs. Molloy was undeniably impressed. The formidable severity of her manner seemed to waver.

"Were you and Soapy mixed up with him?"

"Sure! We were the best pals he had."

"Is he alive?"

"No; died in Buenos Aires the other day."

Mrs. Molloy bit her lower lip thoughtfully.

"Say, it's beginning to look to me like that story of Soapy's was the goods after all. Listen, Chimp, I'd best tell you the whole thing. When I give Soapy the razz for staying out all night like the way he done, he pulled this long spiel about having had a letter from a guy he used to know named Finglass, written on his death-bed, saying that this guy Finglass hadn't been able to get away with the money he'd swiped from this New Asiatic Bank on account the bulls being after him, and he'd had to leave the whole entire lot of it behind, hidden in some house down in the suburbs somewheres. And he told Soapy where the house was, and Soapy claims that what kep' him out so late was he'd been searching the house, trying to locate the stuff. And what I want to know is, was he telling the truth or was he off somewheres at one of these here new gilded night clubs, cutting up with a bunch of janes and doing me wrong?"

Again Mr. Twist seemed to resent the necessity of acting as a favourable witness for a man he obviously disliked. He struggled with his feelings for a space.

"Yes, it's true," he said at length.

"But listen here. This don't seem to me to gee up. If this guy Finglass wanted Soapy to have the money, why did he wait all this time before telling him about it?"

"Thought he might find a chance of sneaking back and getting it himself, of course. But he got into trouble in Argentina almost as soon as he hit the place, and they stowed him away in the cooler; and he only got out in time to write the letters and then make his finish."

"How do you know all that?"

"Finky wrote to me too."

"Oh, did he? Well, then, here's another thing that don't seem to make sense: When he did finally get round to telling Soapy about this money, why couldn't he let him

Sam the Sudden

know where it was? I mean, why didn't he say it's under the mat or poked up the chimney or something, 'stead of leaving him hunt for it like he was playing button, button, where's the button—or something?"

"Because," said Mr. Twist bitterly, "Soapy and me were both pals of his, and he wanted us to share. And to make sure we should get together he told Soapy where the house was and me where the stuff was hidden in the house."

"So you've only to pool your info' to bring home the bacon?" cried Dolly, wide-eyed.

"That's all."

"Then why in time haven't you done it?"

Mr. Twist snorted. It is not easy to classify snorts, but this was one which would have been recognised immediately by any expert as the snort despairing, caused by the contemplation of the depths to which human nature can sink.

"Because," he said, "Soapy, the pig-headed stiff, thinks he can double-cross me and get it alone."

"What?" Mrs. Molloy uttered a cry of wifely pride. "Well, isn't that bright of my sweet old pie-face! I'd never of thought the dear boy would have had sense to think up anything like that."

Mr. Twist was unable to share her pretty enthusiasm.

"A lot it's going to get him!" he said sourly.

"Two million smackers it's going to get him," retorted Dolly.

"Two million smackers nothing! The stuff's hidden in a place where he'd never think of looking in two million years."

"You can't bluff me, Chimp Twist," said Dolly, gazing at him with the cold disdain of a princess confronted with a boll weevil. "If he keeps on looking, it stands to reason——"

She broke off. The door had opened and a man was entering, a fine, handsome, open-faced man of early middle age. At the sight of this person Chimp Twist's eyes narrowed militantly, but Dolly flung herself into his arms with a remorseful cry.

"Oh, Soapy, darling! How I misjudged you!"

The new-comer had had the air of a man weighed down with the maximum amount of sorrow that a human being can bear. This demonstration, however, seemed to remove something of the burden.

"'S all right, sweetness," he said, clasping her to his swelling bosom.

"Was I mean to my angel-face?"

"There, there, honey lamb!"

Chimp Twist looked sourly upon this nauseating scene of marital reconciliation.

"Ah, cut it out!" he growled.

"Chimp's told me everything, baby doll," proceeded Mrs. Molloy. "I know all about that money, and you just keep right along, precious, hunting for it by yourself. I don't mind how often you stay out nights or how late you stay out."

It was a generous dispensation, for which many husbands would have been grateful, but Soapy Molloy merely smiled a twisted, tortured smile of ineffable sadness.

"It's all off, honey bunch," he said, shaking his head. "It's cold, petty. We'll have to let Chimp in on it after all, sweetie-pie. I came here to put my cards on the table and have a show-down."

A quivering silence fell upon the room. Mrs. Molloy was staring at her husband, aghast. As for Chimp, he was completely bewildered. The theory that his old comrade had had a change of heart—that his conscience, putting in some rapid work after getting off to a bad start, had caused him to regret his intention of double-crossing a friend—was too bizarre to be tenable. Soapy Molloy was not the sort of man to have changes of heart. Chimp, in his studies of the motion-picture drama, had once seen a film where a tough egg had been converted by hearing a church organ, but he knew Mr. Molloy well enough to be aware that all the organs in all the churches in London might play in his ear simultaneously without causing him to do anything more than grumble at the noise.

"The house has been taken," said Soapy despondently.

"Taken? What do you mean?"

"Rented."

"Rented? When?"

"I heard this morning. I was in a saloon down Fleet Street way, and two fellows come in and one of them was telling the other how he'd just rented this joint."

Chimp Twist uttered a discordant laugh.

"So that's what's come of your darned smooth double-crossing act!" he said nastily. "Yes, I guess you better had let Chimp in on it. You want a man with brains now, not a guy that never thought up anything smarter than gypping suckers with phony oil stock."

Mr. Molloy bowed his head meekly before the blast. His wife was made of sterner stuff.

"You talk a lot, don't you?" she said coldly.

"And I can do a lot," retorted Mr. Twist, fingering his waxed moustache. "So you'd best come clean, Soapy, and have a show-down, like you say. Where is this joint?"

"Don't you dare tell him before he tells you where the stuff is!" cried Mrs. Molloy.

"Just as you say," said Chimp carelessly. He scribbled a few words on a piece of paper and covered them with his hand. "There! Now you write down your end of it and Dolly can read them both out."

"Have you really thought up a scheme?" asked Mr. Molloy humbly.

109

"I've thought up a dozen."

Mr. Molloy wrote in his turn and Dolly picked up the two papers.

"In the cistern!" she read.

"And the rest of it?" inquired Mr. Twist pressingly.

"Mon Repos, Burberry Road," said Mr. Molloy.

"Ah!" said Chimp. "And if I'd known that a week ago we'd have been worth a million dollars apiece by now."

"Say, listen," said Dolly, who was pensive and had begun to eye Mr. Twist in rather an unpleasant manner. "This stuff old Finglass swiped from the bank, what is it?"

"American bearer securities, sweetie," said her husband, rolling the words round his tongue as if they were vintage port. "As good as dollar bills. What's the dope you've thought up, Chimpie?" he asked, deferentially removing a piece of fluff from his ally's coat sleeve.

"Just a minute!" said Dolly sharply. "If that's so, how can this stuff be in any cistern? It would have melted or something, being all that time in the water."

"It's in a waterproof case, of course," said Chimp.

"Oh, it is, is it?"

"What's the matter, petty?" inquired Mr. Molloy. "You're acting strange."

"Am I? Well, if you want to know, I'm wondering if this guy is putting one over on us. How are we to know he's telling us the right place?"

"Dolly!" said Mr. Twist, deeply pained.

"Dolly!" said Mr. Molloy, not so much pained as apprehensive. He had a very modest opinion of his own chances of thinking of any plan for coping with the situation which had arisen, and everything, it seemed to him, depended upon being polite to Chimp Twist, who was admittedly a man of infinite resource and sagacity.

"If you think that of me——" began Mr. Twist.

"We don't, Chimpie, we don't," interrupted Mr. Molloy hastily. "The madam is a little upset. Don't listen to her. What is this scheme of yours, Chimpie?"

Perhaps Mrs. Molloy's estimate of her husband's talents as a strategist resembled his own. At any rate, she choked down certain words that had presented themselves to her militant mind and stood eyeing Chimp inquiringly.

"Well, I'll tell you," said Chimp. "But first let's get the business end straight. How do we divvy?"

"Why, fifty-fifty, Chimp," stammered Mr. Molloy, stunned at the suggestion implied in his words that any other arrangement could be contemplated. "Me and the madam counting as one, of course."

Chimp laughed sardonically.

"Fifty-fifty nothing! I'm the brains of this concern, and the brains of a concern always get paid highest. Look at Henry Ford! Look at the Archbishop of Canterbury!"

"Do you mean to say," demanded Dolly, "that if Soapy was sitting in with the Archbishop of Canterbury on a plan for skinning a sucker the archbish wouldn't split Even Stephen?"

"It isn't like that at all," retorted Mr. Twist with spirit. "It's more as if Soapy went to the archbishop and asked him to slip him a scheme for skinning the mug."

"Well, in that case," said Mr. Molloy, "I venture to assert that the archbishop would simply say to me, 'Molloy,' he'd say——"

Dolly wearied of a discussion which seemed to her too academic for the waste of valuable moments.

"Sixty-forty," she said brusquely.

"Seventy-thirty," emended Chimp.

"Sixty-five-thirty-five," said Mr. Molloy.

"Right!" said Chimp. "And now I'll tell you what to do. I'll give you five minutes first to see if you can think of it for yourself, and if you can't, I'll ask you not to start beefing because it's so simple and not worth the money."

Five minutes' concentrated meditation produced no brain wave in Mr. Molloy, who, outside his chosen profession of selling valueless oil stock to a trusting public, was not a very gifted man.

"Well, then," said Chimp, "here you are: You go to that fellow who's taken the joint and ask him to let you buy it off him."

"Well, of all the fool propositions!" cried Dolly shrilly, and even Mr. Molloy came near to sneering.

"Not so good, you don't think?" continued Chimp, uncrushed. "Well, then, listen here to the rest of it. Dolly calls on this fellow first. She acts surprised because her father hasn't arrived yet."

"Her what?"

"Her father. Then she starts in vamping this guy all she can. If she hasn't lost her pep since she last tried that sort of thing, the guy ought to be in pretty good shape for Act Two by the time the curtain rings up. That's when you blow in, Soapy."

"Am I her father?" asked Mr. Molloy, a little blankly.

"Sure, you're her father. Why not?"

Mr. Molloy, who was a little sensitive about the difference in age between his bride and himself, considered that Chimp was not displaying his usual tact, but muttered something about greying himself up some at the temples.

"Then what?" asked Dolly.

"Then," said Chimp, "Soapy does a spiel."

Mr. Molloy brightened. He knew himself to be at his best when it came to a spiel.

"Soapy says he was born in this joint—ages and ages ago."

"What do you mean—ages and ages ago?" said Mr. Molloy starting.

"Ages and ages ago," repeated Chimp firmly, "before he had to emigrate to America and leave the dear old place to be sold. He has loving childhood recollections of the lawn where he played as a kiddy, and worships every brick in the place. All his favourite relations pegged out in the rooms upstairs, and all like that. Well, I'm here to say," concluded Chimp emphatically, "that if that guy has any sentiment in him, and if Dolly has done the preliminary work properly, he'll drop."

There was a tense silence.

"It'll work," said Soapy.

"It might work," said Dolly, more doubtfully.

"It will work," said Soapy. "I shall be good. I will have that lobster weeping into his handkerchief inside three minutes."

"A lot depends on Dolly," Chimp reminded him.

"Don't you worry about that," said the lady stoutly. "I'll be good too. But listen here: I've got to dress this act. This is where I have to have that hat with the bird-of-paradise feather that I see in Regent Street this morning."

"How much?" inquired the rest of the syndicate in a single breath.

"Eighteen guineas."

"Eighteen guineas!" said Chimp.

"Eighteen guineas!" said Soapy.

They looked at each other wanly, while Dolly, unheeded, spoke of ships and ha'porths of tar.

"And a new dress," she continued. "And new shoes and a new parasol and new gloves and new——"

"Have a heart, petty," pleaded Mr. Molloy. "Exercise a little discretion, sweetness."

Dolly was firm.

"A girl," she said, "can't do herself justice in a tacky lid. You know that. And you know as well as I do that the first thing a gentleman does is to look at a dame's hoofs. And as for gloves, I simply beg you to cast an eye on these old things I've got on now, and ask your-selves——"

"Oh, all right, all right," said Chimp.

"All right," echoed Mr. Molloy.

Their faces were set grimly. These men were brave, but they were suffering.

CHAPTER XIV
THE CHIRRUP

MR. WRENN looked up from his plate with a sudden start, a wild and febrile glare of horror in his eyes. Old theatre-goers, had any such been present, would have been irresistibly reminded by his demeanour of the late Sir Henry Irving in "The Bells."

It was breakfast time at San Rafael; and, as always at this meal, the air was charged with an electric unrest. It is ever thus at breakfast in the suburbs. The spectre of a fleeting train broods over the feast, turning normally placid men into temporary neuropaths. Meeting Mr. Wrenn in Fleet Street after lunch, you would have set him down as a very pleasant, quiet, elderly gentleman, rather on the mild side. At breakfast, Bengal tigers could have picked up hints from him.

"Zatawittle?" he gasped, speaking in the early morning patois of Suburbia, which is the English language filtered through toast and marmalade.

"Of course, it wasn't a whistle, darling," said Kay soothingly. "I keep telling you you've lots of time."

Partially reassured, Mr. Wrenn went on with his meal.
He finished his toast and reached for his cup.

"Wassatie?"

"Only a quarter-past."

"Sure your washrah?"

"I put it right yesterday."

At this moment there came faintly from afar a sweet,
musical chiming.

"There's the college clock striking the quarter," said Kay.

Mr. Wrenn's fever subsided. If it was only a quarter-
past he was on velvet. He could linger and chat for a
while. He could absolutely dally. He pushed back his
chair and lighted a cigarette with the air of a leisured man.

"Kay, my dear," he said, "I've been thinking—about
this young fellow Shotter."

Kay jumped. By an odd coincidence, she had herself
been thinking of Sam at that moment. It annoyed her to
think of Sam, but she constantly found herself doing it.

"I really think we ought to invite him to dinner one
night."

"No!"

"But he seems so anxious to be friendly. Only yesterday
he asked me if he could drop round some time and borrow
the garden roller. He said he understood that that was
always the first move in the suburbs toward establishing
good neighbourly relations."

"If you ask him to dinner I shall go out."

"I can't understand why you dislike him so much."

"Well, I just do."

"He seems to admire you tremendously."   .

"Does he?"

"He keeps talking about you—asking what you were
like as a child and whether you ever did your hair differently and things of that kind."

115

"Oh!"

"I rather wish you didn't object to him so much. I should like to see something of him out of office hours. I find him a very pleasant fellow myself, and extremely useful in the office. He has taken that Aunt Ysobel page off my hands. You remember how I used to hate having to write that?"

"Is that all he does?"

Mr. Wrenn chuckled.

"By no means," he said amusedly.

"What are you laughing at?"

"I was thinking," explained Mr. Wrenn, "of something that happened yesterday. Cordelia Blair called to see me with one of her usual grievances——"

"Oh, no!" said Kay sympathetically. Her uncle, she knew, was much persecuted by female contributors who called with grievances at the offices of Pyke's *Home Companion;* and of all these gifted creatures, Miss Cordelia Blair was the one he feared most. "What was the trouble this time?"

"Apparently the artist who is illustrating *Hearts Aflame* had drawn Leslie Mordyke in a lounge suit instead of dress clothes."

"Why don't you bite these women's heads off when they come bothering you? You shouldn't be so nice to them."

"I can't, my dear," said Mr. Wrenn plaintively. "I don't know why it is, but the mere sight of a woman novelist who is at all upset seems to take all the heart out of me. I sometimes wish I could edit some paper like *Tiny Tots* or *Our Feathered Chums.* I don't suppose indignant children come charging in on Mason or outraged canaries on Mortimer. . . . But I was telling you—When I heard her voice in the outer office, I acquainted this young fellow Shotter briefly with the facts, and he most nobly volunteered to go out and soothe her."

"I can't imagine him soothing anyone."

"Well, he certainly had the most remarkable effect on Miss Blair. He came back ten minutes later to say that all was well and that she had gone away quite happy."

"Did he tell you how he managed it?"

"No." Another chuckle escaped Mr. Wrenn. "Kay, it isn't possible—you don't imagine—you don't suppose he could conceivably, on such a very slight acquaintance, have kissed her, do you?"

"I should think it very probable."

"Well, I'm bound to own——"

"Don't laugh in that horrible ghoulish way, uncle!"

"I can't help it. I could see nothing, you understand, as I was in the inner office; but there were most certainly sounds that suggested——"

Mr. Wrenn broke off. Again that musical chiming had come faintly to his ears. But this time its effect was the reverse of soothing. He became a thing of furious activity. He ran to and fro, seizing his hat and dropping it, picking it up and dropping his brief case, retrieving the brief case and dropping his stick. By the time he had finally shot out of the front door with his hat on his head, his brief case in his hand and his stick dangling from his arm, it was as if a tornado had passed through the interior of San Rafael, and Kay, having seen him off, went out into the garden to try to recover.

It was a pleasant, sunny morning, and she made for her favourite spot, the shade of the large tree that hung over the edge of the lawn, a noble tree, as spreading as that which once sheltered the Village Blacksmith. Technically, this belonged to Mon Repos, its roots being in the latter's domain; but its branches had grown out over the

fence, and San Rafael, with that injustice which is so marked
a feature of human affairs, got all the benefit of its shade.

Seated under this, with a gentle breeze ruffling her hair,
Kay gave herself up to meditation.

She felt worried and upset and in the grip of one of
her rare moods of despondency. She had schooled herself
to pine as little as possible for the vanished luxury of
Midways, but when she did so pine it was always at this
time of the day. For although she had adjusted herself with
almost complete success to the conditions of life at San
Rafael, she had not yet learned to bear up under the
suburban breakfast.

At Midways the meal had been so leisurely, so orderly,
so spacious, so redolent of all that is most delightful in the
country life of the wealthy; a meal of soft murmurs and
rustling papers, of sunshine falling on silver in the summer,
of crackling fires in winter; a take-your-time meal; a thing
of dignity and comfort. Breakfast at San Rafael was a mere
brutish bolting of food, and it jarred upon her afresh each
morning.

The breeze continued to play in her hair. Birds hopped
upon the grass. Some one down the road was using a lawn
mower. Gradually the feeling of having been jolted and
shaken by some rude force began to pass from Kay, and
she was just reaching the stage where, re-establishing connection with her sense of humour, she would be able to
look upon the amusing side of the recent scramble, when
from somewhere between earth and heaven there spoke a
voice.

"Oo-oo!" said the voice.

Kay was puzzled. Though no ornithologist, she had
become reasonably familiar with the distinctive notes of
such of our feathered chums as haunted the garden of San
Rafael, and this did not appear to be one of them.

118

"I see you," proceeded the voice lovingly. "How's your pore head, dearie?"

The solution of the mystery presented itself at last. Kay raised her eyes and beheld, straddled along a branch almost immediately above her, a lean, stringy man of ruffianly aspect, his naturally unlovely face rendered additionally hideous by an arch and sentimental smile. For a long instant this person goggled at her, and she stared back at him. Then, with a gasp that sounded confusedly apologetic, he scrambled back along the branch like an anthropoid ape, and dropping to earth beyond the fence, galloped blushingly up the garden.

Kay sprang to her feet. She had been feeling soothed, but now a bubbling fury had her in its grip. It was bad enough that outcasts like Sam Shotter should come and camp themselves next door to her. It was bad enough that they should annoy her uncle, a busy man, with foolish questions about what she had been like as a child, and whether she had ever done her hair differently. But when their vile retainers went to the length of climbing trees and chirruping at her out of them, the situation, it seemed to her, passed beyond the limit up to which a spirited girl may reasonably be expected to endure.

She returned to the house, fermenting, and as she reached the hall the front door-bell rang.

Technically, when the front door-bell of San Rafael rang, it was Claire Lippett's duty to answer it; but Claire was upstairs making beds. Kay stalked across the hall, and, having turned the handle, found confronting her a young woman of spectacular appearance, clad in gorgeous raiment and surmounted by a bird-of-paradise-feathered hat so much too good for her that Kay's immediate reaction of beholding it was one of simple and ignoble jealousy. It was the sort of hat she would have liked to be able to

afford herself, and its presence on the dyed hair of another
cemented the prejudice which that other's face and eyes
had aroused within her.

"Does a guy named Shotter live here?" asked the visitor.
Then, with the air of one remembering a part and with
almost excessive refinement, "Could I see Mr. Shotter, if
you please?"

"Mr. Shotter lives next door," said Kay frostily.

"Oh, thank yaw. Thank yaw so much."

"Not at all," said Kay.

She shut the door and went into the drawing-room.
The feeling of being in a world bounded north, east, south
and west by Sam Shotter had thoroughly poisoned her day.

She took pen, ink and paper and wrote viciously for a
few moments.

"Claire," she called.

"'Ullo!" replied a distant voice.

"I'm leaving a note on the hall table. Will you take
it next door some time?"

"Right-ho!" bellowed the obliging Miss Lippett.

CHAPTER XV

VISITORS AT MON REPOS

SAM was preparing to leave for the office when his
visitor arrived. He had, indeed, actually opened the front
door.

"Mr. Shottah?"

"Yes," said Sam. He was surprised to see Mrs. Molloy.
He had not expected visitors at so early a period of his
tenancy. This, he supposed, must be the suburban equivalent
of the county calling on the new-comer. Impressed by the
hat, he assumed Dolly to be one of the old aristocracy of

Valley Fields. A certain challenging jauntiness in her bearing forbade the suspicion that she was collecting funds for charity. "Won't you come in?"

"Thank yaw. Thank yaw so much. The house agent told me your name."

"Cornelius?"

"Gink with a full set of white whiskers. Say, somebody ought to put that baby wise about Gillette's wonderful invention of the safety razor."

Sam agreed that this might be in the public interest, but he began to revise his views about the old aristocracy.

"I'm afraid you'll find the place in rather a mess," he said apologetically, leading the way to the drawing-room. "I've only just moved in."

The visitor replied that, on the contrary, she thought it cute.

"I seem to know this joint by heart," she said. "I've heard so much about it from old pop."

"I don't think I am acquainted with Mr. Popp."

"My father, I mean. He used to live here when he was a tiny kiddy."

"Really? I should have taken you for an American."

"I am American, and don't let anyone tell you different."

"I won't."

"One hundred per cent., that's me."

Sam nodded.

" 'Oh, say, can you see by the dawn's early light?' " he said reverently.

" 'What so proudly'—I never can remember any more."

"No one," Sam reminded her, "knows the words but the Argentines . . ."

". . . And the Portuguese and the Greeks." The lady beamed. "Say, don't tell me you're American too!"

"My mother was."

"Why, this is fine! Pop'll be tickled to death."

"Is your father coming here too?"

"Well, I should say so! You don't think I pay calls on strange gentlemen all by myself, do you?" said the lady archly. "But listen! If you're American, we're sitting pretty, because it's only us Americans that's got real sentiment in them. Ain't it the truth?"

"I don't quite understand. Why do you want me to have sentiment?"

"Pop'll explain all that when he arrives. I'm surprised he hasn't blown in yet. I didn't think I'd get here first." She looked about her. "It seems funny to think of pop as a little kiddy in this very room."

"Your father was English then?"

"Born in England—born here—born in this very house. Just to think of pop playing all them childish games in this very room!"

Sam began to wish that she would stop. Her conversation was beginning to give the place a queer feeling. The room had begun to seem haunted by a peculiar being of middle-aged face and juvenile costume. So much that when she suddenly exclaimed "There's pop!" he had a momentary impression that a whiskered elder in Lord Fauntleroy clothes was about to dance out from behind the sofa.

Then he saw that his visitor was looking out of the window, and, following her gaze, noted upon the front steps a gentleman of majestic port.

"I'll go and let him in," he said.

"Do you live here all alone?" asked the lady, and Sam got the idea that she spoke eagerly.

"Oh, no. I've a man. But he's busy somewhere."

"I see," she said disappointedly.

The glimpse which Sam had caught of the new arrival through the window had been a sketchy one. It was only as he opened the door that he got a full view of him. And having done so, he was a little startled. It is always disconcerting to see a familiar face where one had expected a strange one. This was the man he had seen in the bar that day when he had met Hash in Fleet Street.

"Mr. Shotter?"

"Yes."

It seemed to Sam that the man had aged a good deal since he had seen him last. The fact was that Mr. Molloy, in greying himself up at the temples, had rather overdone the treatment. Still, though stricken in years, he looked a genial, kindly, honest soul.

"My name is Gunn, Mr. Shotter—Thomas G. Gunn."

It had been Mr. Molloy's intention—for he was an artist and liked to do a thing, as he said, properly—to adopt for this interview the pseudonym of J. Felkin Haggenbakker, that seeming to his critical view the sort of name a sentimental millionaire who had made a fortune in Pittsburgh and was now revisiting the home of his boyhood ought to have. The proposal had been vetoed by Dolly, who protested that she did not intend to spend hours of her time in unnecessary study.

"Won't you come in?" said Sam.

He stood aside to let his visitor pass, wondering again where it was that he had originally seen the man. He hated to forget a face and personality which should have been unforgettable. He ushered Mr. Gunn into the drawing-room, still pondering.

"So there you are, pop," said the lady. "Say, pop, isn't it dandy? Mr. Shotter's an American."

Mr. Gunn's frank eyes lit up with gratification.

"Ah! Then you are a man of sentiment, Mr. Shotter.

123

You will understand. You will not think it odd that a man should cherish all through his life a wistful yearning for the place where he was born."

"Not at all," said Sam politely, and might have reminded his visitor that the feeling, a highly creditable one, was shared by practically all America's most eminent song writers.

"Well, that is how I feel, Mr. Shotter," said the other bluffly, "and I am not ashamed to confess it. This house is very dear to me. I was born in it."

"So Miss Gunn was telling me."

"Ah, she has told you? Yes, Mr. Shotter, I am a man who has seen men and cities. I have lived in the hovels of the poor, I have risen till, if I may say so, I am welcomed in the palaces of the rich. But never, rich or poor, have I forgotten this old place and the childhood associations which hallow it."

He paused. His voice had trembled and sunk to a whisper in those last words, and now he turned abruptly and looked out of a window. His shoulders heaved significantly for an instant and something like a stifled sob broke the stillness of the room. But when a moment later he swung round he was himself again, the tough, sturdy old J. Felkin Haggenbakker—or, rather, Thomas G. Gunn —who was so highly respected, and perhaps a little feared, at the Rotary Club in Pittsburgh.

"Well, I must not bore you, Mr. Shotter. You are, no doubt, a busy man. Let me be brief. Mr. Shotter, I want this house."

"You want what?" said Sam, bewildered. He had had no notion that he was going to be swept into the maelstrom of a business transaction.

"Yes, sir, I want this house. And let me tell you that money is no object. I've lots of money." He dismissed

9*

money with a gesture. "I have my whims and I can pay for them. How much for the house, Mr. Shotter?"

Sam felt that it behoved him to keep his head. He had not the remotest intention of selling for all the gold in Pittsburgh a house which, in the first place, did not belong to him and, secondly, was next door to Kay Derrick.

"I'm very sorry——" he began.

Mr. Gunn checked him with an apologetic lift of the hand.

"I was too abrupt," he said. "I rushed the thing. A bad habit of mine. When I was prospecting in Nevada, the boys used to call me Hair-Trigger Gunn. I ought to have stated my position more clearly."

"Oh, I understand your position."

"You realise then that this isn't a house to me; it is a shrine?"

"Yes, yes; but——"

"It contains," said Mr. Gunn with perfect truth, "something very precious to me."

"Yes; but——"

"It is my boyhood that is enshrined here—my innocent, happy, halcyon boyhood. I have played games at my mother's knee in this very room. I have read tales from the Scriptures with her here. It was here that my mother, seated at the piano, used to sing—sing——"

His voice died away again. He blew his nose and turned once more to the window. But though he was under the impression that he had achieved a highly artistic aposiopesis, he could hardly have selected a more unfortunate word to stammer brokenly. Something resembling an electric thrill ran through Sam. Memory, dormant, had responded to the code word.

Sing Sing! He knew now where he had seen this man before.

It is the custom of the Welfare League of America's

most famous penitentiary to alleviate the monotony of the convict's lot by giving periodical performances of plays, produced and acted by the personnel of the prison. When the enterprising burglar isn't burgling, in fact, he is probably memorising the words of some popular lyric for rendition on the next big night.

To one of these performances, some eighteen months back, Sam had been taken by a newspaper friend. The hit of the evening had been this very Thomas G. Gunn, then a mere number, in the rôle of a senator.

Mr. Gunn had resumed his address. He was speaking once more of his mother, and speaking well. But he was not holding his audience. Sam cut in on his eloquence.

"I'm sorry," he said, "but I'm afraid this house is not for sale."

"But, Mr. Shotter——"

"No," said Sam. "I have a very special reason for wishing to stay here, and I intend to remain. And now I'm afraid I must ask you——"

"Suppose I look in this evening and take the matter up again?" pleaded Mr. Gunn, finding with some surprise that he had been edged out on to the steps and making a last stand there.

"It's no use. Besides, I shan't be in this evening. I'm dining out."

"Will anybody be in?" asked Miss Gunn suddenly, breaking a long silence.

"Why, yes," said Sam, somewhat surprised, "the man who works here. Why?"

"I was only thinking that if we called he might show us over the place."

"Oh, I see. Well, good-bye."

"But, say now, listen——"

"Good-bye," said Sam.

126

He closed the door and made his way to the kitchen. Hash, his chair tilted back against the wall, was smoking a thoughtful pipe.

"Who was it, Sam?"

"Somebody wanting to buy the house. Hash, there's something fishy going on."

"Ur?"

"Do you remember me pointing out a man to you in that bar in Fleet Street?"

"Yes."

"Well, it was the same fellow. And do you remember me saying that I was sure I had seen him before somewhere?"

"Yes."

"Well, I've remembered where it was. It was in Sing Sing, and he was serving a sentence there."

Mr. Todhunter's feet came to the floor with a crash.

"There's something darned peculiar about this house, Hash. I slept in it the night I landed, and there was a fellow creeping around with an electric torch. And now this man, whom I know to be a crook, puts up a fake story to make me let him have it. What do you think, Hash?"

"I'll tell you what I think," said Mr. Todhunter, alarmed. "I think I'm going straight out to buy a good watchdog."

"It's a good idea."

"I don't like these bad characters hanging about. I had a cousin in the pawnbroking line what was hit on the 'ead by a burglar with a antique vase. That's what happened to him, all through hearing a noise in the night and coming down to see what it was."

"But what's at the back of all this? What do you make of it?"

"Ah, there you have me," said Hash frankly. "But that don't alter the fact that I'm going to get a dog."

"I should. Get something pretty fierce."

"I'll get a dog," said Hash solemnly, "that'll feed on nails and bite his own mother."

CHAPTER XVI
ASTONISHING STATEMENT OF HASH TODHUNTER

§ 1

THE dinner to which Sam had been bidden that night was at the house of his old friend, Mr. Willoughby Braddock in John Street, Mayfair, and at ten minutes to eight Mr. Braddock was fidgeting about the morning room, interviewing his housekeeper, Mrs. Martha Lippett. His guests would be arriving at any moment, and for the last quarter of an hour, a-twitter with the nervousness of an anxious host, he had been popping about the place on a series of tours of inspection, as jumpy, to quote the words of Sleddon, his butler—whom, by leaping suddenly out from the dimly lit dining-room, he had caused to bite his tongue and nearly drop a tray of glasses—as an old hen. The general consensus of opinion below stairs was that Willoughby Braddock, in his capacity of master of the revels, was making a thorough pest of himself.

"You are absolutely certain that everything is all right, Mrs. Lippett?"

"Everything is quite all right, Master Willie," replied the housekeeper equably.

This redoubtable woman differed from her daughter Claire in being tall and thin and beaked like an eagle. One of the well-known Bromage family of Marshott-in-the-Dale, she had watched with complacent pride the Bromage nose developing in her sons and daughters, and it had always been a secret grief to her that Claire, her favourite,

128

who inherited so much of her forceful and determined character, should have been the only one of her children to take nasally after the inferior, or Lippett, side of the house. Mr. Lippett had been an undistinguished man, hardly fit to mate with a Bromage and certainly not worthy to be resembled in appearance by the best of his daughters.

"You're sure there will be enough to eat?"

"There will be ample to eat."

"How about drinks?" said Mr. Braddock, and was reminded by the word of a grievance which had been rankling within his bosom ever since his last expedition to the dining-room. He pulled down the corners of his white waistcoat and ran his finger round the inside of his collar. "Mrs. Lippett," he said, "I—er—I was outside the dining-room just now——"

"Were you, Master Willie? You must not fuss so. Everything will be quite all right."

"—and I overheard you telling Sleddon not to let me have any champagne to-night," said Mr. Braddock, reddening at the outrageous recollection.

The housekeeper stiffened.

"Yes, I did, Master Willie. And your dear mother, if she were still with us, would have given the very same instructions—after what my daughter Claire told me of what occurred the other night and the disgraceful condition you were in. What your dear mother would have said, I don't know!"

Mrs. Lippett's conversation during the last twenty years of Willoughby Braddock's life had dealt largely with speculations as to what his dear mother would have said of various ventures undertaken or contemplated by him.

"You must fight against the craving, Master Willie. Remember your Uncle George!"

Mr. Braddock groaned in spirit. One of the things that make these old retainers so hard to bear is that they are so often walking editions of the *chroniques scandaleuses* of the family. It sometimes seemed to Mr. Braddock that he could not move a step in any direction without having the awful example of some erring ancestor flung up against him.

"Well, look here," he said, with weak defiance, "I want champagne to-night."

"You will have cider, Master Willie."

"But I hate cider."

"Cider is good for you, Master Willie," said Mrs. Lippett firmly.

The argument was interrupted by the ringing of the door-bell. The housekeeper left the room, and presently Sleddon, the butler, entered, escorting Lord Tilbury.

"Ha, my dear fellow," said Lord Tilbury, bustling in.

He beamed upon his host as genially as the Napoleonic cast of his countenance would permit. He rather liked Willoughby Braddock, as he rather liked all very rich young men.

"How are you?" said Mr. Braddock. "Awfully good of you to come at such short notice."

"My dear fellow!"

He spoke heartily, but he had, as a matter of fact, been a little piqued at being invited to dinner on the morning of the feast. He considered that his eminence entitled him to more formal and reverential treatment. And though he had accepted, having had previous experience of the excellence of Mr. Braddock's cook, he felt that something in the nature of an apology was due to him and was glad that it had been made.

"I asked you at the last moment," explained Mr. Braddock, "because I wasn't sure till this morning that Sam

130

Shotter would be able to come. I thought it would be jolly for him, meeting you out of the office, don't you know."

Lord Tilbury inclined his head. He quite saw the force of the argument that it would be jolly for anyone, meeting him.

"So you know young Shotter?"

"Oh, yes. We were at school together."

"A peculiar young fellow."

"A great lad."

"But—er—a little eccentric, don't you think?"

"Oh, Sam always was a bit of nib," said Mr. Braddock. "At school there used to be some iron bars across the passage outside our dormitory, the idea being to coop us up during the night, don't you know. Sam used to shin over these and go downstairs to the house master's study."

"With what purpose?"

"Oh, just to sit."

Lord Tilbury was regarding his host blankly. Not a day passed, he was ruefully reflecting, but he received some further evidence of the light und unstable character of this young man of whom he had so rashly taken charge.

"It sounds a perfectly imbecile proceeding to me," he said.

"Oh, I don't know, you know," said Mr. Braddock, for the defence. "You see, occasionally there would be a cigar or a plate of biscuits or something left out, and then Sam would scoop them. So it wasn't altogether a waste of time."

Sleddon was entering with a tray.

"Cocktail?" said Mr. Braddock, taking one himself with a defiant glare at his faithful servant, who was trying to keep the tray out of his reach.

"No, I thank you," said Lord Tilbury. "My doctor has

temporarily forbidden me the use of alcoholic beverages. I have been troubled of late with a suspicion of gout."

"Tough luck."

"No doubt I am better without them. I find cider an excellent substitute. . . . Are you expecting many people here to-night?"

"A fairish number. I don't think you know any of them—except, of course, old Wrenn."

"Wrenn? You mean the editor of my *Home Companion?*"

"Yes. He and his niece are coming. She lives with him, you know."

Lord Tilbury started as if a bradawl had been thrust through the cushions of his chair; and for an instant, so powerfully did these words affect him, he had half a mind to bound at the receding Sleddon and, regardless of medical warnings, snatch from him that rejected cocktail. A restorative of some kind seemed to him imperative.

The statement by Mr. Wrenn, delivered in his office on the morning of Sam's arrival, that he possessed no daughter, had had the effect of relieving Lord Tilbury's mind completely. Francie, generally so unerring in these matters, had, he decided, wronged Sam in attributing his occupancy of Mon Repos to a desire to be next door to some designing girl. And now it appeared that she had been right all the time.

He was still staring with dismay at his unconscious host when the rest of the dinner guests began to arrive. They made no impression on his dazed mind. Through a sort of mist, he was aware of a young man with a face like a rabbit, another young man with a face like another rabbit; two small, shingled creatures, one blonde, the other dark, who seemed to be either wives or sisters of these young men; and an unattached female whom Mr. Braddock

132

addressed as Aunt Julia. His Lordship remained aloof, buried in his thoughts and fraternising with none of them.

Then Sam appeared, and a few moments later Sleddon announced Mr. Wrenn and Miss Derrick; and Lord Tilbury, who had been examining a picture by the window, swung round with a jerk.

In a less prejudiced frame of mind he might have approved of Kay; for, like so many other great men, he had a nice eye for feminine beauty, and she was looking particularly attractive in a gold dress which had survived the wreck of Midways. But now that very beauty merely increased his disapproval and alarm. He looked at her with horror. He glared as the good old father in a film glares at the adventuress from whose clutches he is trying to save his only son.

At this moment, however, something happened that sent hope and comfort stealing through his heart. Sam, who had been seized upon by Aunt Julia and had been talking restively to her for some minutes, now contrived by an adroit piece of side-stepping to remove himself from her sphere of influence. He slid swiftly up to Kay, and Lord Tilbury, who was watching her closely, saw her face freeze. She said a perfunctory word or two, and then, turning away, began to talk with great animation to one of the rabbit-faced young men. And Sam, with rather the manner of one who has bumped into a brick wall in the dark, drifted off and was immediately gathered in again by Aunt Julia.

A delightful sensation of relief poured over Lord Tilbury. In the days of his youth when he had attended subscription dances at the Empress Rooms, West Kensington, he had sometimes seen that look on the faces of his partners when he had happened to tread on their dresses. He knew its significance. Such a look could mean but one thing—

that Kay, though living next door to Sam, did not regard him as one of the pleasant features of the neighbourhood. In short, felt Lord Tilbury, if there was anything between these two young people, it was something extremely one-sided; and he went in to dinner with a light heart, prepared to enjoy the cooking of Mr. Braddock's admirable chef as it should be enjoyed.

When, on sitting at the table, he found that Kay was on his right, he was pleased, for he had now come to entertain a feeling of warm esteem for this excellent and sensible girl. It was his practice never to talk while he ate caviare; but when that had been consumed in a holy silence he turned to her, beaming genially.

"I understand you live at Valley Fields, Miss Derrick."

"Yes."

"A charming spot."

"Very."

"The college grounds are very attractive."

"Oh, yes."

"Have you visited the picture gallery?"

"Yes, several times."

Fish arrived—*sole meunière.* It was Lord Tilbury's custom never to talk during the fish course.

"My young friend Shotter is, I believe, a near neighbour of yours," he said, when the *sole meunière* was no more.

"He lives next door."

"Indeed? Then you see a great deal of him, no doubt?"

"I never see him."

"A most delightful young fellow," said Lord Tilbury, sipping cider.

Kay looked at him stonily.

"Do you think so?" she said.

Lord Tilbury's last doubts were removed. He felt that

all was for the best in the best of all possible worlds. Like some joyous reveller out of Rabelais, he raised his glass with a light-hearted flourish. He looked as if he were about to start a drinking chorus.

"Excellent cider, this, Braddock," he boomed genially. "Most excellent."

Willoughby Braddock, who had been eyeing his own supply of that wholesome beverage with sullen dislike, looked at him in pained silence; and Sam, who had been sitting glumly, listening without interest to the prattle of one of the shingled girls, took it upon himself to reply. He was feeling sad and ill used. That incident before dinner had distressed him. Moreover, only a moment ago he had caught Kay's eye for an instant across the table, and it had been cold and disdainful. He welcomed the opportunity of spoiling somebody's life, and particularly that of an old ass like Lord Tilbury, who should have been thinking about the hereafter instead of being so infernally hearty.

"I read a very interesting thing about cider the other day," he said in a loud, compelling voice that stopped one of the rabbit-faced young men in mid-anecdote as if he had been smitten with an axe. "It appears that the farmers down in Devonshire put a dead rat in every barrel——"

"My dear Shotter!"

"——to give it body," went on Sam doggedly. "And the curious thing is that when the barrels are opened, the rats are always found to have completely disappeared—which goes to show the power of the juice."

A wordless exclamation proceeded from Lord Tilbury. He lowered his glass. Mr. Braddock was looking like one filled with a sudden great resolution.

"I read it in Pyke's *Home Companion*," said Sam. "So it must be true."

"A little water, please," said Lord Tilbury stiffly.

"Sleddon," said Mr. Braddock in a voice of thunder, "give me some champagne."

"Sir?" quivered the butler. He cast a swift look over his shoulder, as if seeking the moral support of Mrs. Lippett. But Mrs. Lippett was in the housekeeper's room.

"Sleddon!"

"Yes, sir," said the butler meekly.

Sam was feeling completely restored to his usual sunny self.

"Talking of Pyke's *Home Companion*," he said, "did you take my advice and read that serial of Cordelia Blair's, Lord Tilbury?"

"I did not," replied His Lordship shortly.

"You should. Miss Blair is a very remarkable woman."

Kay raised her eyes.

"A great friend of yours, isn't she?" she said.

"I would hardly say that. I've only met her once."

"But you got on very well with her, I heard."

"I think I endeared myself to her pretty considerably."

"So I understood."

"I gave her a plot for a story," said Sam.

One of the rabbit-faced young men said that he could never understand how fellows—or women, for that matter —thought up ideas for stories—or plays, for the matter of that—or, as a matter of fact, any sort of ideas, for that matter.

"This," Sam explained, "was something that actually happened—to a friend of mine."

The other rabbit-faced young man said that something extremely rummy had once happened to a pal of his. He had forgotten what it was, but it had struck him at the time as distinctly rummy.

"This fellow," said Sam, "was fishing up in Canada. He lived in a sort of shack."

"A what?" asked the blonde shingled girl.

"A hut. And tacked up on the wall of the shack was a photograph of a girl, torn out of an illustrated weekly paper."

"Pretty?" asked the dark shingled girl.

"You bet she was pretty," said Sam devoutly. "Well, this man spent weeks in absolute solitude, with not a soul to talk to—nothing, in fact, to distract his mind from the photograph. The consequence was that he came to look on this girl as—well, you might say an old friend."

"Sleddon," said Mr. Braddock, "more champagne."

"Some months later," proceeded Sam, "the man came over to England. He met the girl. And still looking on her as an old friend, you understand, he lost his head and, two minutes after they had met, he kissed her."

"Must have been rather a soppy kind of a silly sort of idiot," observed the blonde shingled girl critically.

"Perhaps you're right," agreed Sam. "Still, that's what happened."

"I don't see where the story comes in," said one of the rabbit-faced young men.

"Well, naturally, you see, not realising the true state of affairs, the girl was very sore," said Sam.

The rabbit-faced young men looked at each other and shook their heads. The shingled young women raised their eyebrows pityingly.

"No good," said the blonde shingled girl.

"Dud," said the dark shingled girl. "Who's going to believe nowadays that a girl is such a chump as to mind a man's kissing her?"

"Everybody kisses everybody nowadays," said one of the rabbit-faced young men profoundly.

"Girl was making a fuss about nothing," said the other rabbit-faced young man.

"And how does the story end?" asked Aunt Julia.

"It hasn't ended," said Sam. "Not yet."

"Sleddon!" said Mr. Braddock, in a quiet, dangerous voice.

§ 2

It is possible, if you are young and active and in an exhilarated frame of mind, to walk from John Street, Mayfair, to Burberry Road, Valley Fields. Sam did so. His frame of mind was extraordinarily exhilarated. It seemed to him, reviewing recent events, that he had detected in Kay's eyes for an instant a look that resembled the first dawning of spring after a hard winter; and, though not in the costume for athletic feats, he covered the seven miles that separated him from home at a pace which drew derisive comment from the proletariat all along the route. The Surrey-side Londoner is always intrigued by the spectacle of anyone hurrying, and when that person is in dress clothes and a tall hat he expresses himself without reserve.

Sam heard nothing of this ribaldry. Unconscious of the world, he strode along, brushing through Brixton, hurrying through Herne Hill, and presently arrived, warm and happy, at the door of Mon Repos.

He let himself in; and, entering, was aware of a note lying on the hall table.

He opened it absently. The handwriting was strange to him, and feminine:

"DEAR MR. SHOTTER,—I should be much obliged if you would ask your manservant not to chirrup at me out of trees.   "Yours truly,
                                    "KAY DERRICK."

He had to read this curt communication twice before he was able fully to grasp its meaning. When he did so a flood of self-pity poured over Sam. He quivered with commiseration for the hardness of his lot. Here was he, doing all that a man could to establish pleasant neighbourly relations with the house next door, and all the while Hash foiling his every effort by chirruping out of trees from morning till night. It was bitter, bitter.

He was standing there, feeding his surging wrath by a third perusal of the letter, when from the direction of the kitchen there suddenly sounded a long, loud, agonised cry. It was like the wail of a soul in torment; and without stopping to pick up his hat, which he had dropped in the sheer shock of this dreadful sound, he raced down the stairs.

"'Ullo," said Hash, looking up from an evening paper. "Back?"

His placidity amazed Sam. If his ears were any guide, murder had been done in this room only a few seconds before, and here was this iron man reading the racing news without having turned a hair.

"What on earth was that?"

"What was what?"

"That noise."

"Oh, that was Amy," said Hash.

Sam's eye was diverted by movement in progress in the shadows behind the table.

A vast shape was rising from the floor, revealing itself as an enormous dog. It finished rising; and having placed its chin upon the table, stood looking at him with dreamy eyes and a wrinkled forehead, like a shortsighted person trying to recall a face.

"Oh, yes," said Sam, remembering. "So you got him?"

"Her."

"What is he—she?"

"Gawd knows," said Hash simply. It was a problem

139

which he himself had endeavoured idly to solve earlier in the evening. "I've named her after an old aunt of mine. Looks a bit like her."

"She must be an attractive woman."

"She's dead."

"Perhaps it's all for the best," said Sam. He leaned forward and pulled the animal's ears in friendly fashion. Amy simpered in a ladylike way, well pleased. "Would you say she was a bloodhound, Hash?"

"I wouldn't say she was anything, not to swear to."

"A kind of canine cocktail," said Sam. "The sort of thing a Cruft's Show judge dreams about when he has a nightmare."

He observed something lying on the floor; and stooping, found that his overtures to the animal had caused Kay's note to slip from his fingers. He picked it up and eyed Hash sternly. Amy, charmed by his recent attentions, snuffled like water going down the waste pipe of a bath.

"Hash!" said Sam.

"'Ullo?"

"What the devil," demanded Sam forcefully, "do you mean by chirruping at Miss Derrick out of trees?"

"I only said oo-oo, Sam," pleaded Mr. Todhunter.

"You said what?"

"Oo-oo!"

"What on earth did you want to say oo-oo for?"

Much voyaging on the high seas had given Hash's cheeks the consistency of teak, but at this point something resembling a blush played about them.

"I thought it was the girl."

"What girl?"

"The maid. Clara, 'er name is."

"Well, why should you say oo-oo at her?"

Again that faint, fleeting blush coloured Hash's face. Before Sam's revolted eyes he suddenly looked coy.

"Well, it's like this: The 'ole thing is, we're engaged."

"What!"

"Engaged to be married."

"Engaged!"

"Ah!" said Mr. Todhunter. And once more that repellent smirk rendered his features hideous beyond even Nature's liberal specifications concerning them.

Sam sat down. This extraordinary confession had shaken him deeply.

"You're engaged?"

"Ah!"

"But I thought you disliked women."

"So I do—most of 'em."

Another aspect of the matter struck Sam. His astonishment deepened.

"But how did you manage it so soon?"

"Soon?"

"You can't have seen the girl more than about half a dozen times."

Still another mysterious point about this romance presented itself to Sam. He regarded the great lover with frank curiosity.

"And what was the attraction?" he asked. "That's what I can't understand."

"She's a nice girl," argued Hash.

"I don't mean in her; I mean in you. What is there about you that could make this misguided female commit such a rash act? If I were a girl, and you begged me for one little rose from my hair, I wouldn't give it to you."

"But——"

"No," said Sam firmly, "it's no use arguing; I just wouldn't give it to you. What did she see in you?"

"Oh, well——"

"It couldn't have been your looks—we'll dismiss that right away, of course. It couldn't have been your conversation or your intellect, because you haven't any. Then what was it?"

Mr. Todhunter smirked coyly.

"Oh, well, I've got a way with me, Sam—that's how it is."

"A way?"

"Ah!"

"What sort of way?"

"Oh, just a way."

"Have you got it with you now?"

"Naturally I wouldn't 'ave it with me now," said Hash.

"You keep it for special occasions, eh? Well, you haven't yet explained how it all happened."

Mr. Todhunter coughed.

"Well, it was like this, Sam: I see 'er in the garden, and I says 'Ullo!' and she says 'Ullo!' and then she come to the fence and then I come to the fence, and she says 'Ullo!' and I says 'Ullo!' and then I kiss her."

Sam gaped.

"Didn't she object?"

"Object? What would she want to object for? No, indeed! It seemed to break what you might call the ice, and after that everything got kind of nice and matey. And then one thing led to another—see what I mean?"

An aching sense of the injustice of things afflicted Sam.

"Well, it's very strange," he said.

"What's strange?"

"I mean, I knew a man—a fellow—who—er—kissed a girl when he had only just met her, and she was furious."

"Ah," said Hash, leaping instantly at a plausible solution, "but then 'e was probably a chap with a face like

142

Gawd'elpus and hair growing out of his ears. Naturally, no one wouldn't like 'aving some one like that kissing 'em."

Sam went upstairs to bed. Before retiring, he looked at himself in the mirror long and earnestly. He turned his head sideways so that the light shone upon his ears. He was conscious of a strange despondency.

§ 3

Kay lay in bed, thinking. Ever and anon a little chuckle escaped her. She was feeling curiously happy tonight. The world seemed to have become all of a sudden interesting and amusing. An odd, uncontrollable impulse urged her to sing.

She would not in any case have sung for long, for she was a considerate girl, and the recollection would soon have come to her that there were people hard by who were trying to get to sleep. But, as a matter of fact, she sang only a mere bar or two, for even as she began, there came a muffled banging on the wall—a petulant banging. Hash Todhunter loved his Claire, but he was not prepared to put up with this sort of thing. Three doughty buffets he dealt the wall with the heel of a number-eleven shoe.

Kay sang no more. She turned out the light and lay in the darkness, her face set.

Silence fell upon San Rafael and Mon Repos. And then, from somewhere in the recesses of the latter, a strange, bansheelike wailing began. Amy was homesick.

CHAPTER XVII
ACTIVITIES OF THE DOG AMY

THE day that followed Mr. Braddock's dinner party dawned on a world shrouded in wet, white fog. By eight o'clock, however, this had thinned to a soft, pearly veil that

hung clingingly to the tree tops and lingered about the
grass of the lawn in little spider-webs of moisture. And
when Kay Derrick came out into the garden, a quarter of
an hour later, the September sun was already beginning to
pierce the mist with hints of a wonderful day to come.

It was the sort of morning which should have bred
happiness and quiet content, but Kay had woken in a
mood of irritated hostility which fine weather could not
dispel. What had happened overnight had stung her to a
militant resentment, and sleep had not removed this.

Possibly this was because her sleep, like that of every
one else in the neighbourhood, had been disturbed and
intermittent. From midnight until two in the morning the
dog Amy had given a spirited imitation of ten dogs being
torn asunder by red-hot pincers. At two, Hash Todhunter
had risen reluctantly from his bed, and arming himself
with the number-eleven shoe mentioned in the previous
chapter, had reasoned with her. This had produced a
brief respite, but by a quarter to three large numbers of
dogs were once more being massacred on the premises of
Mon Repos, that ill-named house.

At three, Sam went down; and being a young man who
liked dogs, and saw their point of view, tried diplomacy.
This took the shape of the remains of a leg of mutton and
it worked like a charm. Amy finished the leg of mutton
and fell into a surfeited slumber, and peace descended on
Burberry Road.

Kay paced the gravel path with hard feelings, which
were not removed by the appearance a few moments later
of Sam, clad in flannels and a sweater. Sam, his back to
her and his face to the sun, began to fling himself about
in a forceful and hygienic manner; and Kay, interested in
spite of herself, came to the fence to watch him. She was
angry with him, for no girl likes to have her singing criti-

144

cised by bangs upon the wall; but, nevertheless, she could not entirely check a faint feeling of approval as she watched him. A country-bred girl, Kay liked men to be strong and of the open air; and Sam, whatever his moral defects, was a fine physical specimen. He looked fit and hard and sinewy.

Presently, in the course of a complicated movement which involved circular swinging from the waist, his eye fell upon her. He straightened himself and came over to the fence, flushed and tousled and healthy.

"Good morning," he said.

"Good morning," said Kay coldly. "I want to apologise, Mr. Shotter. I'm afraid my singing disturbed you last night."

"Good lord!" said Sam. "Was that you? I thought it was the dog."

"I stopped directly you banged on the wall."

"I didn't bang on any wall. It must have been Hash."

"Hash?"

"Hash Todhunter, the man who cooks for me—and, oh, yes, who chirrups at you out of trees. I got your note and spoke to him about it. He explained that he had mistaken you for your maid, Claire. It's rather a romantic story. He's engaged to her."

"Engaged!"

"That's just what I said when he told me, and in just that tone of voice. I was surprised. I gather, however, that Hash is what you would call a quick worker. He tells me he has a way with him. According to his story, he kissed her, and after that everything was nice and matey."

Kay flushed faintly.

"Oh!" she said.

"Yes," said Sam.

There was a silence. The San Rafael kitten, which had been playing in the grass, approached and rubbed a wet head against Kay's ankle.

145

"Well, I must be going in," said Kay. "Claire is in bed with one of her neuralgic headaches and I have to cook my uncle's breakfast."

"Oh, no, really? Let me lend you Todhunter."

"No, thanks."

"Perhaps you're wise. Apart from dry hash, he's a rotten cook."

"So is Claire."

"Really? What a battle of giants it will be when they start cooking for each other!"

"Yes."

Kay stooped and tickled the kitten under the ear, then walked quickly toward the house. The kitten, having subjected Sam to a long and critical scrutiny, decided that he promised little entertainment to an active-minded cat and galloped off in pursuit of a leaf. Sam sighed and went in to have a bath.

Some little time later, the back door of Mon Repos opened from within as if urged by some irresistible force, and the dog Amy came out to take the morning air.

Dogs are creatures of swiftly changing moods. Only a few hours before, Amy, in the grip of a dreadful depression caused by leaving the public-house where she had spent her girlhood—for, in case the fact is of interest to anyone, Hash had bought her for five shillings from the proprietor of the Blue Anchor at Tulse Hill—had been making the night hideous with her lamentations. Like Niobe, she had mourned and would not be comforted. But now, to judge from her manner and a certain jauntiness in her walk, she had completely resigned herself to the life of exile. She scratched the turf and sniffed the shrubs with the air of a lady of property taking a stroll round her estates. And when Hash, who did not easily forgive, flung an egg at her out of the kitchen window so that it burst before her on the gravel, she ate the remains light-heartedly, as one who feels that the day is beginning well.

The only flaw in the scheme of things seemed to her to consist in a lack of society. By nature sociable, she yearned for company, and for some minutes roamed the garden in quest of it. She found a snail under a laurel bush, but snails are reserved creatures, self-centred and occupied with their own affairs, and this one cut Amy dead, retreating into its shell with a frigid aloofness which made anything in the nature of camaraderie out of the question.

She returned to the path, and became interested in the wooden structure that ran along it. Rearing herself up to a majestic height and placing her paws on this, she looked over and immediately experienced all the emotions of stout Cortez when with eagle eyes he stared at the Pacific. It is not, indeed, too much to say that Amy at that moment felt like some watcher of the skies when a new planet swims into his ken; for not only was there a complete new world on the other side of this wooden structure, but on the grass in the middle of it was a fascinating kitten running round in circles after its tail.

Amy had seen enough. She would have preferred another dog to chat with; but failing that, a kitten made an admirable substitute. She adored kittens. At the Blue Anchor there had been seven, all intimate friends of hers, who looked upon her body as a recreation ground and her massive tail as a perpetual object of the chase. With a heave of her powerful hind legs, she hoisted herself over the fence and, descending on the other side like the delivery of half a ton of coal, bounded at the kitten, full of good feeling. And the kitten, after one brief, shocked stare, charged madly at the fence and scrambled up it into the branches of the tree from which Hash Todhunter had done his recent chirruping.

Amy came to the foot of the tree and looked up, perplexed. She could make nothing of this. It is not given to dogs any more than to men to see themselves as others see them, and it never occurred to her for an instant that there was in her appearance anything that might be alarming to a high-strung young cat. But a dog cannot have a bloodhound-Airedale father and a Great Dane-Labrador mother without acquiring a certain physique. The kitten, peering down through the branches, congratulated itself on a narrow escape from death and climbed higher. And at this point Kay came out into the garden.

"Hullo, dog," said Kay. "What are you doing here?"

Amy was glad to see Kay. She was a shortsighted dog and took her for the daughter of the host of the Blue Anchor who had been wont to give her her meals. She left the tree and galloped toward her. And Kay, who had been brought up with dogs from childhood and knew the correct procedure to be observed when meeting a strange one, welcomed her becomingly. Hash, hurrying out on observing Amy leap the fence, found himself a witness of what practically amounted to a feast of reason and a flow of soul. That is to say, Amy was lying restfully on her back with her legs in the air, and Kay was thumping her chest.

"I hope the dog is not annoying you, lady," said Hash in his best *preux-chevalier* manner.

Kay looked up and perceived the man who had chirruped at her from the tree. Having contracted to marry into San Rafael, he had ceased to be an alien and had become something in the nature of one of the family; so she smiled amiably at him, conscious the while of a passing wonder that Claire's heart should have been ensnared by one who, whatever his merits, was notably deficient in conventional good looks.

"Not at all, thank you," she said. "Is he your dog?"

"She," corrected Hash. "Yes, miss."

"She's a nice dog."

"Yes, miss," said Hash, but with little heartiness.

"I hope she won't frighten my kitten, though. It's out in the garden somewhere. I can hear it mewing."

Amy could hear the mewing too; and, still hopeful that an understanding might be reached, she at once proceeded to the tree and endeavoured to jump to the top of it. In this enterprise she fell short by some fifty feet, but she jumped high enough to send the kitten scrambling into the upper branches.

"Oh!" cried Kay, appreciating the situation.

Hash also appreciated the situation; and being a man of deeds rather than words, vaulted over the fence and kicked Amy in the lower ribbs. Amy, her womanly feelings wounded, shot back into her own garden, where she stood looking plaintively on with her forepaws on the fence. Treatment like this was novel to her, for at the Blue Anchor she had been something of a popular pet; and it seemed to her that she had fallen among tough citizens. She expressed a not unnatural pique by throwing her head back and uttering a loud, moaning cry like an ocean liner in a fog. Hearing which, the kitten, which had been in two minds about risking a descent, climbed higher.

"What shall we do?" said Kay.

"Shut up!" bellowed Hash. "Not you, miss," he hastened to add with a gallant smirk. "I was speaking to the dog." He found a clod of earth and flung it peevishly at Amy, who wrinkled her forehead thoughtfully as it flew by, but made no move. Amy's whole attitude now was that of one who has got a front-row seat and means to keep it. "The 'ole thing 'ere," explained Hash, "is that that there cat is scared to come down, bein' frightened of this 'ere dog."

And having cleared up what might otherwise have remained a permanent mystery, he plucked a blade of grass and chewed reflectively.

"I wonder," said Kay, with an ingratiating smile, "if you would mind climbing up and getting her."

Hash stared at her amazedly. Her smile, which was wont to have so much effect on so many people, left him cold. It was the silliest suggestion he had ever heard in his life.

"Me?" he said, marvelling. "You mean me?"

"Yes."

"Climb up this 'ere tree and fetch that there cat?"

"Yes."

"Lady," said Hash, "do you think I'm an acrobat or something?"

Kay bit her lip. Then, looking over the fence, she observed Sam approaching.

"Anything wrong?" said Sam.

Kay regarded him with mixed feelings. She had an uneasy foreboding that it might be injudicious to put herself under an obligation to a young man so obviously belonging to the class of those who, given an inch, take an ell. On the other hand, the kitten, mewing piteously, had plainly got itself into a situation from which only skilled assistance could release it. She eyed Sam doubtfully.

"Your dog has frightened my kitten up the tree," she said.

A wave of emotion poured over Sam. Only yesterday he had been correcting the proofs of a short story designed for a forthcoming issue of Pyke's *Home Companion*—"Celia's Airman," by Louise G. Boffin—and had curled his lip with superior masculine scorn at what had seemed to him the naïve sentimentality of its central theme. Celia had quarrelled with her lover, a young wing commander in the air force, and they had become reconciled owing to the latter saving her canary. In a mad moment in which his critical faculties must have been completely blurred, Sam had thought the situation far-fetched; but now he offered up a silent apology to Miss Boffin, realising that it was from the sheer, stark facts of life that she had drawn her inspiration.

"You want her brought down?"

"Yes, I do."

"Leave it to me," said Sam. "Leave it absolutely to me—leave the whole thing entirely and completely to me."

"It's awfully good of you."

"Not at all," said Sam tenderly. "There is nothing I wouldn't do for you—nothing. I was saying to myself only just now——"

"I shouldn't," said Hash heavily. "Only go breaking your neck. What we ought to do 'ere is to stand under the tree and chirrup."

Sam frowned.

"You appear to me, Hash," he said with some severity, "to think that your mission in life is to chirrup. If you devoted half the time to work that you do to practising your chirruping, Mon Repos would be a better and a sweeter place."

He hoisted himself into the tree and began to climb rapidly. So much progress did he make that when, a few moments later, Kay called to him, he could not distinguish her words. He scrambled down again.

"What did you say?" he asked.

"I only said take care," said Kay.

"Oh!" said Sam.

He resumed his climb. Hash followed him with a pessimistic eye.

"A cousin of mine broke two ribs playing this sort of silly game," he said moodily. "Light-haired feller named

151

George Turner. Had a job pruning the ellums on a gentle-man's place down Chigwell way. Two ribs he broke, besides a number of contusions."

He was aggrieved to find that Kay was not giving that attention to the story which its drama and human interest deserved.

"Two ribs," he repeated in a louder voice. "Also cuts, scratches and contusions. Ellums are treacherous things. You think the branches is all right, but lean your weight on 'em and they snap. That's an ellum he's climbin' now."

"Oh, be quiet!" said Kay nervously. She was follow-ing Sam's movements as tensely as ever Celia followed her airman's. It did look horribly dangerous, what he was doing.

"The proper thing we ought to have done 'ere was to have took a blanket and a ladder and a pole and to have held the blanket spread out and climbed the ladder and prodded at that there cat with the pole, same as they do at fires," said Hash, casting an unwarrantable slur on the humane methods of the fire brigade.

"Oh, well done!" cried Kay.

Sam was now operating in the topmost branches, and the kitten, not being able to retreat farther, had just come within reach of his groping hand. Having regarded him suspiciously for some moments and registered a formal protest against the proceedings by making a noise like an exploding soda-water bottle, it now allowed itself to be picked up and buttoned into his coat.

"Splendid!" shouted Kay.

"What?" bellowed Sam, peering down.

"I said splendid!" roared Kay.

"The lady said splendid!" yelled Hash, in a voice strengthened by long practice in announcing dinner in the midst of hurricanes. He turned to Kay with a mournful

152

shake of the head, his bearing that of the man who has tried to put a brave face on the matter, but feels the uselessness of affecting further optimism. "It's now that's the dangerous part, miss," he said. "The coming down, what I mean. I don't say the climbing up of one of these 'ere ellums is safe—not what you would call safe; but it's when you're coming down that the nasty accidents occur. My cousin was coming down when he broke his two ribs and got all them contusions. George Turner his name was—a light-haired feller, and he broke two ribs and had to have seven stitches sewed in him."

"Oh!" cried Kay.

"Ah!" said Hash.

He spoke with something of the smug self-satisfaction of the prophet whose predicted disasters come off as per schedule. Half-way down the tree, Sam, like Mr. Turner, had found proof of the treachery of ellums. He had rested his weight on a branch which looked solid, felt solid and should have been solid, and it had snapped under him. For one breathless moment he seemed to be about to shoot down like Lucifer, then he snatched another bough and checked his fall.

This time the bough held. It was as if the elm, having played its practical joke and failed, had become discouraged. Hash, with something of the feelings of a spectator in the gallery at a melodrama who sees the big scene fall flat, watched his friend and employer reach the lowest branch and drop safely to the ground. The record of George Turner still remained a mark for other climbers to shoot at.

Kay was not a girl who wept easily, but she felt strangely close to tears. She removed the agitated kitten from Sam's coat and put it on the grass, where it immediately made another spirited attempt to climb the tree.

Foiled in this, it raced for the coal cellar and disappeared from the social life of San Rafael until late in the afternoon.

"Your poor hands!" said Kay.

Sam regarded his palms with some surprise. In the excitement of the recent passage he had been unaware of injury.

"It's all right," he said. "Only skinned a little."

Hash would have none of this airy indifference.

"Ah," he said, "and the next thing you know you'll be getting dirt into 'em and going down with lockjaw. I had an uncle what got dirt into a cut 'and, and three days later we were buying our blacks for him."

"Oh!" gasped Kay.

"Two and a half really," said Hash. "Because he expired toward evening."

"I'll run and get a sponge and a basin," said Kay in agitation.

"That's awfully good of you," said Sam. O woman, he felt, in our hours of ease uncertain, coy and hard to please; when pain and anguish wring the brow, a ministering angel thou.

And he nearly said as much.

"You don't want to do that, miss," said Hash. "Much simpler for him to come indoors and put 'em under the tap."

"Perhaps that would be better," agreed Kay.

Sam regarded his practical-minded subordinate with something of the injured loathing which his cooking had occasionally caused to appear on the faces of dainty feeders in the fo'c'sle of the *Araminta*.

"This isn't your busy day, Hash, I take it?" he said coldly.

"Pardon?"

"I said you seem to be taking life pretty easily. Why

Sam the Sudden

don't you do a little work sometimes? If you imagine you're a lily of the field, look in the glass and adjust that impression."

Hash drew himself up, wounded.

"I'm only stayin' 'ere to 'elp and encourage," he said stiffly. "Now that what I might call the peril is over, there's nothing to keep me."

"Nothing," agreed Sam cordially.

"I'll be going."

"You know your way," said Sam. He turned to Kay. "Hash is an ass," he said. "Put them under the tap, indeed. These hands need careful dressing."

"Perhaps they do," Kay agreed.

"They most certainly do."

"Shall we go in, then?"

"Without delay," said Sam.

"There," said Kay, some ten minutes later. "I think that will be all right."

The finest efforts of the most skilful surgeon could not have evoked more enthusiasm from her patient. Sam regarded his bathed and sticking-plastered hands with an admiration that was almost ecstatic.

"You've had training in this sort of thing," he said.

"No."

"You've never been a nurse?"

"Never."

"Then," said Sam, "it is pure genius. It is just one of those cases of an amazing natural gift. You've probably saved my life. Oh, yes, you have! Remember what Hash said about lockjaw."

"But I thought you thought Hash was an ass."

"In many ways, yes," said Sam. "But on some points he has a certain rugged common sense. He——"

"Won't you be awfully late for the office?"

"For the what? Oh! Well, yes, I suppose I ought to be going there. But I've got to have breakfast first."

"Well, hurry, then. My uncle will be wondering what has become of you."

"Yes. What a delightful man your uncle is!"

"Yes, isn't he! Good-bye."

"I don't know when I've met a man I respected more."

"This will be wonderful news for him."

"So kind."

"Yes."

"So patient with me."

"I expect he needs to be."

"The sort of man it's a treat to work with."

"If you hurry you'll be able to work with him all the sooner."

"Yes," said Sam; "yes. Er—is there any message I can give him?"

"No, thanks."

"Ah! Well, then look here," said Sam. "Would you care to come and have lunch somewhere to-day?"

Kay hesitated. Then her eyes fell on those sticking-plastered hands and she melted. After all, when a young man has been displaying great heroism in her service, a girl must do the decent thing.

"I should like to," she said.

"The Savoy Grill at 1.30?"

"All right. Are you going to bring my uncle along?"

Sam started.

"Why—er—that would be splendid, wouldn't it?"

"Oh, I forgot. He's lunching with a man to-day at the Press Club."

"Is he?" said Sam. "Is he really?"

His affection and respect for Mr. Matthew Wrenn increased to an almost overwhelming degree. He went back

11*

to Mon Repos feeling that it was the presence in the world
of men like Matthew Wrenn that gave the lie to pessimism
concerning the future of the human race.

Kay, meanwhile, in her rôle of understudy to Claire
Lippett, who had just issued a bulletin to the effect that
the neuralgic pains were diminishing and that she hoped
to be up and about by midday, proceeded to an energetic
dusting of the house. As a rule, she hated this sort of
work, but to-day a strange feeling of gaiety stimulated her.
She found herself looking forward to the lunch at the Savoy
with something of the eagerness which, as a child, she had
felt at the approach of a party. Reluctant to attribute this
to the charms of a young man whom less than twenty-four
hours ago she had heartily disliked, she decided that it
must be the prospect of once more enjoying good cooking
in pleasant surroundings that was causing her excitement.
Until recently she had taken her midday meal at the home
of Mrs. Winnington-Bates, and, as with a celebrated chewing
gum, the taste lingered.

She finished her operations in the dining-room and made
her way to the drawing-room. Here the photograph of herself on the mantelpiece attracted her attention. She picked
it up and stood gazing at it earnestly.

A sharp double rap on the front door broke in on her
reflections. It was the postman with the second delivery,
and he had rapped because among his letters for San Rafael
was one addressed to Kay on which the writer had omitted
to place a stamp. Kay paid the twopence and took the
letter back with her to the drawing-room, hoping that the
interest of its contents would justify the financial outlay.

Inspecting them, she decided that they did. The letter
was from Willoughby Braddock; and Mr. Braddock, both
writing and expressing himself rather badly, desired to
know if Kay could see her way to marrying him.

CHAPTER XVIII
DISCUSSION AT A LUNCHEON-TABLE

THE little lobby of the Savoy grill-room that opens on to Savoy Court is a restful place for meditation; and Kay, arriving there at twenty minutes past one, was glad that she was early. She needed solitude, and regretted that in another ten minutes Sam would come in and deprive her of it. Ever since she had received his letter she had been pondering deeply on the matter of Willoughby Braddock, but had not yet succeeded in reaching a definite conclusion either in his favour or against him.

In his favour stood the fact that he had been a pleasant factor in her life as far back as she could remember. She had bird's-nested with him on spring afternoons, she had played the mild card games of childhood with him on winter evenings, and—as has been stated—she had sat in trees and criticised with incisive power his habit of wearing bed socks. These things count. Marrying Willoughby would undeniably impart a sort of restful continuity to life. On the other hand——

"Hullo!"

A young man, entering the lobby, had halted before her. For a moment she supposed that it was Sam, come to bid her to the feast; then, emerging from her thoughts, she looked up and perceived that blot on the body politic, Claude Winnington-Bates.

He was looking down at her with a sort of sheepish impudence, as a man will when he encounters unexpectedly a girl who in the not distant past has blacked his eye with a heavy volume of theological speculation. He was a slim young man, dressed in the height of fashion. His mouth

158

was small and furtive, his eyes flickered with a kind of stupid slyness, and his hair, which mounted his head in a series of ridges or terraces, shone with the unguent affected by the young lads of the town. A messy spectacle.

"Hullo," he said. "Waiting for someone?"

For a brief, wistful instant Kay wished that the years could roll back, making her young enough to be permitted to say some of the things she had said to Willoughby Braddock on that summer morning long ago when the topic of bed socks had come up between them. Being now of an age of discretion, and so debarred from that rich eloquence, she contented herself with looking through him and saying nothing.

The treatment was not effective. Claude sat down on the lounge beside her.

"I say, you know," he urged, "there's no need to be ratty. I mean to say——"

Kay abandoned her policy of silence.

"Mr. Bates," she said, "do you remember a boy who was at school with you named Shotter?"

"Sam Shotter?" said Claude, delighted at her chattiness. "Oh, yes, rather. I remember Sam Shotter. Rather a bad show, that. I saw him the other night and he was absolutely——"

"He's coming here in a minute or two. And if he finds you sitting on this lounge and I explain to him that you have been annoying me, he will probably tear you into little bits. I should go if I were you."

Claude Bates went. Indeed, the verb but feebly expresses the celerity of his movement. One moment he was lolling on the lounge; the next he had ceased to be and the lobby was absolutely free from him. Kay, looking over her shoulder into the grill-room, observed him drop into a chair and mop his forehead with a handkerchief.

She returned to her thoughts.

The advent of Claude had given them a new turn; or, rather, it had brought prominently before her mind what until then had only lurked at the back of it—the matter of Willoughby Braddock's financial status. Willoughby Braddock was a very rich man; the girl who became Mrs. Willoughby Braddock would be a very rich woman. She would, that is to say, step automatically into a position in life where the prowling Claude Bateses of the world would cease to be an annoyance. And this was beyond a doubt another point in Mr. Braddock's favour.

Willoughby, moreover, was rich in the right way, in the Midways fashion, with the richness that went with old grey-stone houses and old green parks and all the comfortable joy of the English country. He could give her the kind of life she had grown up in and loved. But on the other hand——

Kay stared thoughtfully before her; and, staring, was aware of Sam hurrying through the swing door.

"I'm not late, am I?" said Sam anxiously.

"No, I don't think so."

"Then come along. Golly, what a corking day!"

He shepherded her solicitously into the grill-room and made for a table by the large window that looks out on to the court. A cloak-room waiter, who had padded silently upon their trail, collected his hat and stick and withdrew with the air of a leopard that has made a good kill.

"Nice-looking chap," said Sam, following him with an appreciative eye.

"You seem to be approving of everything and everybody this morning."

"I am. This is the maddest, merriest day of all the glad New Year, and you can quote me as saying so. Now then, what is it to be?"

160

Having finished his ordering, a task which he approached on a lavish scale, Sam leaned forward and gazed fondly at his guest.

"Gosh!" he said rapturously. "I never thought, when I was sitting in that fishing hut staring at your photograph, that only a month or two later I'd be having lunch with you at the Savoy."

Kay was a little startled. Her brief acquaintance with him had taught her that Sam was a man of what might be called direct methods, but she had never expected that he would be quite so direct as this. In his lexicon there appeared to be no such words as "reticence" and "finesse."

"What fishing hut was that?" she asked, feeling rather like a fireman turning a leaky hose on a briskly burning warehouse full of explosives.

"You wouldn't know it. It's the third on the left as you enter Canada."

"Are you fond of fishing?"

"Yes. But we won't talk about that, if you don't mind. Let's stick to the photograph."

"You keep talking about a photograph and I don't in the least know what you mean."

"The photograph I was speaking of at dinner last night."

"Oh, the one your friend found—of some girl."

"It wasn't a friend; it was me. And it wasn't some girl; it was you."

Here the waiter intruded, bearing *hors d'œuvres.* Kay lingered over her selection, but the passage of time had not the effect of diverting her host from his chosen topic. Kay began to feel that nothing short of an earthquake would do that, and probably not even an earthquake unless it completely wrecked the grill-room.

"I remember the first time I saw that photograph."

"I wonder which it was," said Kay casually.

"It was———"

"So long as it wasn't the one of me sitting in a sea shell at the age of two, I don't mind."

"It was———"

. "They told me that if I was very good and sat very still, I should see a bird come out of the camera. I don't believe it ever did. And why they let me appear in a costume like that, even at the age of two, I can't imagine."

"It was the one of you in a riding habit, standing by your horse."

"Oh, that one? . . . I think I will take eggs after all."

"Eggs? What eggs?"

. "I don't know. *Œufs à la* something, weren't they?"

"Wait!" said Sam. He spoke as one groping his way through a maze. "Somehow or other we seem to have got on to the subject of eggs. I don't want to talk about eggs."

"Though I'm not positive it was à la something. I believe it was *œufs marseillaises* or some word like that. Anyhow, just call the waiter and say eggs."

Sam called the waiter and said eggs. The waiter appear┐ not only to understand but to be gratified.

The first time I saw that photograph———" he resumed.

"I wonder why they call those eggs *œufs marseillaises,*" said Kay pensively. "Do you think it's a special sort of egg they have in Marseilles?"

"I couldn't say. You know," said Sam, "I'm not really frightfully interested in eggs."

"Have you ever been in Marseilles?"

"Yes, I went there once with the *Araminta.*"

"Who is Araminta?"

"The *Araminta.* A tramp steamer I've made one or two trips on."

"What fun! Tell me all about your trips on the *Araminta.*"

"There's nothing to tell."

162

—

"Was that where you met the man you call Hash?"

"Yes. He was the cook. Weren't you surprised," said Sam, beginning to see his way, "when you heard that he was engaged to Claire?"

"Yes," said Kay, regretting that she had shown interest in tramp steamers.

"It just shows———"

"I suppose the drawback to going about on small boats like that is the food. It's difficult to get fresh vegetables, I should think—and eggs."

"Life isn't all eggs," said Sam desperately.

The head waiter, a paternal man, halted at the table and inquired if everything was to the satisfaction of the lady and gentleman. The lady replied brightly that everything was perfect. The gentleman grunted.

"They're very nice here," said Kay. "They make you feel as if they were fond of you."

"If they weren't nice to you," said Sam vehemently, "they ought to be shot. And I'd like to see the fellow who wouldn't be fond of you."

Kay began to have a sense of defeat, not unlike that which comes to a scientific boxer who has held off a rushing opponent for several rounds and feels himself weakening.

"The first time I saw that photograph," said Sam, "was one night when I had come in tired out after a day's fishing."

"Talking about fish———"

"It was pretty dark in the hut, with only an oil lamp on the table, and I didn't notice it at first. Then, when I was having a smoke after dinner, my eye caught something tacked up on the wall. I went across to have a look, and, by Jove, I nearly dropped the lamp!"

"Why?"

"Why? Because it was such a shock."

"So hideous?"

"So lovely, so radiant, so beautiful, so marvellous."

"I see."

"So heavenly, so———"

"Yes? There's Claude Bates over at that table."

The effect of these words on her companion was so electrical that it seemed to Kay that she had at last discovered a theme which would take his mind off other and disconcerting topics. Sam turned a dull crimson; his eyes hardened; his jaw protruded; he struggled for speech.

"The tick! The blister! The blighter! The worm! The pest! The hound! The bounder!" he cried. "Where is he?"

He twisted round in his chair, and having located the companion of his boyhood, gazed at the back of his ridged and shining head with a malevolent scowl. Then, taking up a hard and nobbly roll, he poised it lovingly.

"You mustn't!"

"Just this one!"

"No!"

"Very well."

Sam threw down the roll with resignation. Kay looked at him in alarm.

"I had no idea you disliked him so much as that!"

"He ought to have his neck broken."

"Haven't you forgiven him yet for stealing jam sandwiches at school?"

"It has nothing whatever to do with jam sandwiches. If you really want to know why I loathe and detest the little beast, it is because he had the nerve—the audacity—the insolence—the immortal rind to—to—er"—he choked—"to kiss you. Blast him!" said Sam, wholly forgetting the dictates of all good etiquette books respecting the kind of language suitable in the presence of the other sex.

Kay gasped. It is embarrassing for a girl to find what she had supposed to be her most intimate private affairs suddenly become, to all appearances, public property.

"How do you know that?" she exclaimed.

"Your uncle told me this morning."

"He had no business to."

"Well, he did. And what it all boils down to," said Sam, "is this—will you marry me?"

"Will I—what?"

"Marry me."

For a moment Kay stared speechlessly; then, throwing her head back, she gave out a short, sharp scream of laughter which made a luncher at the next table stab himself in the cheek with an oyster fork. The luncher looked at her reproachfully. So did Sam.

"You seem amused," he said coldly.

"Of course I'm amused," said Kay.

Her eyes were sparkling, and that little dimple on her chin which had so excited Sam's admiration when seen in photographic reproduction had become a large dimple. Sam tickled her sense of humour. He appealed to her in precisely the same way as the dog Amy had appealed to her in the garden that morning.

"I don't see why," said Sam. "There's nothing funny about it. It's monstrous that you should be going about at the mercy of every bounder who takes it into his head to insult you. The idea of a fellow with marcelled hair having the crust to——"

He paused. He simply could not mention that awful word again.

"—kiss me?" said Kay. "Well, you did.".

"That," said Sam with dignity, "was different. That was—er—well, in short, different. The fact remains that you need somebody to look after you, to protect you."

165

"And you chivalrously offer to do it? I call that awfully nice of you, but—well, don't you think it's rather absurd?"

"I see nothing absurd in it at all."

"How many times have you seen me in your life?"

"Thousands!"

"What? Oh, I was forgetting the photograph. But do photographs really count?"

"Yes."

"Mine can't have counted much, if the first thing you did was to tell your friend Cordelia Blair about it and say she might use it as a story."

"I didn't. I only said that at dinner to—to introduce the subject. As if I would have dreamed of talking about you to anybody! And she isn't a friend of mine."

"But you kissed her."

"I did not kiss her."

"My uncle insists that you did. He says he heard horrible sounds of Bohemian revelry going on in the outer office and then you came in and said the lady was soothed."

"Your uncle talks too much," said Sam severely.

"Just what I was thinking a little while ago. But still, if he tells you my secrets, it's only fair that he should tell me yours."

Sam swallowed somewhat convulsively.

"If you really want to know what happened, I'll tell you. I did not kiss that ghastly Blair pipsqueak. She kissed me."

"What!"

"She kissed me," repeated Sam doggedly. "I had been laying it on pretty thick about how much I admired her work, and suddenly she said 'Oh, you dear boy!' and flung her loathsome arms round my neck. What could I do? I might have uppercut her as she bored in, but, short of that, there wasn't any way of stopping her."

166

A look of shocked sympathy came into Kay's face.

"It's monstrous," she said, "that you should be going about at the mercy of every female novelist who takes it into her head to insult you. You need somebody to look after you, to protect you——"

Sams dignity, never a very durable article, collapsed.

"You're quite right," he said. "Well then——"

Kay shook her head.

"No, I'm not going to volunteer. Whatever your friend Cordelia Blair may say in her stories, girls don't marry men they've only seen twice in their lives."

"This is the fourth time you've seen me."

"Or even four times."

"I knew a man in America who met a girl at a party one night and married her next morning."

"And they were divorced the week after, I should think. No, Mr. Shotter——"

"You may call me Sam."

"I suppose I ought to after this. No, Sam, I will not marry you. Thanks ever so much for asking me, of course."

"Not at all."

"I don't know you well enough."

"I feel as if I had known you all my life."

"Do you?"

"I feel as if we had been destined for each other from the beginning of time."

"Perhaps you were a king in Babylon and I was a Christian slave."

"I shouldn't wonde:. And what is more, I'll tell you something. When I was in America, before I had ever dreamed of coming over to England, a palmist told me that I was shortly about to take a long journey, at the end of which I should meet a fair girl."

"You can't believe what those palmists say."

"Ah, but everything else that this one told me was absolutely true."

"Yes?"

"Yes. She said I had a rare spiritual nature and a sterling character and was beloved by all; but that people meeting me for the first time sometimes failed to appreciate me——"

"I certainly did."

"—because I had such hidden depths."

"Oh, was that the reason?"

"Well, that shows you."

"Did she tell you anything else?"

"Something about bewaring of a dark man, but nothing of importance. Still, I don't call it a bad fifty cents' worth."

"Did she say that you were going to marry this girl?"

"She did—explicitly."

"Then the idea, as I understand it, is that you want me to marry you so that you won't feel you wasted your fifty cents. Is that it?"

"Not precisely. You are overlooking the fact that I love you." He looked at her reproachfully. "Don't laugh."

"Was I laughing?"

"You were."

"I'm sorry. I oughtn't to mock a strong man's love, ought I?"

"You oughtn't to mock anybody's love. Love's a very wonderful thing. It even made Hash look almost beautiful for a moment, and that's going some."

"When is it going to make you look beautiful?"

"Hasn't it?"

"Not yet."

"You must be patient."

"I'll try to be, and in the meantime let us face this

168

situation. Do you know what a girl in a Cordelia Blair story would do if she were in my place?"

"Something darned silly, I expect."

"Not at all. She would do something very pretty and touching. She would look at the man and smile tremulously and say, 'I'm sorry, so—so sorry. You have paid me the greatest compliment a man can pay a woman. But it cannot be. So shall we be pals—just real pals?'"

"And he would redden and go to Africa, I suppose?"

"No. I should think he would just hang about and hope that some day she might change her mind. Girls often do, you know."

She smiled and put out her hand. Sam, with a cold glance at the head waiter, whom he considered to be standing much too near and looking much too paternal, took it. He did more—he squeezed it. And an elderly gentleman of Napoleonic presence, who had been lunching with a Cabinet minister in the main dining-room and was now walking through the court on his way back to his office, saw the proceedings through the large window and halted, spellbound.

For a long instant he stood there, gaping. He saw Kay smile. He saw Sam take her hand. He saw Sam smile. He saw Sam hold her hand. And then it seemed to him that he had seen enough. Abandoning his intention of walking down Fleet Street, he hailed a cab.

"There's Lord Tilbury," said Kay, looking out.

"Yes?" said Sam. He was not interested in Lord Tilbury.

"Going back to work, I suppose. Isn't it about time you were?"

"Perhaps it is. You wouldn't care to come along and have a chat with your uncle?"

"I may look in later. Just now I want to go to that.

169

messenger-boy office in Northumberland Avenue and send
off a note."

"Important?"

"It is, rather," said Kay.   "Willoughby Braddock
wanted me to do something, and now I find that I shan't
be able to."

CHAPTER XIX

LORD TILBURY ENGAGES AN ALLY

§ 1

ALTHOUGH Lord Tilbury had not seen much of what
had passed between Kay and Sam at the luncheon table,
he had seen quite enough; and as he drove back to Tilbury House in his cab he was thinking hard and bitter
thoughts of the duplicity of the modern girl. Here, he
reflected, was one who, encountered at dinner on a given
night, had as good as stated in set terms that she thoroughly
disliked Sam Shotter. And on the very next afternoon,
there she was, lunching with this same Sam Shotter, smiling at this same Sam Shotter, and allowing this same
Shotter to press her hand. It all looked very black to
Lord Tilbury, and the only solution that presented itself
to him was that the girl's apparent dislike of Sam on the
previous night had been caused by a lovers' quarrel. He
knew all about lovers' quarrels, for his papers were full of
stories, both short and in serial form, that dealt with nothing else. Oh, woman, woman! about summed up Lord
Tilbury's view of the affair.

He was, he perceived, in an extraordinarily difficult
position. As he had explained to his sister Frances on the
occasion of Sam's first visit to the Mammoth Publishing
Company, a certain tactfulness and diplomacy in the hand-

Sam the Sudden   170

ling of that disturbing young man were essential. He had not been able, during his visit to America, to ascertain exactly how Sam stood in the estimation of his uncle. The impression Lord Tilbury had got was that Mr. Pynsent was fond of him. If, therefore, any unpleasantness should occur which might lead to a breach between Sam and the Mammoth Publishing Company, Mr. Pynsent might be expected to take his nephew's side, and this would be disastrous. Any steps, accordingly, which were to be taken in connection with foiling the young man's love affair must be taken subtly and with stealth.

That such steps were necessary it never occurred to Lord Tilbury for an instant to doubt. His only standard when it came to judging his fellow creatures was the money standard, and it would have seemed ridiculous to him to suppose that any charm or moral worth that Kay might possess could neutralise the fact that she had not a penny in the world. He took it for granted that Mr. Pynsent would see eye to eye with him in this matter.

In these circumstances the helplessness of his position tormented him. He paced the room in an agony of spirit. The very first move in his campaign must obviously be to keep a watchful eye on Sam and note what progress this deplorable affair of his was having. But Sam was in Valley Fields and he was in London. What he required, felt Lord Tilbury, as he ploughed to and fro over the carpet, his thumbs tucked into the armholes of his waistcoat, his habit when in thought, was an ally. But what ally?

A secret-service man. But what secret-service man? A properly accredited spy, who, introduced by some means into the young man's house, could look, listen and make daily reports on his behaviour.

But what spy?

And then, suddenly, as he continued to perambulate,

inspiration came to Lord Tilbury. It seemed to him that the job in hand might have been created to order for young Pilbeam.

Among the numerous publications which had their being in Tilbury House was that popular weekly, *Society Spice,* a paper devoted to the exploitation of the shadier side of London life and edited by one whom the proprietor of the Mammoth had long looked on as the brightest and most promising of his young men—Percy Pilbeam, to wit, as enterprising a human ferret as ever wrote a Things-We-Want-to-Know-Don't-You-Know paragraph. Young Pilbeam would handle this business as it should be handled.

It was the sort of commission which he had undertaken before and carried through with complete success, reflected Lord Tilbury, recalling how only a few months back Percy Pilbeam, in order to obtain material for his paper, had gone for three weeks as valet to one of the smart set—the happy conclusion of the venture being that admirable Country-House Cesspools series which had done so much for the rural circulation of *Society Spice.*

His hand was on the buzzer to summon this eager young spirit, when a disturbing thought occurred to him, and instead of sending for Percy Pilbeam, he sent for Sam Shotter.

"Ah, Shotter, I—ah—— Do you happen to know young Pilbeam?" said His Lordship.

"The editor of *Society Spice?*"

"Exactly."

"I know him by sight."

"You know him by sight, eh? Ah? You know him, eh? Exactly. Quite so. I was only wondering. A charming young fellow. You should cultivate his acquaintance. That is all, Shotter."

Sam, with a passing suspicion that the strain of conducting a great business had been too much for his employer, returned to his work; and Lord Tilbury, walking with bent brows to the window, stood looking out, once more deep in thought.

The fact that Sam was acquainted with Pilbeam was just one of those little accidents which so often upset the brilliantly conceived plans of great generals, and it left His Lordship at something of a loss. Pilbeam was a man he could have trusted in a delicate affair like this, and now that he was ruled out, where else was an adequate agent to be found?

It was at this point in his meditations that his eyes, roving restlessly, were suddenly attracted by a sign on a window immediately opposite:

THE TILBURY DETECTIVE AGENCY LTD.

J. Sheringham Adair, Mgr.

Large and Efficient Staff

Such was the sign, and Lord Tilbury read and re-read it with bulging eyes. It thrilled him like a direct answer to prayer.

A moment later he had seized his hat, and without pausing to wait for the lift, was leaping down the stairs like some chamois of the Alps that bounds from crag to crag. He reached the lobby and, at a rate of speed almost dangerous in a man of his build and sedentary habits, whizzed across the street.

§ 2

Although, with the single exception of a woman who had lost her Pekingese dog, there had never yet been a client on the premises of the Tilbury Detective Agency, it was Chimp Twist's practice to repair daily to his office and remain there for an hour or two every afternoon. If questioned, he would have replied that he might just as well be there as anywhere; and he felt, moreover, that it looked well for him to be seen going in and out—a theory which was supported by the fact that only a couple of days back the policeman on the beat had touched his helmet to him. To have policemen touching themselves on the helmet instead of him on the shoulder was a novel and agreeable experience to Chimp.

This afternoon he was sitting, as usual, with the solitaire pack laid out on the table before him, but his mind was not on the game. He was musing on Soapy Molloy's story of his failure to persuade Sam to evacuate Mon Repos.

To an extent, this failure had complicated matters; and yet there was a bright side. To have walked in and collected the late Edward Finglass' legacy without let or hindrance would have been agreeable; but, on the other hand, it would have involved sharing with Soapy and his bride; and Chimp was by nature one of those men who, when there is money about, instinctively dislike seeing even a portion of it get away from them. It seemed to him that a man of his admitted ingenuity might very well evolve some scheme by which the Molloy family could be successfully excluded from all participation in the treasure.

It only required a little thought, felt Chimp; and he was still thinking when a confused noise without announced the arrival of Lord Tilbury.

The opening of the door was followed by a silence. Lord Tilbury was not built for speed, and the rapidity with which he had crossed the street and mounted four flights of stairs had left him in a condition where he was able only to sink into a chair and pant like a spent seal. As for Chimp, he was too deeply moved to speak. Even when lying back in a chair and saying "Woof!" Lord Tilbury still

174

retained the unmistakable look of one to whom bank managers grovel, and the sudden apparition of such a man affected him like a miracle. He felt as if he had been fishing idly for minnows and landed a tarpon.

Being, however, a man of resource, he soon recovered himself. Placing a foot on a button beneath the table, he caused a sharp ringing to pervade the office.

"Excuse me," he said, politely but with a busy man's curtness, as he took up the telephone. "Yes? Yes? Yes, this is the Tilbury Detective Agency. . . . Scotland Yard? Right, I'll hold the wire."

He placed a hand over the transmitter and turned to Lord Tilbury.

"Always bothering me," he said.

"Woof!" said Lord Tilbury.

Mr. Twist renewed his attention to the telephone.

"Hullo! . . . Sir John? Good afternoon. . . . Yes. . . . Yes. . . . We are doing our best, Sir John. We are always anxious to oblige headquarters. . . . Yes. . . . Yes. . . . Very well, Sir John. Good-bye."

He replaced the receiver and was at Lord Tilbury's disposal.

"If the Yard would get rid of their antiquated system and give more scope to men of brains," he said, not bitterly but with a touch of annoyance, "they would not always have to be appealing to us to help them out. Did you know that a man cannot be a detective at Scotland Yard unless he is over a certain height?"

"You surprise me," said Lord Tilbury, who was now feeling better.

"Five-foot-nine, I believe it is. Could there be an absurder regulation?"

"It sounds ridiculous."

"And is," said Chimp severely. "I am five-foot-seven.

175

myself. Wilbraham and Donahue, the best men on my staff, are an inch and half an inch shorter. You cannot gauge brains by height."

"No, indeed," said Lord Tilbury, who was five-feet-six. "Look at Napoleon! And Nelson!"

"Exactly," said Chimp. "Battling Nelson. A very good case in point. And Tom Sharkey was a short man too. . . . Well, what was it you wished to consult me about, Mr.——— I have not your name."

Lord Tilbury hesitated.

"I take it that I may rely on your complete discretion, Mr. Adair?"

"Nothing that you tell me in this room will go any farther," said Chimp, with dignity.

"I am Lord Tilbury," said His Lordship, looking like a man unveiling a statue of himself.

"The proprietor of the joint across the way?"

"Exactly," said Lord Tilbury a little shortly.

He had expected his name to cause more emotion, and he did not like hearing the Mammoth Publishing Company described as "the joint across the way."

He would have been gratified had he known that his companion had experienced considerable emotion and that it was only by a strong effort that he had contrived to conceal it. He might have been less pleased if he had been aware that Chimp was confidently expecting him to reveal some disgraceful secret which would act as the foundation for future blackmail. For although, in establishing his detective agency, Chimp Twist had been animated chiefly by the desire to conceal his more important movements, he had never lost sight of the fact that there were possibilities in such an institution.

"And what can I do for you, Lord Tilbury?" he asked, putting his finger tips together.

176

His Lordship bent closer.

"I want a man watched."

Once again his companion was barely able to conceal his elation. This sounded exceptionally promising. Though only an imitation private detective, Chimp Twist had a genuine private detective's soul. He could imagine but one reason why men should want men watched.

"A boy on the staff of Tilbury House."

"Ah!" said Chimp, more convinced than ever. "Good-looking fellow, I suppose?"

Lord Tilbury considered. He had never had occasion to form an opinion of Sam's looks.

"Yes," he said.

"One of these lounge lizards, eh? One of these parlour tarantulas? I know the sort—know 'em well. One of these slithery young-feller-me-lads with educated feet and shiny hair. And when did the dirty work start?"

"I beg your pardon?"

"When did you first suspect this young man of alienating Lady Tilbury's affections?"

"Lady Tilbury? I don't understand you. I am a widower."

"Eh? Then what's this fellow done?" said Chimp, feeling at sea again.

Lord Tilbury coughed.

"I had better tell you the whole position. This boy is the nephew of a business acquaintance of mine in America, with whom I am in the process of conducting some very delicate negotiations. He, the boy, is over here at the moment, working on my staff, and I am, you will understand, practically responsible to his uncle for his behaviour. That is to say, should he do anything of which his uncle might disapprove, the blame will fall on me, and these negotiations—these very delicate negotiations—will undoubtedly be broken off. My American acquaintance is a peculiar man, you understand."

"Well?"

"Well, I have just discovered that the boy is conducting a clandestine love affair with a girl of humble circumstances who resides in the suburb."

"A Tooting tooti-frooti," translated Chimp, nodding, "I see."

"A what?" asked Lord Tilbury, a little blankly.

"A belle of Balham—Bertha from Brixton."

"She lives at Valley Fields. And this boy Shotter has taken the house next door to her. I beg your pardon?"

"Nothing," said Chimp in a thick voice.

"I thought you spoke."

"No." Chimp swallowed feverishly. "Did you say hotter?"

"Shotter."

"Taken a house in Valley Fields?"

"Yes. In Burberry Road. Mon Repos is the name."

"Ah!" said Chimp, expelling a deep breath.

"You see the position? All that can be done at present is to institute a close watch on the boy. It may be that I have allowed myself to become unduly alarmed. Possibly he does not contemplate so serious a step as marriage with this young woman. Nevertheless, I should be decidedly relieved if I felt that there was someone in his house watching his movements and making daily reports to me."

"I'll take this case," said Chimp.

"Good! You will put a competent man on it?"

"I wouldn't trust it to one of my staff, not even Wilbraham or Donahue. I'll take it on myself."

"That is very good of you, Mr. Adair."

"A pleasure," said Chimp.

"And now arises a difficult point. How do you propose to make your entry into young Shotter's household?"

"Easy as pie. Odd-job man."

"Odd-job man?"

"They always want odd-job men down in the suburbs. Fellows who'll do the dirty work that the help kicks at. Listen here; you tell this young man that I'm a fellow that once worked for you and ask him to engage me as a personal favour. That'll cinch it. He won't like to refuse the boss—what I mean."

"True," said Lord Tilbury. "True. But it will necessitate something in the nature of a change of costume," he went on, looking at the other's shining tweeds.

"Don't you fret about that. I'll dress the part."

"And what name would you suggest taking? Not your own, of course?"

"I've always called myself Twist before."

"Twist? Excellent! Then suppose you come to my office in half an hour's time."

"Sure!"

"I am much obliged, Mr. Adair."

"Not at all," said Chimp handsomely. "Not a-tall! Don't mention it. Only too pleased."

§ 3

Sam, when the summons came for him to go to his employer's office, was reading with no small complacency a little thing of his own in the issue of Pyke's *Home Companion* which would be on the bookstalls next morning. It was signed Aunt Ysobel, and it gave some most admirable counsel to Worried (Upper Sydenham) who had noticed of late a growing coldness toward her on the part of her betrothed.

He had just finished reading this, marvelling, as authors will when they see their work in print, at the purity of his style and the soundness of his reasoning, when the telephone rang and he learned that Lord Tilbury desired his presence. He hastened to the holy of holies and found there not only His Lordship but a little man with a waxed moustache, to which he took an instant dislike.

"Ah, Shotter," said Lord Tilbury.

There was a pause. Lord Tilbury, one hand resting on the back of his chair, the fingers of the other in the fold of his waistcoat, stood looking like a Victorian uncle being photographed. The little man fingered the waxed moustache. And Sam glanced from Lord Tilbury to the moustache inquiringly and with distaste. He had never seen a moustache he disliked more.

"Ah, Shotter," said Lord Tilbury, "this is a man named Twist, who was at one time in my employment."

"Odd-job man," interpolated the waxed-moustached one.

"As odd-job man," said Lord Tilbury.

"Ah?" said Sam.

"He is now out of work."

Sam, looking at Mr. Twist, considered that this spoke well for the rugged good sense of the employers of London.

"I have nothing to offer him myself," continued Lord Tilbury, "so it occurred to me that you might possibly have room for him in your new house."

"Me?" said Sam.

"I should take it as a personal favour to myself if you would engage Twist. I naturally dislike the idea of an old and—er—faithful employee of mine being out of work."

Mr. Twist's foresight was justified. Put in this way, the request was one that Sam found it difficult to refuse.

"Oh, well, in that case——"

"Excellent! No doubt you will find plenty of little things for him to do about your house and garden."

"He can wash the dog," said Sam, inspired. The question of the bathing of Amy was rapidly thrusting itself into the forefront of the domestic politics of Mon Repos.

"Exactly! And chop wood and run errands and what not."

"There's just one thing," said Sam, who had been eyeing his new assistant with growing aversion. "That moustache must come off."

"What?" cried Chimp, stricken to the core.

"Right off at the roots," said Sam sternly. "I will not have a thing like that about the place, attracting the moths."

Lord Tilbury sighed. He found this young man's eccentricities increasingly hard to bear. With that sad wistfulness which the Greeks called *pothos* and the Romans *desiderium,* he thought of the happy days, only a few weeks back, when he had been a peaceful, care-free man, ignorant of Sam's very existence. He had had his troubles then, no doubt; but how small and trivial they seemed now.

"I suppose Twist will shave off his moustache if you wish it," he said wearily.

Chancing to catch that eminent private investigator's eye, he was surprised to note its glazed and despairing expression. The man had the air of one who has received a death sentence.

"Shave it?" quavered Chimp, fondling the growth tenderly. "Shave my moustache?"

"Shave it," said Sam firmly. "Hew it down. Raze it to the soil and sow salt upon the foundations."

"Very good, sir," said Chimp lugubriously.

"That is settled then," said Lord Tilbury, relieved. "So you will enter Mr. Shotter's employment immediately, Twist."

Chimp nodded a mournful nod.

"You will find Twist thoroughly satisfactory, I am sure. He is quiet, sober, respectful and hard-working."

"Ah, that's bad," said Sam.

Lord Tilbury heaved another sigh.

CHAPTER XX
TROUBLE IN THE SYNDICATE

WHEN Chimp Twist left Tilbury House, he turned westward along the Embankment, for he had an appointment to meet his colleagues of the syndicate at the Lyons teashop in Green Street, Leicester Square. The depression which had swept over him on hearing Sam's dreadful edict had not lasted long. Men of Mr. Twist's mode of life are generally resilient. They have to be.

After all, he felt, it would be churlish of him, in the face of this almost supernatural slice of luck, to grumble at the one crumpled rose leaf. Besides, it would only take him about a couple of days to get away with the treasure of Mon Repos, and then he could go into retirement and grow his moustache again. For there is this about moustaches, as about whiskers—though of these Mr. Twist, to do him justice, had never been guilty—that, like truth, though crushed to earth, they will rise. A little patience and his moustache would rise on stepping-stones of its dead self to higher things. Yes, when the fields were white with daisies it would return. Pondering thus, Chimp Twist walked briskly to the end of the Embankment, turned up Northumberland Avenue, and reaching his destination, found Mr. and Mrs. Molloy waiting for him at a table in a far corner.

It was quiet in the tea-shop at this hour, and the tryst

had been arranged with that fact in mind. For this was in all essentials a board meeting of the syndicate, and business men and women do not like to have their talk interrupted by noisy strangers clamorous for food. With the exception of a woman in a black silk dress with bugles who, incredible as it may seem, had ordered cocoa and sparkling limado simultaneously and was washing down a meal of Cambridge sausages and pastry with alternate draughts of both liquids, the place was empty.

Soapy and his bride, Chimp perceived, were looking grave, even gloomy; and in the process of crossing the room he forced his own face into an expression in sympathy with theirs. It would not do, he realised, to allow his joyous excitement to become manifest at what was practically a post-mortem. For the meeting had been convened to sit upon the failure of his recent scheme and he suspected the possibility of a vote of censure. He therefore sat down with a heavy seriousness befitting the occasion; and having ordered a cup of coffee, replied to his companions' questioning glances with a sorrowful shake of the head.

"Nothing stirring," he said.

"You haven't doped out another scheme?" said Dolly, bending her shapely brows in a frown.

"Not yet."

"Then," demanded the lady heatedly, "where does this sixty-five-thirty-five stuff come in? That's what I'd like to know."

"Me, too," said Mr. Molloy with spirit. It occurred to Chimp that a little informal discussion must have been indulged in by his colleagues of the board previous to his arrival, for their unanimity was wonderful.

"You threw a lot of bull about being the brains of the concern," said Dolly accusingly, "and said that, being the brains of the concern, you had ought to be paid highest.

And now you blow in and admit that you haven't any more ideas than a rabbit."

"Not so many," said Mr. Molloy, who liked rabbits and had kept them as a child.

Chimp stirred his coffee thoughtfully. He was meditating on what a difference a very brief time can make in the fortunes of man. But for that amazing incursion of Lord Tilbury, he would have been approaching this interview in an extremely less happy frame of mind. For it was plain that the temper of the shareholders was stormy.

"You're quite right, Dolly," he said humbly, "quite right. I'm not so good as I thought I was."

This handsome admission should have had the effect proverbially attributed to soft words, but it served only to fan the flame.

"Then where do you get off with this sixty-five-thirty-five?"

"I don't," said Chimp. "I don't, Dolly." The man's humility was touching. "That's all cold. We split fifty-fifty, that's what we do."

Soft words may fail, but figures never. Dolly uttered a cry that caused the woman in the bugles to spill her cocoa, and Mr. Molloy shook as with a palsy.

"Now you're talking," said Dolly.

"Now," said Mr. Molloy, "you are talking."

"Well, that's that," said Chimp. "Now let's get down to it and see what we can do."

"I might go to the joint and have another talk with that guy," suggested Mr. Molloy.

"No sense in that," said Chimp, somewhat perturbed. It did not at all suit his plans to have his old friend roaming about in the neighbourhood of Mon Repos while he was in residence.

"I don't know so much," said Mr. Molloy thoughtfully.

184

"I didn't seem to get going quite good that last time. The fellow had me out on the sidewalk before I could pull a real spiel. If I tried again——"

"It wouldn't be any use," said Chimp. "This guy Shotter told you himself he had a special reason for staying on."

"You don't think he's wise to the stuff being there?" said Dolly, alarmed.

"No, no," said Chimp. "Nothing like that. There's a dame next door he's kind of stuck on."

"How do you know?"

Chimp gulped. He felt like a man who discovers himself on the brink of a precipice.

"I—I was snooping around down there and I saw 'em," he said.

"What were you doing down there?" asked Dolly suspiciously.

"Just looking around, Dolly, just looking around."

"Oh!"

The silence which followed was so embarrassing to a sensitive man that Chimp swallowed his coffee hastily and rose.

"Going?" said Mr. Molloy coldly.

"Just remembered I've got a date."

"When do we meet again?"

"No sense in meeting for the next day or two."

"Why not?"

"Well, a fellow wants time to think. I'll give you a ring."

"You'll be at your office to-morrow?"

"Not to-morrow."

"Day after?"

"Maybe not the day after. I'm moving around some."

"Where?"

"Oh, all around."

"Doing what?"

Chimp's self-control gave way.

"Say, what's eating you?" he demanded. "Where do you get this stuff of prying and poking into a man's affairs? Can't a fellow have a little privacy sometimes?"

"Sure!" said Mr. Molloy. "Sure!"

"Sure!" said Mrs. Molloy. "Sure!"

"Well, good-bye," said Chimp.

"Good-bye," said Mr. Molloy.

"God bless you," said Mrs. Molloy, with a little click of her teeth.

Chimp left the tea shop. It was not a dignified exit, and he was aware of it with every step that he took. He was also aware of the eyes of his two colleagues boring into his retreating back. Still, what did it matter, argued Chimp Twist, even if that stiff, Soapy, and his wife had suspicions of him? They could not know. And all he needed was a clear day or two and they could suspect all they pleased. Nevertheless, he regretted that unfortunate slip.

The door had hardly closed behind him when Dolly put her suspicions into words.

"Soapy!"

"Yes, petty?"

"That bird is aiming to double-cross us."

"You said it!"

"I wondered why he switched to that fifty-fifty proposition so smooth. And when he let it out that he'd been snooping around down there, I knew. He's got some little game of his own on, that's what he's got. He's planning to try and scoop that stuff by himself and leave us flat."

"The low hound!" said Mr. Molloy virtuously.

"We got to get action, Soapy, or we'll be left. To think of that little Chimp doing us dirt just goes against my better nature. How would it be if you was to go down to-night and do some more porch climbing? Once you were in you could get the stuff easy. It wouldn't be a case of hunting around same as last time."

"Well, sweetie," said Mr. Molloy frankly, "I'll tell you. I'm not so strong for that burgling stuff. It's not my line and I don't like it. It's awful dark and lonesome in that joint at three o'clock in the morning. All the time I was there I kep' looking over my shoulder, expecting old Finky's ghost to sneak up on me and breathe down the back of my neck."

"Be a man, honey!"

"I'm a man all right, petty, but I'm temperamental."

"Well, then——" said Dolly, and breaking off abruptly, plunged into thought.

Mr. Molloy watched her fondly and hopefully. He had a great respect for her woman's resourcefulness, and it seemed to him from the occasional gleam in her vivid eyes that something was doing.

"I've got it!"

"You have?"

"Yes, sir!"

"There is none like her, none," Mr. Molloy's glistening eye seemed to say. "Give us an earful, baby," he begged emotionally.

Dolly bent closer and lowered her voice to a whisper. The woman in the bugles, torpid with much limado, was out of ear-shot, but a waitress was hovering nôt far away.

"Listen! We got to wait till the guy Shotter is out of the house."

"But he's got a man. You told me that yourself."

"Sure he's got a man, but if you'll only listen I'll tell you. We wait till this fellow Shotter is out——"

"How do we know he's out?"

"We ask at the front door, of course. Say, listen, Soapy, for the love of Pete don't keep interrupting! We go to the house. You go round to the back door."

"Why?"

"I'll soak you one in a minute," exclaimed Dolly despairingly.

"All right, sweetness. Sorry. Didn't mean to butt in. Keep talking. You have the floor."

"You go round to the back door and wait, keeping your eye on the front steps, where I'll be. I ring the bell and the hired man comes. I say, 'Is Mr. Shotter at home?' If he says yes, I'll go in and make some sort of spiel about something. But if he's not, I'll give you the high sign and you slip in at the back door; and then when the man comes down into the kitchen again you're waiting and you bean him one with a sandbag. Then you tie him up and come along to the front door and let me in and we go up and grab that stuff. How about it?"

"I bean him one?" said Mr. Molloy doubtfully.

"Cert'nly you bean him one."

"I couldn't do it, petty," said Mr. Molloy. "I've never beaned anyone in my life."

Dolly exhibited the impatience which all wives, from Lady Macbeth downward through the ages, have felt when their schemes appear in danger of being thwarted by the pusillanimity of a husband.

The words, "Infirm of purpose, give me the sandbag!" seemed to be trembling on her lips.

"You poor cake eater!" she cried with justifiable vigour. "You talk as if it needed a college education to lean a stuffed eelskin on a guy's head. Of course you can do it. You're behind the kitchen door, see?—and he comes in, see?—and you sim'ly bust him one, see? A feller with one arm and no legs could do it. And say, if you want something to brace you up, think of all that money lying in the cistern, just waiting for us to come and dip for it!"

"Ah!" said Mr. Molloy, brightening.

CHAPTER XXI
AUNT YSOBEL POINTS THE WAY

§ 1

CLAIRE LIPPETT sat in the kitchen of San Rafael, reading Pyke's *Home Companion*. It was Mr. Wrenn's kindly custom to bring back a copy for her each week on the day of publication, thus saving her an outlay of twopence. She was alone in the house, for Kay was up in London doing some shopping, and Mr. Wrenn, having come in and handed over the current number, had gone off for a game of chess with his friend, Cornelius.

She was not expecting to be alone long. Muffins lay on the table, all ready to be toasted; a cake which she had made herself stood beside them; and there was also a new tin of anchovy paste—all of which dainties were designed for the delectation of Hash Todhunter, her fiancé, who would shortly be coming to tea.

As a rule, Pyke's *Home Companion* absorbed Claire's undivided attention, for she was one of its most devoted supporters; but this evening she found her mind wandering, for there was that upon it which not even Cordelia Blair's "Hearts Aflame" could conjure away.

Claire was worried.

On the previous day a cloud had fallen on her life, not exactly blotting out the sunshine, but seeming to threaten some such eclipse in the near future. She had taken Hash to John Street for a formal presentation to her mother, and

It was on the way home that she had first observed the approach of the cloud.

Hash's manner had seemed to her peculiar. A girl who has just become romantically betrothed to a man does not expect that man, when they are sitting close together on the top of an omnibus, to talk moodily of the unwisdom of hasty marriages.

It pains and surprises her when he mentions friends of his who, plunging hot-headedly into matrimony, spent years of subsequent regret. And when, staring woodenly before him, he bids her look at Samson, Doctor Crippen and other celebrities who were not fortunate in their domestic lives, she feels a certain alarm.

And such had been the trend of Hash Todhunter's conversation, coming home from John Street. Claire, recalling the more outstanding of his dicta, felt puzzled and unhappy, and not even the fact that Cordelia Blair had got her hero into a ruined mill with villains lurking on the ground floor and dynamite stored in the basement could enchain her interest. She turned the page listlessly and found herself confronted by Aunt Ysobel's Chats With My Girls.

In spite of herself, Claire's spirits rose a little. She never failed to read every word that Aunt Ysobel wrote, for she considered that lady a complete guide to all mundane difficulties. Nor was this an unduly flattering opinion, for Aunt Ysobel was indeed like some wise pilot, gently steering the storm-tossed barks of her fellow men and women through the shoals and sunken rocks of the ocean of life. If you wanted to know whether to blow on your tea or allow it to cool of itself in God's good time, Aunt Ysobel would tell you. If, approaching her on a deeper subject, you desired to ascertain the true significance of the dark young man's offer of flowers, she could tell you that too—even attributing to each individual bloom a hidden and esoteric meaning which it would have been astonished to find that it possessed.

Should a lady shake hands or bow on parting with a gentleman whom she has met only once? Could a gentleman present a lady with a pound of chocolates without committing himself to anything unduly definite? Must mother always come along? Did you say "Miss Jones—Mr. Smith" or "Mr. Smith—Miss Jones," when introducing friends? And arising from this question did Mr. Smith on such an occasion say, "Pleased to meet you" or "Happy, I'm sure"?

Aunt Ysobel was right there every time with the correct answer. And everything she wrote had a universal message.

It was so to-day. Scarcely had Claire begun to read, when her eye was caught by a paragraph headed Worried (Upper Sydenham).

"Coo!" said Claire.

The passage ran as follows:

"WORRIED (Upper Sydenham). You tell me, dear, that the man to whom you are betrothed seems to you to be growing cold, and you ask me what you had better do. Well, dear, there is only one thing you can do, and I give this advice to all my girl friends who come to me with this trouble. You must test this man. You see, he may not really be growing cold; he may merely have some private business worry on his mind which causes him to seem distrait. If you test him you will soon learn the truth. What I suggest may seem to you at first a wee bit unladylike, but try it all the same. Pretend to show a liking for some other gentleman friend of yours. Even flirt with him a teeny-weeny bit.

"You will soon discover then if this young man really cares for you still. If he does he will exhibit agitation,

He may even go to the length of becoming violent. In the olden days, you know, knights used to joust for the love of their lady. Try Herbert or George, or whatever his name is, out for a week, and see if you can work him up to the jousting stage."

Claire laid down the paper with trembling hands. The thing might have been written for her personal benefit. There was no getting away from Aunt Ysobel. She touched the spot every time.

Of course, there were difficulties. It was all very well for Aunt Ysobel to recommend flirting with some other male member of your circle, but suppose your circle was so restricted that there were no available victims. From the standpoint of dashing male society, Burberry Road was at the moment passing through rather a lean time. The postman was an elderly man who, if he stopped to exchange a word, talked only of his son in Canada. The baker's representative, on the other hand, was a mere boy, and so was the butcher's. Besides, she might smile upon these by the hour and Hash would never see her. It was all very complex, and she was still pondering upon the problem when a whistle from without announced the arrival of her guest.

The chill of yesterday still hung over Mr. Todhunter's demeanour. He was not precisely cold, but he was most certainly not warm. He managed somehow to achieve a kind of intermediate temperature. He was rather like a broiled fish that has been lying too long on a plate.

He kissed Claire. That is to say, technically the thing was a kiss. But it was not the kiss of other days.

"What's up?" asked Claire, hurt.

"Nothing's up."

"Yes, there is something up."

192

"No, there ain't anything up."

"Yes, there is."

"No, there ain't."

"Well, then," said Claire, "what's up?"

These intellectual exchanges seemed to have the effect of cementing Mr. Todhunter's gloom. He relapsed into a dark silence, and Claire, her chin dangerously elevated, prepared tea.

Tea did not thaw the guest. He ate a muffin, sampled the cake and drank deeply; but he still remained that strange, moody figure who rather reminded Claire of the old earl in "Hearts Aflame." But then the old earl had had good reason for looking like a man who has drained the wine of life and is now unwillingly facing the lees, because he had driven his only daughter from his door, and, though mistaken in this view, supposed that she had died of consumption in Australia. (It was really another girl.) But why Hash should look like one who has drained the four ale of life and found a dead mouse at the bottom of the pewter, Claire did not know, and she quivered with a sense of injury.

However, she was a hostess. ("A hostess, dears, must never, never permit her private feelings to get the better of her"—Aunt Ysobel.)

"Would you like a nice fresh lettuce?" she asked. It might be, she felt, that this would just make the difference.

"Ah!" said Hash. He had a weakness for lettuces.

"I'll go down the garden and cut you one."

He did not offer to accompany her, and that in itself was significant. It was with a heart bowed down that Claire took her knife and made her way along the gravel path. So preoccupied was she that she did not cast even a glance over the fence till she was aware suddenly of a strange moaning sound proceeding from the domain of Mon Repos.

This excited her curiosity. She stopped, listened, and finally looked.

The garden of Mon Repos presented an animated spectacle. Sam was watering a flower bed, and not far away the dog Amy, knee-deep in a tub, was being bathed by a small, clean-shaven man who was a stranger to Claire.

Both of them seemed to be having a rough passage. Amy, as is the habit of her species on these occasions, was conveying the impression of being at death's door and far from resigned. Her mournful eyes stared hopelessly at the sky, her brow was wrinkled with a perplexed sorrow, and at intervals she uttered a stricken wail. On these occasions she in addition shook herself petulantly, and Chimp Twist —for, as Miss Blair would have said, it was he—was always well within range.

Claire stopped, transfixed. She had had no notion that the staff of Mon Repos had been augmented, and it seemed to her that Chimp had been sent from heaven. Here, right on the spot, in daily association with Hash, was the desired male. She smiled dazzlingly upon Chimp.

"Hullo," she said.

"Hullo," said Chimp.

He spoke moodily, for he was feeling moody. There, might be golden rewards at the end of this venture of his, but he perceived already that they would have to be earned. Last night Hash Todhunter had won six shillings from him at stud poker, and Chimp was a thrifty man. Moreover, Hash slept in the top back room, and when not in it, locked the door.

This latter fact may seem to offer little material for gloom on Chimp's part, but it was, indeed, the root of all his troubles. In informing Mr. and Mrs. Molloy that the plunder of the late Edward Finglass was hidden in the cistern of Mon Repos, Chimp Twist had been guilty of subterfuge—pardonable, perhaps, for your man of affairs must take these little business precautions, but nevertheless subterfuge. In the letter which, after carefully memorising, he had just as carefully destroyed, Mr. Finglass had revealed that the proceeds of his flutter with the New Asiatic Bank might be found not in the cistern but rather by anyone who procured a chisel and raised the third board from the window in the top back room. Chimp had not foreseen that this top back room would be occupied by a short-tempered cook who, should he discover people prizing up his floor with chisels, would scarcely fail to make himself unpleasant. That was why Mr. Twist spoke moodily to Claire, and who shall blame him?

Claire was not discouraged. She had cast Chimp for the rôle of stalking horse and he was going to be it.

"Is the doggie having his bath?" she asked archly.

"I think they're splitting it about fifty-fifty," said Sam, adding himself to the conversation.

Claire perceived that this was, indeed, so.

"Oh, you are wet," she cried. "You'll catch cold. Would you like a nice cup of hot tea?"

Something approaching gratitude appeared in Chimp's mournful face.

"Thank you, miss," he said. "I would."

"We're spoiling you," said Sam.

He sauntered down the garden, plying his hose, and Claire hurried back to her kitchen.

"Where's my nice lettuce?" demanded Hash.

"Haven't got it yet. I've come in to get a cup of hot tea and a slice of cake for that young man next door. He's got so wet washing that big dog."

It was some little time before she returned.

"I've been having a talk with that young man," she said. "He liked his tea very much."

"Did he?" said Hash shortly. "Ho, did he? Where's my lettuce?"

Claire uttered an exclamation.

"There! If I haven't gone and forgotten it!"

Hash rose, a set look on his face.

"Never mind," he said. "Never mind."

"You aren't going?"

"Yes, I am."

"What, already?"

"Yes, already."

"Well, if you must," said Claire. "I like Mr. Twist," she went on pensively. "He's what I call a perfect gentleman."

"He's what I call a perisher," said Hash sourly.

"Nice way he's got of speaking. His Christian name's Alexander. Do you call him that or Aleck?"

"If you care to 'ear what I call him," replied Hash with frigid politeness, "you can come and listen at our kitchen door."

"Why, you surely aren't jealous!" cried Claire, wide-eyed.

"Who, me?" said Hash bitterly.

It was some few minutes later that Sam, watering his garden like a good householder, heard sounds of tumult from within. Turning off his hose, he hastened toward the house and reached it in time to observe the back door open with some violence and his new odd-job man emerge at a high rate of speed. A crockery implement of the kind used in kitchens followed the odd-job man, bursting like a shell against the brick wall which bounded the estate of Mon Repos. The odd-job man himself, heading for the street, disappeared, and Sam, going into the kitchen, found Mr. Todhunter fuming.

"Little tiff?" inquired Sam.

Hash gave vent to a few sailorly oaths.

"He's been flirting with my girl and I've been telling him off."

Sam clicked his tongue.

"Boys will be boys," he said. "But, Hash, didn't I gather from certain words you let fall when you came home last night that your ardour was beginning to wane a trifle?"

"Ur?"

"I say, from the way you spoke last night about the folly of hasty marriages, I imagined that you had begun to experience certain regrets. In other words, you gave me the impression of a man who would be glad to be free from sentimental entanglements. Yet here you are positively —yes, by Jove, positively jousting!"

"What say?"

"I was quoting from a little thing I dashed off up at the office recently. Have you changed your mind about hasty marriages, then?"

Hash frowned perplexedly at the stove. He was not a man who found it easy to put his thoughts into words.

"Well, it's like this: I saw her mother yesterday."

"Ah! That is a treat I have not had."

"Do you think girls get like their mothers, Sam?"

"Sometimes."

Hash shivered.

"Well, the 'ole thing is, when I'm away from the girl I get to thinking about her."

"Very properly," said Sam. "Absence, it has been well said, makes the heart grow fonder."

"Thinking of her mother, I mean."

"Oh, of her mother?"

"And then I wish I was well out of it all, you understand. But then again, when I'm settin' with 'er with my arm round 'er little waist——"

"You are still speaking of the mother?"

"No, the girl."

"Oh, the girl?"

"And when I'm lookin' at her and she's lookin' at me, it's different. It's—well, it's what I may call different. She's got a way of tossing her chin up, Sam, and waggling of 'er 'air——"

Sam nodded.

"I know," he said, "I know. They have, haven't they? Confirmed hair wagglers, all of them. Well, Hash, if you will listen to the advice of an old lady with girl friends in every part of England—and Scotland, too, for that matter; you will find a communication from Bonnie Lassie (Glasgow) in this very issue—I would say, Risk the mother. And meanwhile, Hash, refrain, if possible, from slaying our odd-job man. He may not be much to look at, but he is uncommonly useful. Never forget that in a few days we may want Amy washed again."

He bestowed an encouraging nod upon his companion and went out into the garden. He was just picking up his hose when a scuffling sound from the other side of the fence attracted his attention. It was followed by a sharp exclamation, and he recognised Kay's voice.

It was growing dark now, but it was not too dark for Sam to see, if only sketchily, what was in progress in the garden of San Rafael. Shrouded though the whole scene was in an evening mist, he perceived a male figure. He also perceived the figure of Kay. The male figure appeared either to be giving Kay a lesson in jiu-jitsu or else embracing her against her will. From the sound of her voice, he put the latter construction on the affair, and it seemed to him that, in the inspired words of the typewriter, now was the time for all good men to come to the aid of the party.

Sam was a man of action. Several policies were open to him. He could ignore the affair altogether; he could shout reproof at the aggressor from a distance; he could climb the fence and run to the rescue. None of these operations appealed to him. It was his rule in life to act swiftly and to think, if at all, later. In his simple, direct fashion, therefore, he lifted the hose and sent a stream of water shooting at the now closely entangled pair.

§ 2

The treatment was instantaneously effective. The male member of the combination, receiving several gallons of the Valley Fields Water Company's best stuff on the side of his head and then distributed at random over his person, seemed to understand with a lightning quickness that something in the nature of reinforcements had arrived. Hastily picking up his hat, which had fallen off, he stood not upon the order of his going, but ran. The darkness closed upon him, and Sam, with a certain smug complacency inevitable in your knight-errant who has borne himself notably well in a difficult situation, turned off the hose and stood waiting while Kay crossed the lawn.

"Who was our guest?" he asked.

Kay seemed a little shaken. She was breathing quickly.

"It was Claude Bates," she said, and her voice quivered.

So did Sam's.

"Claude Bates!" he cried distractedly. "If I had known that, I would have chased him all the way back to London, kicking him violently."

"I wish you had."

"How on earth did that fellow come to be here?"

"I met him outside Victoria Station. I suppose he got into the train and followed me."

"The hound!"

"I suddenly found him out here in the garden."

"The blister!"

"Do you think somebody will kill him some day?" asked Kay wistfully.

"I shall have a very poor opinion of the public spirit of the modern Englishman," Sam assured her, "if that loathsome leprous growth is permitted to infest London for long. But in the meantime," he said, lowering his voice tenderly, "doesn't it occur to you that this thing has been sent for a purpose? Surely it is intended as a proof of the truth of what I was saying at lunch, that you need——"

"Yes," said Kay; "but we'll talk about that some other time, if you don't mind. I suppose you know you've soaked me to the skin."

"You?" said Sam incredulously.

"Yes, me."

"You don't mean Bates?"

"No, I do not mean Bates. Feel my arm if you don't believe me."

Sam extended a reverent hand.

"What an extraordinarily beautiful arm you have," he said.

"An extraordinarily wet arm."

"Yes, you are wet," Sam acknowledged. "Well, all I can say is that I am extremely sorry. I acted for the best; impulsively, let us say—mistakenly it may be—but still with the best intentions."

"I should hate to be anywhere near when you are doing your worst. Well, things like this, I suppose, must be——"

"——after a famous victory. Exactly!"

"I must run in and change."

"Wait!" said Sam. "We must get this thing straight. You will admit now, I imagine, that you need a strong man's protection?"

"I don't admit anything of the kind."

"You don't?"

"No."

"But surely, with Claude Bateses surging around you on every side, dogging your footsteps, forcing their way into your very garden, you must acknowledge——"

"I shall catch cold."

"Of course! What am I thinking of? You must run in at once."

"Yes."

"But wait!" said Sam. "I want to get to the bottom of this. What makes you think that you and I were not designed for each other from the beginning of time? I've been thinking very deeply about the whole thing, and it beats me why you can't see it. To start with, we are so much alike, we have the same tastes——"

"Have we?"

"Most certainly. To take a single instance, we both dislike Claude Bates. Then there is your love, which I share, for a life in the country. The birds, the breeze, the trees, the bees—you love them and so do I. It is my one ambition to amass enough money to enable me to buy a farm and settle down. You would like that."

"You seem to know a lot about me."

"I have my information from your uncle."

"Don't you and uncle ever do any work at the office? You seem to spend your whole time talking."

"In the process of getting together a paper like Pyke's *Home Companion,* there come times when a little rest, a little folding of the hands, is essential. Otherwise the machine would break down. On these occasions we chat, and when we chat we naturally talk about you."

"Why?"

"Because there is no other subject in which I am in the least interested. Well, then, returning to what I was saying, we are so much alike——"

"They say that people should marry their opposites."

"Pyke's *Home Companion* has exploded that view. Replying to Anxious (Wigan) in this very issue, Aunt Ysobel says just the contrary."

"I've often wondered who Aunt Ysobel was."

"It would be foreign to the policy of Pyke's *Home Companion* to reveal office secrets. You may take it from me that Aunt Ysobel is the goods. She knows. You might say she knows everything."

"I wonder if she knows I'm getting pneumonia."

"Good heavens! I was forgetting. I mustn't keep you standing here for another instant."

"No. Good-bye."

"Wait!" said Sam. "While we are on the subject of Aunt Ysobel, I wonder if you have seen her ruling this week in the case of Romeo (Middlesbrough)?"

"I haven't read this week's number."

"Ah! Well, the gist of what she says—I quote from memory—is that there is nothing wrong in a young man taking a girl to the theatre, provided that it is a matinée performance. On the contrary, the girl will consider it a pretty and delicate attention. Now to-morrow will be Saturday, and I have in my possession two seats for the Winter Garden. Will you come?"

"Does Aunt Ysobel say what the significance is if the girl accepts?"

"It implies that she is beginning to return—slightly, it may be, but still perceptibly—the gentleman's esteem."

"I see. Rather serious. I must think this over."

"Certainly. And now, if I may suggest it, you really ought to be going in and changing your dress. You are very wet."

"So I am. You seem to know everything—like Aunt Ysobel."

"There is a resemblance, perhaps," said Sam.

Hash Todhunter met Sam as he re-entered Mon Repos.

"Oh, there you are," said Hash. "There was some people calling, wanting to see you, a minute ago."

"Really? Who?"

"Well, it was a young female party that come to the door, but I thought I saw a kind of thickset feller hanging about down on the drive."

"My old friends, Thomas G. and Miss Gunn, no doubt. A persistent couple. Did they leave any message?"

"No. She asked if you was in, and when I told her you was around somewhere she said it didn't matter."

§ 3

That night. The apartments of Lord Tilbury.

"Yes? Yes? This is Lord Tilbury speaking. . . . Ah, is that you, Twist? Have you anything to report?"

"The young woman's cook has just been round with a message. The young woman is going with Mr. Shotter to the theatre to-morrow afternoon."

"Cor!" said Lord Tilbury.

He replaced the receiver. He remained for a moment in the deepest thought. Then, swiftly reaching a decision, he went to the desk and took out a cable form.

The wording of the cable gave him some little trouble. The first version was so condensed that he could not understand it himself. He destroyed the form and decided that this was no time for that economy which is instinctive even to the richest men when writing cables. Taking another form and recklessly dashing the expense, he informed Mr. Pynsent that, in spite of the writer's almost fatherly care, his nephew Samuel had most unfortunately sneaked off surreptitiously and become entangled with a young woman residing in the suburbs. He desired Mr. Pynsent to instruct him in this matter.

The composition satisfied him. It was a good piece of work. He rang for an underling and sent him with it to the cable office.

CHAPTER XXII

STORMY TIMES AT MON REPOS

§ 1

THERE are few pleasanter things in life than to sit under one's own roof-tree and smoke that first pipe of the morning which so sets the seal on the charms of breakfast. Sam, as he watched Hash clearing away the remains of as goodly a dish of bacon and eggs and as fragrant a pot of coffee as ever man had consumed, felt an uplifted thrill of well-being. It was Saturday morning, and a darned good Saturday morning at that—mild enough to permit of an open window, yet crisp enough to justify a glowing fire.

"Hash," said Sam, "have you ever felt an almost overwhelming desire to break into song?"

"No," said Hash, after consideration.

"You have never found yourself irresistibly compelled to render some old Provençal *chansonnette* breathing of love and youth and romance?"

"No, I ain't."

"Perhaps it's as well. You wouldn't be good at it, and one must consider the neighbours. But I may tell you that I am feeling the urge to-day. What's that thing of Browning's that you're always quoting? Ah, yes!"

> 'The morning's at seven;
> The hillside's dew-pearled.
> God's in His heaven;
> All's right with the world.'

That is how I feel."

"How'd you like this bacon?" inquired Hash, picking up a derelict slice and holding it against the light as if it were some rare *objet d'art*.

Sam perceived that his audience was not attuned to the lyrical note.

"I am too spiritual to be much of a judge of these things," he said; "but as far as I could gather, it seemed all right."

"Ha'penny a pound cheaper than the last," said Hash with sober triumph.

"Indeed? Well, as I was saying, life seems decidedly tolerable to-day. I am taking Miss Derrick to the theatre this afternoon, so I shall not be back until lateish. Before I go, therefore, I have something to say to you, Hash. I noticed a disposition on your part yesterday to try to disintegrate our odd-job man. This must not be allowed to grow upon you. When I return this evening I shall expect to find him all in one piece."

"That's all right, Sam," replied Mr. Todhunter cordially. "All that 'appened there was that I let myself get what I might call rather 'asty. I been thinking it over, and I've got nothing against the feller."

This was true. Sleep, which knits up the ravelled sleeve of care, had done much to soothe the troubled spirit of Hash Todhunter. The healing effect of a night's slumber had been to convince him that he had wronged Claire. He proceeded to get Sam's expert views on this.

"Suppose it was this way, Sam: Suppose a feller's young lady went and give another feller a cup of hot tea and cut him a slice of cake. That wouldn't 'ave to mean that she was flirting with 'im, would it?"

"Not at all," said Sam warmly. "Far from it. I would call it evidence of the kind heart rather than the frivolous mind."

"Ah!"

"I may be dangerously modern," said Sam, "but my view—and I give it fearlessly—is that a girl may cut many a slice of cake and still remain a good, sweet, womanly woman."

"You see," argued Hash, "he was wet."

"Who was wet?"

"This feller Twist. Along of washing the dog. And Clara, she took and give him a nice cup of hot tea and a slice of cake. Upset me at the time, I'll own, but I see where maybe I done 'er an injustice."

"You certainly did, Hash. That girl is always doing that sort of thing out of pure nobility of nature. Why, the first morning I was here she gave me a complete breakfast—eggs, bacon, toast, coffee, marmalade and everything."

"No; did she?"

"You bet she did. She's a jewel, and you're lucky to get her."

"Ah!" said Hash with fervour.

He gathered up the tray alertly and bore it downstairs to the kitchen, where Chimp Twist eyed him warily. Although on his return to the house on the previous night Chimp had suffered no injury at Hash's hands, he attributed this solely to the intervention of Sam, who had insisted on a formal reconciliation; and he had just heard the front door bang behind Sam. A nervous man who shrank from personal violence, particularly when it promised to be so one-sided as in his present society, Chimp felt apprehensive. He was reassured by the geniality of his companion's manner.

"Nice day," said Hash.

"Lovely," said Chimp, relieved.

"'As that dog 'ad 'er breakfast?"

"She was eating a shoe when I saw her last,"

206

"Ah, well, maybe that'll do her till dinner-time. Nice dog."

"Yes, yes."

"Nice weather."

"Yes, yes."

"If the rain 'olds off it'll be a regular nice day."

"It certainly will."

"And if it rains," continued Hash, sunnily optimistic, "I see by the paper that the farmers need it."

It was a scene which would have rejoiced the heart of Henry Ford or any other confirmed peacemaker; and Chimp, swift, in his canny fashion, to take advantage of his companion's miraculous cordiality, put a tentative question:

"Sleep well last night?"

"Like a top."

"So did I. Say," said Chimp enthusiastically, "that's a swell bed I've got."

"Ah?"

"Yes, sir, that's one swell bed. And a dandy room too. And I been thinking it over, and it don't seem right that I should have that dandy room and that swell bed, seeing that I came here after you. So what say we exchange?"

"Change rooms?"

"Yes, sir; you have my swell big front room and I have your poky little back room."

The one fault which undoes diplomatists more than any other is the temptation to be too elaborate. If it had been merely a case of exchanging rooms, as two medieval monarchs, celebrating a truce, might have exchanged chargers and suits of armour, Hash would probably have consented. He would have thought it silly, but he would have done it by way of a gesture indicating his opinion of the world's excellence this morning and of his desire to show Mr. Twist that he had forgiven him and wished him well. But the way the other put it made it impossible for any man feeling as generous and amiable as he did to become a party to a scheme for turning this charming fellow out of a swell front room and putting him in a poky back one.

"Couldn't do it," he said.

"I cert'nly wish you would."

"No," said Hash. "No; couldn't do it."

Chimp sighed and returned to his solitaire. Hash, full of the milk of human kindness, went out into the garden. It had occurred to him that at about this time of day Claire generally took a breather in the open after the rough work of making the beds. She was strolling up and down the gravel path.

"Hullo," she said.

"Hullo," said Hash. "Nice day."

A considerable proportion of the pathos of life comes from the misunderstandings that arise between male and female through the inability of a man with an untrained voice to convey the emotions underlying his words. Hash supposed that he had spoken in a way that would show Claire that he considered her an angel of light and a credit to her sex. If he was slightly more formal than usual, that was because he was feeling embarrassed at the thought of the injustice he had done her at their last meeting.

Claire, however, noting the formality—for it was customary with him to couch his morning's greeting in some such phrase as "Hullo, ugly!" or "What cheer, face!"—attributed it to that growing coldness of which she had recently become aware. Her heart sank. She became provocative.

"How's Mr. Twist this morning?"

"Oh, he's fine."

"Not been quarrelling with him, have you?"

"Who, me?" cried Hash, shocked. "Why, him and me is the best of friends!"

"Oh?"

"We just been having a chat."

"About me?"

"No; about the weather and the dog and how well we slept last night."

Claire scraped at the gravel with the toe of her shoe.

"Oh! Well, I've got to go and wash my dishes," she said. "Goo' mornin'."

§ 2

Hash Todhunter was not a swift-thinking man. Nor was he one of those practised amateurs of the sex who can read volumes in a woman's glance and see in a flash exactly what she means when she scrapes arabesques on a gravel path with the toe of her shoe. For some three hours and more, therefore, he remained in a state of perfect content. And then suddenly, while smoking a placid after-luncheon pipe, his mood changed and there began to seep into the hinterlands of his mind the idea that in Claire's manner at their recent meeting there had been something decidedly peculiar.

He brooded over this; and as the lunch which he had cooked and eaten fought what was for the moment a winning battle with his organs of digestion, there crept over him a sombre alarm. Slowly, but with a persistence not to be denied, the jealousy of which sleep had cured him began to return. He blew out a cloud of tobacco smoke and through it stared bleakly at Chimp Twist, who was in a reverie on the other side of the kitchen table.

It came to him, not for the first time, that he did not like Chimp's looks. Handsome not even his mother could have called Chimp Twist; and yet there was about him a

certain something calculated to inspire uneasiness in an
engaged man. He had that expression in his eyes which
home wreckers wear in the movies. A human snake, if
ever there was one, felt Hash, as his interior mechanism
strove vainly to overcome that which he had thrust upon it.

Nor did his recollection of Claire's conversation bring
any reassurance. So brief it had been that he could remember everything she had said. And it had all been
about that black-hearted little object across the table.

"How's Mr. Twist this morning?" A significant question. "Not been quarrelling with him, have you?" A fishy
remark. And then he had said that they had been having
a chat, and she had asked, "About me?"

So moved was Hash by the recollection of this that
he took the pipe out of his mouth and addressed his
companion with an abruptness that was almost violent:
"Hey!"

Chimp looked up with a start. He had been pondering whether it might not possibly come within the scope
of an odd-job man's duties to put a ladder against the
back of the house and climb up it and slap a coat of paint
on the window frame of the top back room. Then, when
Hash was cooking dinner——

"Hullo?" he said, blinking. He was surprised to see
that the other, who had been geniality itself during lunch,
was regarding him with a cold and suspicious hostility.

"Want to ask you something," said Hash.

"Spill it," said Chimp, and smiled nervously.

It was an unfortunate thing for him to have done, for
he did not look his best when smiling. It seemed to Hash
that his smile was furtive and cunning.

"Want to know," said Hash, "if there are any larks
on?"

"Eh?"

"You and my young lady next door—there's nothing what you might call between you, is there?"

"'Course not!" cried Chimp in agitation.

"Well," said Hash weightily, "there better hadn't be. See?"

He rose, feeling a little better, and, his suspicions being momentarily quieted, he proceeded to the garden, where he chirruped for a while over the fence.

This producing no response, he climbed the fence and peeped in through the kitchen window of San Rafael. The kitchen was empty.

"Gone for a walk," diagnosed Hash, and felt a sense of injury. If Claire wanted to go for a walk, why hadn't she asked him to come too? He did not like it. It seemed to him that love must have grown cold. He returned to Mon Repos and embarrassed the sensitive Mr. Twist by staring at him for twenty minutes almost without a blink.

Claire had not gone for a walk. She had taken the 12.10 train to Victoria and had proceeded thence to Mr. Braddock's house in John Street. It was her intention to put the facts before her mother and from that experienced woman to seek advice in this momentous crisis of her life. Her faith in Aunt Ysobel had not weakened, but there is never any harm done by getting the opinion of a second specialist. For Claire's uneasiness had been growing ever since that talk with Hash across the fence that morning. His manner had seemed to her peculiar. Nor did her recollection of his conversation bring any reassurance.

"How's Mr. Twist this morning?" she had asked. And instead of looking like one about to joust, he had replied heartily: "Oh, he's fine." A disturbing remark.

And then he had gone on to say that he and Chimp

were the best of friends. It was with tight lips and hard
eyes that Claire, replying absently to the paternal badinage
of Sleddon, the butler, made her way into her mother's
presence. Mrs. Lippett, consulted, proved uncompromisingly
pro-Aunt Ysobel.

"That's what I call a sensible woman, Clara."

"Claire," corrected her daughter mechanically.

"She knows."

"That's what I think."

"Ah, she's suffered, that woman has," said Mrs. Lippett.
"You can see that. Stands to reason she couldn't know
so much about life if she hadn't suffered."

"Then you'd go on testing him?" said Claire anxiously.

"Test him more and more," said Mrs. Lippett. "There's
no other way. You've got to remember, dearie, that your
Clarence is a sailor, and sailors has to be handled firm.
They say sailors don't care. I say they must be made to
care. That's what I say."

Claire made the return journey on an omnibus.

For purposes of thought there is nothing like a ride on
the top of an omnibus. By four o'clock, when the vehicle
put her down at the corner of Burberry Road, her resolution was as chilled steel and she had got her next move
all planned out. She went into the kitchen for a few moments, and coming out into the garden, perceived Hash
roaming the lawn of Mon Repos.

"Hi!" she called, and into her voice managed to project a note of care-free liveliness.

"Where you been?" inquired Hash.

"I been up seeing mother. . . . Is Mr. Twist indoors?"

"What do you want with Mr. Twist?"

"Just wanted to give him this—something I promised
him."

This was an envelope, lilac in colour and scent, and

212

Hash, taking it and gazing upon it as he might have gazed upon an adder nestling in his palm, made a disturbing discovery.

"There's something inside this."

"Of course there is. If there wasn't, what 'ud I be giving it him for?"

Hash's fingers kneaded the envelope restlessly.

"What you writing to him about?"

"Never mind."

"There's something else inside this 'ere envelope besides a letter. There's something that sort of crinkles when you squeeze it."

"Just a little present I promised to give him."

A monstrous suspicion flamed in Hash Todhunter's mind. It seemed inconceivable, and yet—— He tore open the envelope and found his suspicion fulfilled. Between his fingers there dangled a lock of tow-coloured hair.

"When you've finished opening other people's letters——" said Claire.

She looked at him, hopefully at first, and then with a growing despair. For Hash's face was wooden and expressionless.

"I'm glad," said Hash huskily at length. "I been worried, but now I'm not worried. I been worried because I been worrying about you and me not being suited to one another and 'aving acted 'asty; but now I'm not worried, because I see there's another feller you're fond of, so the worry about what was to be done and everything don't worry me no more. He's in the kitchen," said Hash in a gentle rumble. "I'll give him this and explain 'ow it come to be opened in error."

Nothing could have exceeded the dignity of his manner, but there are moments when women chafe at masculine dignity.

213

"Aren't you going to knock his head off?" demanded
Claire distractedly.

"Me?" said Hash, looking as nearly as he could like
the picture of Saint Sebastian in the Louvre. "Me? Why
should I knock the pore feller's 'ead off? I'm glad. Because
I been worried, and now I'm not worried—see what I
mean?"

Before Claire's horrified eyes and through a world that
rocked and danced, he strode toward the kitchen of Mon
Repos, bearing the envelope daintily between finger and
thumb. He seemed calm and at peace. He looked as if
he might be humming.

Inside the kitchen, however, his manner changed.
Chimp Twist, glancing up from his solitaire, observed in
the doorway, staring down at him, a face that seemed to
his excited imagination to have been equipped with searchlights instead of eyes. Beneath these searchlights was a
mouth that appeared to be gnashing its teeth. And from
this mouth, in a brief interval of gnashing, proceeded dreadful words.

The first that can be printed were the words: "Put
'em up!"

Mr. Twist, rising, slid like an eel to the other side of
the table.

"What's the matter?" he demanded in considerable
agitation.

"I'll show you what's the matter," said Hash, after
another verbal interlude which no compositor would be
allowed by his union to set up. "Come out from behind
that table like a man and put your 'ands up!"

Mr. Twist rejected this invitation.

"I'm going to take your 'ead," continued Hash, sketch-
ing out his plans, "and I'm going to pull it off, and
then——"

214

What he proposed to do after this did not intrigue Chimp. He foiled a sudden dash with an inspired leap.

"Come 'ere," said Hash coaxingly.

His mind clearing a little, he perceived that the root of the trouble, the obstacle which was standing in the way of his aims, was the table. It was a heavy table, but with a sharp heave he tilted it on its side and pushed it toward the stove. Chimp, his first line of defence thus demolished, shot into the open, and Hash was about to make another offensive movement when the dog Amy, who had been out in the garden making a connoisseur's inspection of the dustbin, strolled in and observed with pleasure that a romp was in progress.

Amy was by nature a thoughtful dog. Most of her time, when she was not eating or sleeping, she spent in wandering about with wrinkled forehead, puzzling over the cosmos. But she could unbend. Like so many philosophers, she loved an occasional frolic, and this one appeared to be of exceptional promise.

The next moment Hash, leaping forward, found his movements impeded by what seemed like several yards of dog. It was hard for him to tell without sorting the tangle out whether she was between his legs or leaning on his shoulders. Certainly she was licking his face; but on the other hand, he had just kicked her with a good deal of violence, which seemed to indicate that she was on a lower level.

"Get out!" cried Hash.

The remark was addressed to Amy, but the advice it contained was so admirable that Chimp Twist acted on it without hesitation. In the swirl of events he had found himself with a clear path to the door, and along this path he shot without delay. And not until he had put the entire length of Burberry Road between him and his apparently insane aggressor did he pause.

Then he mopped his forehead and said "Gee!"

It seemed to Chimp Twist that a long walk was indicated—a walk so long that by the time he reached Mon Repos again, Sam, his preserver, would have returned and would be on the spot to protect him.

Hash, meanwhile, raged, baffled. He had extricated himself from Amy and had rushed out into the road, but long ere that his victim had disappeared. He went back, to try to find Amy and rebuke her, but Amy had disappeared too. In spite of her general dreaminess, there was sterling common sense in Amy. She knew when and when not to be among those present.

Hash returned to his kitchen and remained there, seething. He had been seething for perhaps a quarter of an hour, when the front door-bell rang. He climbed the stairs gloomily; and such was his disturbed frame of mind that not even the undeniable good looks of the visitor who had rung could soothe him.

"Mr. Shotter in?"

He recognised her now. It was the young party who had called on the previous evening, asking for Sam. And, as on that occasion, he seemed to see through the growing darkness the same sturdy male person hovering about in the shadows.

"No, miss, he ain't."

"Expecting him back soon?"

"No, miss, I ain't. He's gone to the theatre, to a mati-nay."

"Ah," said the lady, "is that so?" And she made a sudden, curious gesture with her parasol.

"Sorry," said Hash, melting a little, for her eyes were very bright.

"Can't be helped. You all alone here then?"

"Yes."

"Tough luck."

"Oh, I don't mind, miss," said Hash, pleased by her sympathy.

"Well, I won't keep you. 'Devening."

"'Evening, miss."

Hash closed the door. Whistling a little, for his visitor had lightened somehow the depression which was gnawing at him, he descended the stairs and entered the kitchen.

Something which appeared at first acquaintance to be the ceiling, the upper part of the house and a ton of bricks thrown in for good measure hit Hash on the head, and he subsided gently on the floor.

§ 3

Soapy Molloy came to the front door and opened it. He was a little pale, and he breathed heavily.

"All right?" said his wife eagerly.

"All right."

"Tied him up?"

"With a clothes-line."

"How about if he hollers?"

"I've put a duster in his mouth."

"At-a-boy!" said Mrs. Molloy. "Then let's get action."

They climbed the stairs to where the cistern stood, and Mr. Molloy, removing his coat, rolled up his sleeves.

Some minutes passed, and then Mr. Molloy, red in the face and wet in the arm, made a remark.

"But it must be there!" cried his wife.

"It isn't."

"You haven't looked."

"I've looked everywhere. There couldn't be a tooth-

pick in that thing without I'd have found it." He expelled
a long breath, his face bleak. "Know what I think?"

"What?"

"That little oil-can, Chimp, has slipped one over on
us—told us the wrong place."

The plausibility of this theory was so obvious that Mrs.
Molloy made no attempt to refute it. She bit her lip in
silence.

"Then let's you and me get busy and find the right
place," she said at length, with the splendid fortitude of a
great woman. "We know the stuff's in the house somewheres, and we got the place to ourselves."

"It's taking a chance," said Mr. Molloy doubtfully.
"Suppose somebody was to come and find us here."

"Well, then, all you would do would be to just simply
haul off and bust them one, same as you did the hired
man."

"'M, yes," said Mr. Molloy.

CHAPTER XXIII
SOAPY MOLLOY'S BUSY AFTERNOON

§ 1

THE unwelcome discovery of the perfidy of Chimp Twist
had been made by Mr. Molloy and his bride at about
twenty minutes past four. At 4.30 a natty two-seater car
drew up at the gate of San Rafael and Willoughby Braddock alighted. Driving aimlessly about the streets of London some forty minutes earlier, and feeling rather at a loose
end, it had occurred to him that a pleasant way of passing
the evening would be to go down to Valley Fields and get
Kay to give him a cup of tea.

Mr. Braddock was in a mood of the serenest happiness.

And if this seems strange, seeing that only recently he had had a proposal of marriage rejected, it should be explained that he had regretted that hasty proposal within two seconds of dropping the letter in the letter box. And he had come to the conclusion that, much as he liked Kay, what had induced him to offer her his hand and heart had been the fact that he had had a good deal of champagne at dinner and that its after effects had consisted of a sort of wistful melancholy which had removed for the time his fundamental distaste for matrimony. He did not want matrimony; he wanted adventure. He had not yet entirely abandoned hope that some miracle might occur to remove Mrs. Lippett from the scheme of things, and when that happened, he wished to be free.

Yes, felt Willoughby Braddock, everything had turned out extremely well. He pushed open the gate of San Rafael with the debonair flourish of a man without entanglements. As he did so, the front door opened and Mr. Wrenn came out.

"Oh, hullo," said Mr. Braddock. "Kay in?"

"I am afraid not," said Mr. Wrenn. "She has gone to the theatre." Politeness to a visitor wrestled with the itch to be away. "I fear I have an engagement also, for which I am already a little late. I promised Cornelius——"

"That's all right. I'll go in next door and have a chat with Sam Shotter."

"He has gone to the theatre with Kay."

"A wash-out, in short," said Mr. Braddock with undiminished cheerfulness. "Right-ho! Then I'll pop."

"But, my dear fellow, you mustn't run away like this," said Mr. Wrenn with remorse. "Why don't you come in and have a cup of tea and wait for Kay? Claire will bring you some if you ring."

"Something in that," agreed Mr. Braddock. "Sound, very sound."

He spoke a few genial words of farewell and proceeded to the drawing-room, where he rang the bell. Nothing ensuing, he went to the top of the kitchen stairs and called down.

"I say!" Silence from below. "I say!" fluted Mr. Braddock once more, and now it seemed to him that the silence had been broken by a sound—a rummy sound—a sound that was like somebody sobbing.

He went down the stairs. It was somebody sobbing.

Bunched up on a chair, with her face buried in her arms, that weird girl Clara was crying like the dickens.

"I say!" said Mr. Braddock.

There is this peculiar quality about tears—that they can wash away in a moment the animosity of a lifetime. ' For years Willoughby Braddock had been on terms of distant hostility with this girl. Even apart from the fact that that affair of the onion had not ceased to rankle in his bosom, there had been other causes of war between them. Mr. Braddock still suspected that it was Claire who, when on the occasion of his eighteenth birthday he had called at Midways in a top hat, had flung a stone at that treasured object from the recesses of a shrubbery. One of those things impossible of proof, the outrage had been allowed to become an historic mystery; but Willoughby Braddock had always believed the hidden hand to be Claire's, and his attitude toward her from that day had been one of stiff disapproval.

But now, seeing her weeping and broken before him, with all the infernal cheek which he so deprecated swept away on a wave of woe, his heart softened. It has been a matter of much speculation among historians what

15*

Wellington would have done if Napoleon had cried at Waterloo.

"I say," said Mr. Braddock, "what's the matter? Anything up?"

The sound of his voice seemed to penetrate Claire's grief. She sat up and looked at him damply.

"Oh, Mr. Braddock," she moaned, "I'm so wretched! I am so miserable, Mr. Braddock!"

"There, there!" said Willoughby Braddock.

"How was I to know?"

"Know what?"

"I couldn't tell."

"Tell which?"

"I never had a notion he would act like that."

"Who would like what?"

"Hash."

"You've spoiled the hash?" said Mr. Braddock, still out of his depth.

"My Hash—Clarence. He took it the wrong way."

At last Mr. Braddock began to see daylight. She had cooked hash for this Clarence, whoever he might be, and he had swallowed it in so erratic a manner that it had choked him.

"Is he dead?" he asked in a hushed voice.

A piercing scream rang through the kitchen.

"Oh! Oh! Oh!"

"My dear old soul!"

"He wouldn't do that, would he?"

"Do what?"

"Oh, Mr. Braddock, do say he wouldn't do that!"

"What do you mean by 'that'?"

"Go and kill himself."

"Who?"

"Hash."

Willoughby Braddock removed the perfectly folded silk handkerchief from his breast pocket and passed it across his forehead.

"Look here," he said limply, "you couldn't tell me the whole thing from the beginning in a few simple words, could you?"

He listened with interest as Claire related the events of the day.

"Then Clarence is Hash?" he said.

"Yes."

"And Hash is Clarence?"

"Yes; everyone calls him Hash."

"That was what was puzzling me," said Mr. Braddock, relieved. "That was the snag that I got up against all the time. Now that that is clear, we can begin to examine this thing in a calm and judicial spirit. Let's see if I've got it straight. You read this stuff in the paper and started testing him—is that right?"

"Yes. And instead of jousting, he just turned all cold-like and broke off the engagement."

"I see. Well, dash it, the thing's simple. All you want is for some polished man of the world to take the blighter aside and apprise him of the facts. Shall I pop round and see him now?"

Claire's tear-stained face lit up as if a light had been switched on behind her eyes.

"Oh, if you only would!"

"Of course I will—like a shot."

"Oh, you are good! I'm sorry I threw that onion at you, Mr. Braddock."

"Faults on both sides," said Mr. Braddock magnanimously. "Now you stop crying, like a good girl, and powder your nose and all that, and I'll have the lad round all present and correct in a couple of minutes."

222

He patted Claire's head in a brotherly fashion, and trotted out through the back door.

A few minutes later, Mr. and Mrs. Molloy, searching feverishly in the drawing-room of Mon Repos, heard a distant tinkle and looked at each other with a wild surmise.

"It's the back door-bell," said Dolly.

"I told you," said Mr. Molloy sombrely. "I knew this would happen. What'll we do?"

Mrs. Molloy was not the woman to be shaken for long.

"Why, go downstairs and answer it," she said. "It's prob'ly only a tradesman come with a loaf of bread or something. He'll think you're the help."

"And if he doesn't," replied Mr. Molloy with some bitterness, "I suppose I bust him one with the meat axe. Looks to me as if I shall have to lay out the whole darned population of this blamed place before I'm through."

"Sweetie mustn't be cross."

"Sweetie's about fed up," said Mr. Molloy sombrely.

§ 2

Expecting, when he opened the back door, to see a tradesman with a basket on his arm, Soapy Molloy found no balm to his nervous system in the apparition of a young man of the leisured classes in a faultlessly cut grey suit. He gaped at Mr. Braddock.

"Hullo," said Mr. Braddock.

"Hullo," said Soapy.

"Are you Hash?" inquired the ambassador.

"Pardon?"

"Is your name Clarence?"

In happier circumstances Soapy would have denied the charge indignantly; but now he decided that it was politic to be whatever anyone wished him to be.

"That's me, brother," he said.

Mr. Braddock greatly disliked being called brother, but he made no comment.

"Well, I just buzzed round," he said, "to tell you that everything's all right."

Soapy was far from agreeing with him. He was almost equally far from understanding a word that this inexplicable visitor was saying. He coughed loudly to drown a strangled sound that had proceeded from the gagged and bound Hash, whom he had deposited in a corner by the range.

"That's good," he said.

"About the girl, I mean. Clara, you know. I was in the kitchen next door a moment ago, and she was crying and howling and all that because she thought you didn't love her any more."

"Too bad," said Mr. Molloy.

"It seems," went on Mr. Braddock, "that she read something in a paper, written by some silly ass, which said that she ought to test your affection by pretending to flirt with some other cove. And when she did, you broke off the engagement. And the gist, if you understand me, of what I buzzed round to say is that she loves you still and was only fooling when she sent that other bloke the lock of hair."

"Ah?" said Mr. Molloy.

"So it's all right, isn't it?"

"It's all right by me," said Mr. Molloy, wishing—for it sounded interesting—that he knew what all this was about.

"Then that's that, what?"

"You said it, brother."

Mr. Braddock paused. He seemed disappointed at a certain lack of emotion on his companion's part.

"She's rather expecting you to dash round right away, you know—fold her in your arms, and all that."

224

This was a complication which Soapy had not foreseen.

"Well, I'll tell you," he said. "I've a lot of work to do around this house and I don't quite see how I can get away. Say, listen, brother, you tell her I'll be round later on in the evening."

"All right. I'm glad everything's satisfactory. She's a nice girl really."

"None better," said Mr. Molloy generously.

"I still think she threw a stone at my top hat that day, but dash it," said Mr. Braddock warmly, "let the dead past bury its dead, what?"

"Couldn't do a wiser thing," said Mr. Molloy.

He closed the door, and having breathed a little stertorously, mounted the stairs.

"Who was it?" called Dolly.

"Some nut babbling about a girl."

"Oh? Well, I'm having a hunt round in the best bedroom. You go on looking in the drawing-room."

Soapy turned his steps toward the drawing-room, but he did not reach it. For as he was preparing to cross the threshold, the front door-bell rang.

It seemed to Soapy that he was being called upon to endure more than man was ever intended to bear. That, at least, was his view as he dragged his reluctant feet to the door. It was only when he opened it that he realised that he had underestimated the malevolence of fate. Standing on the top step was a policeman.

"Hell!" cried Soapy. And while we blame him for the intemperate ejaculation, we must in fairness admit that the situation seemed to call for some such remark. He stood goggling, a chill like the stroke of an icy finger running down his spine.

"Evening, sir," said the policeman. "Mr. Shotter?"

Soapy's breath returned.

"That's me," he said huskily. This thing, coming so soon after his unrehearsed impersonation of Hash Todhunter, made him feel the sort of dizzy feeling which a small-part actor must experience who has to open a play as Jervis, a footman, and then rush up to his dressing-room, make a complete change and return five minutes later as Lord George Spelvin, one of Lady Hemmingway's guests at The Towers.

The policeman fumbled in the recesses of his costume.

"Noo resident, sir, I think?"

"Yes."

"Then you will doubtless be glad," said the policeman, shutting his eyes and beginning to speak with great rapidity, as if he were giving evidence in court, "of the opportunity to support a charitibulorganisation which is not only most deserving in itself but is connected with a body of men to 'oom you as a nouse'older will be the first to admit that you owe the safety of your person and the tranquillity of your home. The police," explained the officer, opening his eyes.

Mr. Molloy did not look on the force in quite this light, but he could not hurt the man's feelings by saying so.

"This charitibulorganisationtowhichIallude," resumed the constable, shutting his eyes again, "is the Policeman's Orphanage, for which I have been told off—one of several others—to sell tickets for the annual concert of, to be 'eld at the Oddfellows' 'All in Ogilvy Street on the coming sixteenth prox. Tickets, which may be purchased in any quantity or number, consist of the five-shilling ticket, the three-shilling ticket, the two-shilling ticket, the one-shilling ticket and the sixpenny ticket." He opened his eyes. "May I have the pleasure of selling you and your good lady a couple of the five-shilling?"

226

"If I may add such weight as I possess to the request, I should certainly advocate the purchase, Mr. Shotter. It is a most excellent and deserving charity."

The speaker was a gentleman in clerical dress who had appeared from nowhere and was standing at the constable's side. His voice caused Soapy a certain relief; for when, a moment before, a second dark figure had suddenly manifested itself on the top step, he had feared that the strain of the larger life was causing him to see double.

"I take it that I am addressing Mr. Shotter?" continued the new-comer. He was a hatchet-faced man with penetrating eyes and for one awful moment he had looked to Soapy exactly like Sherlock Holmes. "I have just taken up my duties as vicar of this parish, and I am making a little preliminary round of visits so that I may become acquainted with my parishioners. Mr. Cornelius, the house agent, very kindly gave me a list of names. May I introduce myself?—the Rev. Aubrey Jerningham."

It has been well said that the world knows little of its greatest men. This name, which would have thrilled Kay Derrick, made no impression upon Soapy Molloy. He was not a great reader; and when he did read, it was something a little lighter and more on the zippy side than *Is There a Hell?*

"How do?" he said gruffly.

"And 'ow many of the five-shilling may I sell you and your good lady?" inquired the constable. His respect for the cloth had kept him silent through the recent conversation, but now he seemed to imply that business is business.

"It is a most excellent charity," said the Rev. Aubrey, edging past Soapy in spite of that sufferer's feeble effort to block the way. "And I understand that several highly competent performers will appear on the platform. I am right, am I not, officer?"

"Yes, sir, you are quite right. In the first part of the programme Constable Purvis will render 'The 'Oly City' —no, I'm a liar, 'Asleep on the Deep'; Constable Jukes will render imitations of well-known footlight celebrities 'oo are familiar to you all; Inspector Oakshott will render conjuring tricks; Constable——"

"An excellent evening's entertainment, in fact," said the Rev. Aubrey. "I am taking the chair, I may mention."

"And the vicar is taking the chair," said the policeman, swift to seize upon this added attraction. "So 'ow many of the five-shilling may I sell you and your good lady, sir?"

Soapy, like Chimp, was a thrifty man; and apart from the expense, his whole soul shrank from doing anything even remotely calculated to encourage the force. Nevertheless, he perceived that there was no escape and decided that it remained only to save as much as possible from the wreck.

"Gimme one," he said, and the words seemed to be torn from him.

"One only?" said the constable disappointedly. "'Ow about your good lady?"

"I'm not married."

"'Ow about your sister?"

"I haven't a sister."

"Then 'ow about if you 'appen to meet one of your gentlemen friends at the club and he expresses a wish to come along?"

"Gimme one!" said Soapy.

The policeman gave him one, received the money, returned a few genial words of thanks and withdrew. Soapy, going back into the house, was acutely disturbed to find that the vicar had come too.

"A most deserving charity," said the vicar.

Soapy eyed him bleakly. How did one get rid of

228.

vicars? Short of employing his bride's universal panacea and hauling off and busting him one, Soapy could not imagine.

"Have you been a resident of Valley Fields long, Mr. Shotter?"

"No."

"I hope we shall see much of each other."

"Do you?" said Soapy wanly.

"The first duty of a clergyman, in my opinion——"

Mr. Molloy had no notion of what constituted the first duty of a clergyman, and he was destined never to find out. For at this moment there came from the regions above, the clear musical voice of a woman.

"Sweet-ee!"

Mr. Molloy started violently. So did the Rev. Aubrey Jerningham.

"I'm in the bedroom, honey bunch. Come right on up."

A dull flush reddened the Rev. Aubrey's ascetic face.

"I understood you to say that you were not married, Mr. Shotter," he said in a metallic voice.

"No—er—ah——"

He caught the Rev. Aubrey's eye. He was looking as Sherlock Holmes might have looked had he discovered Doctor Watson stealing his watch.

"No—I—er—ah——"

It is not given to every man always to do the right thing in trying circumstances. Mr. Molloy may be said at this point definitely to have committed a social blunder. Winking a hideous, distorted wink, he raised the forefinger of his right hand and with a gruesome archness drove it smartly in between his visitor's third and fourth ribs.

"Oh, well, you know how it is," he said thickly.

The Rev. Aubrey Jerningham quivered from head to heel. He drew himself up and looked at Soapy. The

finger had given him considerable physical pain, but it
was the spiritual anguish that hurt the more.

"I do, indeed, know how it is," he said.

"Man of the world," said Soapy, relieved.

"I will wish you good evening, Mr. Shotter," said the
Rev. Aubrey.

The front door banged. Dolly appeared on the landing.

"Why don't you come up?" she said.

"Because I'm going to lie down," said Soapy, breathing
heavily.

"What do you mean?"

"I want a rest. I need a rest, and I'm going to have
it." Dolly descended to the hall.

"Why, you're looking all in, precious!"

"'All in' is right. If I don't ease off for a coupla
minutes, you'll have to send for an ambulance."

"Well, I don't know as I won't take a spell myself.
It's kinda dusty work, hunting around. I'll go take a
breath of air outside at the back. . . . Was that somebody
else calling just now?"

"Yes, it was."

"Gee! These people round these parts don't seem to
have any homes of their own, do they? Well, I'll be back
in a moment, honey. There's a sort of greenhouse place
by the back door. Quite likely old Finglass may have
buried the stuff there."

§ 3

The Rev. Aubrey Jerningham crossed the little strip of
gravel that served both Mon Repos and San Rafael as a
drive and mounted the steps to Mr. Wrenn's front door.
He was still quivering.

"Mr. Wrenn?" he asked of the well-dressed young man
who answered the ring.

Mr. Braddock shook his head.

This was the second time in the last five minutes that he had been taken for the owner of San Rafael; for while the vicar had worked down Burberry Road from the top, the policeman had started at the bottom and worked up.

"Sorry," he said. "Mr. Wrenn's out."

"I will come in and wait," said the Rev. Aubrey.

"Absolutely," said Mr. Braddock.

He led the way to the drawing-room, feeling something of the embarrassment, though in a slighter degree, which this holy man had inspired in Soapy Molloy. He did not know much about vicars, and rather wondered how he was to keep the conversation going.

"Offer you a cup of tea?"

"No, thank you."

"I'm afraid," said Mr. Braddock apologetically, "I don't know where they keep the whisky."

"I never touch spirits."

Conversation languished. Willoughby Braddock began to find his companion a little damping. Not matey. Seemed to be brooding on something, or Mr. Braddock was very much mistaken.

"You're a clergyman, aren't you, and all that?" he said, after a pause of some moments.

"I am. My name is the Rev. Aubrey Jerningham. I have just taken up my duties as vicar of this parish."

"Ah? Jolly spot."

"Where every prospect pleases," said the Rev. Aubrey, "and only man is vile."

Silence fell once more. Mr. Braddock searched in his mind for genial chatter, and found that he was rather short on clerical small talk.

He thought for a moment of asking his visitor why it was that bishops wore those rummy bootlace-looking things

on their hats—a problem that had always perplexed him;
but decided that the other might take offence at being
urged to give away professional secrets.

"How's the choir coming along?" he asked.

"The choir is quite satisfactory."

"That's good. Organ all right?"

"Quite, thank you."

"Fine!" said Mr. Braddock, feeling that things were
beginning to move. "You know, down where I live, in
Wiltshire, the local padres always seem to have the deuce
of a lot of trouble with their organs. Their church organs,
I mean, of course. I'm always getting touched for contribu-
tions to organ funds. Why is that? I've often wondered."

The Rev. Aubrey Jerningham forbore to follow him into
this field of speculation.

"Then you do not live here, Mr.——"

"Braddock's my name—Willoughby Braddock. Oh, no,
I don't live here. Just calling. Friend of the family."

"Ah? Then you are not acquainted with the—gentleman who lives next door—Mr. Shotter?"

"Oh, yes, I am! Sam Shotter? He's one of my best
pals. Known him for years and years and years."

"Indeed? I cannot compliment you upon your choice
of associates."

"Why, what's wrong with Sam?" demanded Mr.
Braddock.

"Only this, Mr. Braddock," said the Rev. Aubrey, his
suppressed wrath boiling over like a kettle: "He is living
a life of open sin."

"Open which?"

"Open sin. In the heart of my parish."

"I don't get this. How do you mean—open sin?"

"I have it from this man Shotter's own lips that he is
a bachelor."

"Yes, that's right."

"And yet a few minutes ago I called at his house and found that there was a woman residing there."

"A woman?"

"A woman."

"But there can't be. Sam's not that sort of chap. Did you see her?"

"I did not wait to see her. I heard her voice."

"I've got it," said Mr. Braddock acutely. "She must have been a caller; some casual popper-in, you know."

"In that case, what would she be doing in his bedroom?"

"In his bedroom?"

"In—his—bedroom! I came here to warn Mr. Wrenn, who, I understand from Mr. Cornelius, has a young niece, to be most careful to allow nothing in the shape of neighbourly relations between the two houses. Do you think that Mr. Wrenn will be returning shortly?"

"I couldn't say. But look here," said Mr. Braddock, troubled, "there must be some mistake."

"You do not know where he is, by any chance?"

"No—yes, I do, though. He said something about going to see Cornelius. I think they play chess together or something. . A game," said Mr. Braddock, "which I have never been able to get the hang of. But then I'm not awfully good at those brainy games."

"I will go to Mr. Cornelius' house," said the Rev. Aubrey, rising.

"You don't play mah-jongg, do you?" asked Mr. Braddock. "Now, there's a game that I——"

"If he is not there, I will return."

Left alone, Willoughby Braddock found that his appetite for tea had deserted him. Claire, grateful for his services, had rather extended herself over the buttered toast, but it had no appeal for him. He lighted a cigarette and went out to fiddle with the machinery of his two-seater, always an assistance to thought.

But even the carburettor, which had one of those fascinating ailments to which carburettors are subject, yielded him no balm. He was thoroughly upset and worried.

He climbed into the car and gave himself up to gloomy meditation, and presently voices down the road announced the return of Kay and Sam.

They were chatting away in the friendliest possible fashion —from where he sat, Willoughby Braddock could hear Kay's clear laugh ringing out happily—and it seemed to Mr. Braddock, though he was no austerer moralist than the rest of his generation, that things were in a position only to be described as a bit thick. He climbed down and waited on the pavement.

"Why, hullo, Willoughby," said Kay. "This is fine. Have you just arrived? Come in and have some tea."

"I've had tea, thanks. That girl Clara gave me some, thanks. . . . I say, Sam, could I have a word with you?"

"Say on," said Sam.

"In private, I mean. You don't mind, Kay?"

"Not a bit. I'll go in and order tea."

Kay disappeared into the house; and Sam, looking at Mr. Braddock, observed with some surprise that his face had turned a vivid red and that his eyes were fastened upon him in a reproachful stare.

"What's up?" he asked, concerned.

Willoughby Braddock cleared his throat.

"You know, Sam——"

"But I don't," said Sam, as he paused.

"——you know, Sam, I'm not a—nobody would call me a——dash it, now I've forgotten the word!"

"Beauty?" hazarded Sam.

"It's on the tip of my tongue—Puritan. That's the word I want. I'm not a Puritan. Not strait-laced, you know. But, really, honestly, Sam, old man—I mean, dash it all!"

Sam stroked his chin thoughtfully.

"I still don't quite get it, Bradder," he said. "What exactly is the trouble?"

"Well, I mean, on the premises, old boy, absolutely on the premises—is it playing the game? I mean, next door to people who are pals of mine and taking Kay to the theatre and generally going on as if nothing was wrong."

"Well, what is wrong?" asked Sam patiently.

"Well, when it comes to the vicar beetling in and complaining about women in your bedroom——"

"What?"

"He said he heard her."

"Heard a woman in my bedroom?"

"Yes."

"He must be crazy. When?"

"Just now."

"This beats me."

"Well, that was what he said, anyway. Dashed unpleasant he was about it, too. Oh, and there's another thing, Sam. I wish you'd ask that man of yours not to call me brother. He——"

"Great Cæsar!" said Sam.

He took Willoughby Braddock by the arm and urged him toward the steps. His face wore a purposeful look.

"You go in, like a good chap, and talk to Kay," he said. "Tell her I'll be in in a minute. There's something I've got to look into."

"Yes, but listen——"

"Run along!"

"But I don't understand."

"Push off!"

Yielding to superior force, Willoughby Braddock entered San Rafael, walking pensively. And Sam, stepping off the gravel on to the grass, moved with a stealthy tread toward his home. Vague but lively suspicions were filling his mind.

He had reached the foot of the steps and paused to listen, when the evening air was suddenly split by a sharp feminine scream. This was followed by a joyous barking. And this in its turn was followed by the abrupt appearance of a flying figure, racing toward the gate. It was moving swiftly and the light was dim, but Sam had no difficulty in recognising his old acquaintance Miss Gunn, of Pittsburgh. She fled rapidly through the gate and out into Burberry Road, while Amy, looking in the dusk like a small elephant, gambolled about her, uttering strange canine noises.

Dolly slammed the gate, but gates meant nothing to Amy. She poured herself over it and the two passed into the darkness.

Sam's jaw set grimly. He moved with noiseless steps to the door of Mon Repos and took out his key.

CHAPTER XXIV
MAINLY ABOUT TROUSERS

§ 1

THE meeting between Amy and Mrs. Molloy had taken place owing to the resolve of the latter to search the small conservatory which stood outside the back door. She had told Soapy that she thought the missing bonds might be hidden there. They were not, but Amy was. The conservatory was a favourite sleeping porch of Amy's, and thither she had repaired on discovering that her frolicsome overtures to Hash had been taken in the wrong spirit.

Mrs. Molloy's feelings, on groping about in the dark and suddenly poking her hand into the cavernous mouth of the largest dog she had ever encountered, have perhaps been sufficiently indicated by the description of her subsequent movements. Iron-nerved woman though she was, this was too much for her.

The single scream which she emitted, previous to saving her breath for the race for life, penetrated only faintly to where Mr. Molloy sat taking a rest on the sofa in the drawing-room. He heard it, but it had no message for him. He was feeling a little better now, and his ganglions, though not having ceased to vibrate with uncomfortable rapidity, were beginning to simmer down. He decided to give himself another couple of minutes of repose.

It was toward the middle of the second minute that the door opened quietly and Sam came in. He stood looking at the recumbent Mr. Molloy for a moment.

"Comfortable?" he said.

Soapy shot off the sofa with a sort of gurgling whoop. Of all the disturbing events of that afternoon, this one had got more surely in among his nerve centres than any other. He had not heard the door open, and Sam's voice had been the first intimation that he was no longer alone.

"I'm afraid I startled you," said Sam.

The exigencies of a difficult profession had made Soapy Molloy a quick thinker. Frequently in the course of a busy life he had found himself in positions where a split second was all that was allowed him for forming a complete plan of action. His trained mind answered to the present emergency like a machine.

"You certainly did startle me," he said bluffly in his

best Thomas G. Gunn manner. "You startled the daylights out of me. So here you are at last, Mr. Shotter."

"Yes, here I am."

"I have been waiting quite some little time. I'm afraid you caught me on the point of going to sleep."

He chuckled, as a man will when the laugh is on him.

"I should imagine," said Sam, "that it would take a smart man to catch you asleep."

Mr. Molloy chuckled again.

"Just what the boys used to say of me in Denver City." He paused and looked at Sam a little anxiously. "Say, you do remember me, Mr. Shotter?"

"I certainly do."

"You remember my calling here the other day to see my old home?"

"I remember you before that—when you were in Sing Sing."

He turned away to light the gas, and Mr. Molloy was glad of the interval for thought afforded by this action.

"Sing Sing?"

"Yes."

"You were never there."

"I went there to see a show in which you took an important part. I forget what your number was."

"And what of it?"

"Eh?"

Mr. Molloy drew himself up with considerable dignity.

"What of it?" he repeated. "What if I was for a brief period—owing to a prejudiced judge and a packed jury—in the place you mention? I decline to have the fact taken as a slur on my character. You are an American, Mr. Shotter, and you know that there is unfortunately a dark side to American politics. My fearless efforts on behalf of

238

the party of reform and progress brought me into open hostility with a gang of unscrupulous men, who did not hesitate to have me arrested on a trumped-up charge and——"

"All this," said Sam, "would go a lot stronger with me if I hadn't found you burgling my house."

It would have been difficult to say whether the expression that swept over Mr. Molloy's fine face was more largely indignation or amazement.

"Burgling your house? Are you insane? I called here in the hope of seeing you, was informed that you were not at home, and was invited by your manservant, a most civil fellow, to await your return. Burgling your house, indeed! If I were, would you have found me lying on the sofa?"

"Hash let you in?"

Such was the magnetic quality of the personality of one who had often sold large blocks of shares in nonexistent oil wells to Scotchmen, that Sam was beginning in spite of himself to be doubtful.

"If Hash is the name of your manservant, most certainly he let me in. He admitted me by the front door in the perfectly normal and conventional manner customary when gentlemen pay calls."

"Where is Hash?"

"Why ask me?"

Sam went to the door. The generous indignation of his visitor had caused him to waver, but it had not altogether convinced him.

"Hash!" he called.

"He appears to be out."

"Hash!"

"Gone for a walk, no doubt."

"Hash!" shouted Sam.

From the regions below there came an eager answering cry.

"Hi! Help!"

It had been a long and arduous task for Hash Todhunter to expel from his mouth the duster which Soapy Molloy had rammed into it with such earnest care, but he had accomplished it at last, and his voice sounded to Mr. Molloy like a knell.

"He appears to be in, after all," he said feebly.

Sam had turned and was regarding him fixedly, and Soapy noted with a sinking heart the athletic set of his shoulders and the large muscularity of his hands. "Haul off and bust him one!" his wife's gentle voice seemed to whisper in his ear; but eyeing Sam, he knew that any such project was but a Utopian dream. Sam had the unmistakable look of one who, if busted, would infallibly bust in return and bust disintegratingly.

"You tied him up, I suppose," said Sam, with a menacing calm.

Soapy said nothing. There is a time for words and a time for silence.

Sam looked at him in some perplexity. He had begun to see that he was faced with the rather delicate problem of how to be in two places at the same time. He must, of course, at once go down to the kitchen and release Hash. But if he did that, would not this marauder immediately escape by the front door? And if he took him down with him to the kitchen, the probability was that he would escape by the back door. While if he merely left him in this room and locked the door, he would proceed at once to depart by the window.

It was a nice problem, but all problems are capable of solution. Sam solved this one in a spasm of pure inspiration. He pointed a menacing finger at Soapy.

"Take off those trousers!" he said.

Soapy gaped. The intellectual pressure of the conversation had become too much for him.

"Trousers?" he faltered.

"Trousers. You know perfectly well what trousers are," said Sam, "and it's no good pretending you don't. Take them off!"

"Take off my trousers?"

"Good Lord!" said Sam with sudden petulance. "What's the matter with the man? You do it every night, don't you? You do it whenever you take a Turkish bath, don't you? Where's the difficulty? Peel them off and don't waste time."

"But——"

"Listen!" said Sam. "If those trousers are not delivered to me f.o.b. inside of thirty seconds, I'll bust you one!"

He had them in eighteen.

"Now," said Sam, "I think you'll find it a little difficult to get away." He gathered up the garments, draped them over his arm and went down to the kitchen.

§ 2

Love is the master passion. It had come to Hash Todhunter late, but, like measles, the more violently for the delay. A natural inclination to go upstairs and rend his recent aggressor limb from limb faded before the more imperious urge to dash across to San Rafael and see Claire. It was the first thing of which he spoke when Sam, with the aid of a carving knife, had cut his bonds.

"I got to see 'er!"

"Are you hurt, Hash?"

"No, 'e only 'it me on the 'ead. I got to see 'er, Sam."

"Claire?"

241

"Ah! The pore little angel, crying 'er ruddy eyes out. The gentleman was saying all about it."

"What gentleman?"

"A gentleman come to the back door and told that perisher all about how the pore little thing was howling and weeping and all, thinking 'e was me."

"Have you had a quarrel with Claire?"

"We 'ad words. I got to see 'er."

"You shall. Can you walk?"

"Of course I can walk. Why shouldn't I walk?"

"Come along then."

In spite of his assurance, however, Hash found his cramped limbs hard to steer. Sam had to lend an arm, and their progress was slow.

"Sam," said Hash, after a pause which had been intended primarily for massage, but which had plainly been accompanied by thought, "do you know anything about getting married?"

"Only that it is an excellent thing to do."

"I mean, 'ow quick can a feller get married?"

"Like a flash, I believe. At any rate, if he goes to a registrar's."

"I'm going to a registrar's then. I've 'ad enough of these what I mignt call misunderstandings."

"Brave words, Hash! How are the legs?"

"The legs are all right. It's her mother I'm thinking of."

"You always seem to be thinking of her mother. Are you quite sure that you've picked the right one of the family?"

Hash had halted again, and his face was that of a man whose soul was a battlefield.

"Sam, 'er mother wants to come and live with us when we're married."

"Well, why not?"

"Ah, you ain't seen 'er, Sam! She's got a hooked nose and an eye like one of these animal trainers. Still——"

The battle appeared to be resumed once more.

"Oh, well!" said Hash. He mused for a while. "You've got to look at it all round, you know."

"Exactly."

"And there's this to think of: She says she'll buy a pub for us."

"Pubs are pubs," agreed Sam.

"I've always wanted to have a pub of my own."

"Then I shouldn't hesitate."

Hash suddenly saw the poetic side of the vision.

"Won't my little Clara look a treat, standing behind a bar, serving the drinks and singing out 'Time, gentlemen, please!' Can't you see her scraping the froth off the mugs?"

He fell into a rapt silence, and said no more while Sam escorted him through the back door of San Rafael and led him into the kitchen.

There, rightly considering that the sacred scene of reunion was not for his eyes, Sam turned away. Gently depositing the nether garments of Mr. Molloy on the table, he left them together and made his way to the drawing-room.

§ 3

The first thing he heard as he opened the door was Kay's voice.

"I don't care," she was saying. "I simply don't believe it."

He went in and discovered that she was addressing her uncle, Mr. Wrenn, and the white-bearded Mr. Cornelius. They were standing together by the mantelpiece, their attitude the sheepish and browbeaten one of men who have been rash enough to argue with a woman. Mr. Wrenn was fiddling with his tie, and Mr. Cornelius looked like a druid who is having a little unpleasantness with the widow of the deceased.

Sam's entrance was the signal for an awkward silence.

"Hullo, Mr. Wrenn," said Sam. "Good evening, Mr. Cornelius."

Mr. Wrenn looked at Mr. Cornelius. Mr. Cornelius looked at Mr. Wrenn.

"Say something," said Mr. Cornelius' eye to Mr. Wrenn. "You are her uncle."

"You say something," retorted Mr. Wrenn's eye to Mr. Cornelius. "You have a white beard."

"I'm sorry I've been such a time," said Sam to Kay. "I have had a little domestic trouble. I found a gentleman burgling my house."

"What?"

"There had been a lady there, too, but she was leaving as I arrived."

"A lady!"

"Well, let us call her a young female party."

Kay swung round on Mr. Wrenn, her eyes gleaming with the light that shines only in the eyes of girls who are entitled to say "I told you so!" to elderly relatives. Mr. Wrenn avoided her gaze. Mr. Cornelius plucked at his beard and registered astonishment.

"Burgling your house? What for?"

"That's what's puzzling me. These two people seem extraordinarily interested in Mon Repos. They called some days ago and wanted to buy the place, and now I find them burgling it."

"Good heavens!" cried Mr. Cornelius. "I wonder! Can it be possible?"

"I shouldn't wonder. It might," said Sam. "What?"

"Do you remember my telling you, Mr. Shotter, when you came to me about the lease of the house, that a well-known criminal had once lived there?"

"Yes."

"A man named Finglass. Do you remember Finglass, Wrenn?"

"No; he must have been before my time."

"How long have you been here?"

"About three years and a half."

"Ah, then it was before your time. This man robbed the New Asiatic Bank of something like four hundred thousand pounds' worth of securities. He was never caught, and presumably fled the country. You will find the whole story in my history of Valley Fields. Can it be possible that Finglass hid the bonds in Mon Repos and was unable to get back there and remove them?"

"You said it!" cried Sam enthusiastically.

"It would account for the anxiety of these people to obtain access to the house."

"Why, of course!" said Kay.

"It sounds extremely likely," said Mr. Wrenn. "Was the man tall and thin, with a strong cast in the left eye?"

"No; a square-faced sort of fellow."

"Then it would not be Finglass himself. No doubt some other criminal, some associate of his, who had learned from him that the bonds were hidden in the house. I wish I had my history here," said Mr. Cornelius. "Several pages of it are devoted to Finglass."

"I'll tell you what," said Sam, "Go and get it."

"Shall I?"

"Yes, do."

"Very well. Will you come with me, Wrenn?"

245

"Certainly he will," said Sam warmly. "Mr. Wrenn would like a breath of fresh air."

With considerable satisfaction he heard the front door close on the non-essential members of the party.

"What an extraordinary thing!" said Kay.

"Yes," said Sam, drawing his chair closer. "The aspect of the affair that strikes me——"

"What became of the man?"

"He's all right. I left him in the drawing-room."

"But he'll escape."

"Oh, no."

"Why not?"

"Well, he won't."

"But all he's got to do is walk out of the door."

"Yes, but he won't do it." Sam drew his chair still closer. "I was saying that the aspect of the affair that strikes me most forcibly is that now I shall be in a position to marry and do it properly."

"Are you thinking of marrying someone?"

"I think of nothing else. Well, now, to look into this. The bank will probably give a ten per cent reward for the return of the stuff. Even five per cent would be a nice little sum. That fixes the financial end of the thing. So now——"

"You seem very certain that you will find this money."

"Oh, I shall find it, have no fear. If it's there——"

"Yes, but perhaps it isn't."

"I feel sure that it is. So now let's make our plans. We will buy a farm somewhere, don't you think?"

"I have no objection to your buying a farm."

"I said we. We will buy a farm, and there settle down and live to a ripe old age on milk, honey and the produce of the soil. You will wear a gingham gown, I shall grow a beard. We will keep dogs, pigeons, cats, sheep, fowls, horses, cows and a tortoise for the garden. Good for the snails," explained Sam.

"Bad for them, I should think. Are you fond of tortoises?"

"Aren't you?"

"Not very."

"Then," said Sam magnanimously, "we will waive the tortoise."

"It sounds like a forgotten sport of the past—Waving The Tortoise."

"To resume. We decide on the farm. Right! Now where is it to be? You are a Wiltshire girl, so no doubt will prefer that county. I can't offer to buy back Midways for you, I'm afraid, unless on second thoughts I decide to stick to the entire proceeds instead of handing them back to the bank—we shall have to talk that over later—but isn't there some old grey-stone, honeysuckle-covered place on the famous Braddock estates?"

"Good heavens!"

"What's the matter?"

"You said you had left that man in your drawing-room."

"Well?"

"I've suddenly remembered that I sent Willoughby over to Mon Repos ten minutes ago to find out why you were so long. He's probably being murdered."

"Oh, I shouldn't think so. To go back to what I was saying——"

"You must go and see at once."

"Do you really think it's necessary?"

"Of course it is."

"Oh, very well."

Sam rose reluctantly. Life, he felt with considerable peevishness, was one long round of interruptions. He went round to the door of Mon Repos and let himself in with his key. A rumble of voices proceeding from the drawing-room greeted him as he entered. He banged the door, and a moment later Mr. Braddock came out, looking a little flustered.

"Oh, there you are, Sam! I was just coming round to fetch you."

"Anything wrong?"

"It depends on what you call wrong." Mr. Braddock closed the drawing-room door carefully. "You know Lord Tilbury?"

"Of course I know Lord Tilbury."

"Well, he's in there," said Willoughby Braddock, jerking an awed thumb toward the drawing-room, "and he hasn't got any trousers on."

CHAPTER XXV
SAM HEARS BAD NEWS

SAM uttered a cry of exceeding bitterness. Nothing is more galling to your strategist than to find that some small, unforeseen accident has occurred and undone all his schemes. The one thing for which he had omitted to allow was the possibility of some trousered caller wandering in during his absence and supplying Mr. Molloy with the means of escape.

"So he's gone, I suppose?" he said morosely.

"No, he's still here," said Mr. Braddock. "In the drawing-room."

"The man, I mean."

"What man?"

"The other man."

248

"What other man?" asked Mr. Braddock, whose exacting afternoon had begun to sap his mental powers.

"Oh, never mind," said Sam impatiently. "What did Lord Tilbury want, coming down here, confound him?"

"Came to see you about something, I should think," surmised Mr. Braddock.

"Didn't he tell you what it was?"

"No. As a matter of fact, we've been chatting mostly about trousers. You haven't got a spare pair in the house by any chance, have you?"

"Of course I have—upstairs."

"Then I wish," said Mr. Braddock earnestly, "that you would dig them out and give them to the old boy. He's been trying for the last ten minutes to get me to lend him mine, and it simply can't be done. I've got to be getting back to town soon to dress for dinner, and you can say what you like, a fellow buzzing along in a two-seater without any trousers on looks conspicuous."

"Darn that fool, coming down here at just this time!" said Sam, still aggrieved. "What exactly happened?"

"Well, he's a bit on the incoherent side; but as far as I can make it out, that man of yours, the chap who called me brother, seems to have gone completely off his onion. Old Tilbury rang the front door-bell, and there was a bit of a pause, and then this chap opened the door and old Tilbury went in, and then he happened to look at him and saw that he hadn't any trousers on."

"That struck him as strange, of course?"

"Apparently he hadn't much time to think about it, for the bloke immediately held him up with a gun."

"He hadn't got a gun."

"Well, old Tilbury asserts that he was shoving something against his pocket from inside."

"His finger, or a pipe."

"No, I say, really!" Mr. Braddock's voice betrayed the utmost astonishment and admiration. "Would that be it? I call that clever."

"Well, he hadn't a gun when I caught him or he would have used it on me. What happened then?"

"How do you mean—caught him?"

"I found him burgling the house."

"Was that chap who called me brother a burglar?" cried Mr. Braddock, amazed. "I thought he was your man."

"Well, he wasn't. What happened next?"

"The bloke proceeded to de-bag old Tilbury. Then shoving on the trousers, he started to leg it. Old Tilbury at this juncture appears to have said 'Hi! What about me?' or words to that effect; upon which the bloke replied, 'Use your own judgment!' and passed into the night. When I came in, old Tilbury was in the drawing-room, wearing the evening paper as a sort of kilt and not looking too dashed pleased with things in general."

"Well, come along and see him."

"Not me," said Mr. Braddock. "I've had ten minutes of him and it has sufficed. Also, I've got to be buzzing up to town. I'm dining out. Besides, it's you he wants to see, not me."

"I wonder what he wants to see me about."

"Must be something important to bring him charging down here. Well, I'll be moving, old boy. Mustn't keep you. Thanks for a very pleasant afternoon."

Willoughby Braddock took his departure; and Sam, having gone to his bedroom and found a pair of grey flannel trousers, returned to the lower regions and went into the drawing-room.

He had not expected to find his visitor in anything

approaching a mood of sunniness, but he was unprepared for the red glare of hate and hostility in the eyes which seared their way through him as he entered. It almost seemed as if Lord Tilbury imagined the distressing happenings of the last quarter of an hour to be Sam's fault.

"So there you are!" said Lord Tilbury.

He had been standing with an air of coyness behind the sofa; but now, as he observed the trousers over Sam's arm, he swooped forward feverishly and wrenched them from him. He pulled them on, muttering thickly to himself; and this done, drew himself up and glared at his host once more with that same militant expression of loathing.

He seemed keenly alive to the fact that he was not looking his best. Sam was a long-legged man, and in the case of Lord Tilbury, Nature, having equipped him with an out-size in brains, had not bothered much about his lower limbs. The borrowed trousers fell in loose folds about his ankles, brushing the floor. Nor did they harmonise very satisfactorily with the upper portion of a morning suit. Seeing him, Sam could not check a faint smile of appreciation.

Lord Tilbury saw the smile, and it had the effect of increasing his fury to the point where bubbling rage becomes a sort of frozen calm.

"You are amused," he said tensely.

"No, no! Just thinking of something."

"Cor!" said Lord Tilbury.

Sam perceived that a frank and soothing explanation must be his first step. After that, and only after that, could he begin to institute inquiries as to why His Lordship had honoured him with this visit.

"That fellow who stole your trousers——"

"I have no wish to discuss him," said Lord Tilbury with hauteur. "The fact that you employ a lunatic manservant causes me no surprise."

"He wasn't my manservant. He was a burglar."

"A burglar? Roaming at large about the house? Did you know he was here?"

"Oh, yes. I caught him and made him take his trousers off, and then I went next door to tea."

Lord Tilbury expelled a long breath.

"Indeed? You went next door to tea?"

"Yes."

"Leaving this—this criminal——"

"Well, I knew he couldn't get away. Oh, I had reasoned it all out. Your happening to turn up was just a bit of bad luck. Was there anything you wanted to see me about?" asked Sam, feeling that the sooner this interview terminated the pleasanter it would be.

Lord Tilbury puffed out his cheeks and stood smouldering for a moment. In the agitation of the recent occurrences, he had almost forgotten the tragedy which had sent him hurrying down to Mon Repos.

"Yes, there was," he said. He sizzled for another brief instant. "I may begin by telling you," he said, "that your uncle, Mr. Pynsent, when he sent you here to join my staff, practically placed me *in loco parentis* with respect to you."

"An excellent idea," said Sam courteously.

"An abominable idea! It was an iniquitous thing to demand of a busy man that he should take charge of a person of a character so erratic, so undisciplined, so—er—eccentric as to border closely upon the insane."

"Insane?" said Sam. He was wounded to the quick by the injustice of these harsh words. From first to last, he could think of no action of his that had not been in-

17*

spired and guided throughout by the dictates of pure reason. "Who, me?"

"Yes, you! It was a monstrous responsibility to give any man, and I consented to undertake it only because—er——"

"I know. My uncle told me," said Sam, to help him out. "You had some business deal on, and you wanted to keep in with him."

Lord Tilbury showed no gratitude for this kindly prompting.

"Well," he said bitterly, "it may interest you to know that the deal to which you refer has fallen through."

"Oh, I'm sorry to hear that," said Sam sympathetically. "That's tough luck. I'm afraid my uncle is a queer sort of fellow to do business with."

"I received a cable from him this afternoon, informing me that he had changed his mind and would be unable to meet me in the matter."

"Too bad," said Sam. "I really am sorry."

"And it is entirely owing to you, you may be pleased to learn."

"Me? Why, what have I done?"

"I will tell you what you have done. Mr. Pynsent's cable was in answer to one from me, in which I informed him that you were in the process of becoming entangled with a girl."

"What!"

"You need not trouble to deny it. I saw you with my own eyes lunching together at the Savoy, and I happen to know that this afternoon you took her to the theatre."

Sam looked at him dizzily.

"You aren't—you can't by any chance be referring to Miss Derrick?"

253

"Of course I am referring to Miss Derrick."

So stupendous was Sam's amazement that anybody could describe what was probably the world's greatest and most beautiful romance as "becoming entangled with a girl" that he could only gape.

"I cabled to Mr. Pynsent, informing him of the circumstances and asking for instructions."

"You did what?" Sam's stupor of astonishment had passed away, whirled to the four winds on a tempestuous rush of homicidal fury. "You mean to tell me that you had the—the nerve—the insolence——" He gulped. Being a young man usually quick to express his rare bursts of anger in terms of action, he looked longingly at Lord Tilbury, regretting that the latter's age and physique disqualified him as a candidate for assault and battery. "Do you mean to tell me——" He swallowed rapidly. The thought of this awful little man spying upon Kay and smirching her with his loathly innuendoes made mere words inadequate.

"I informed Mr. Pynsent that you were conducting a clandestine love affair, and asked him what I was to do."

To Sam, like some blessed inspiration, there came a memory of a scene that had occurred in his presence abaft the fiddley of the tramp steamer *Araminta* when that vessel was two days out of New York. A dreamy able-bodied seaman, thoughts of home or beer having temporarily taken his mind off his job, had chanced to wander backward on to the foot of the bos'n while the latter was crossing the deck with a full pot of paint in his hands. And the bos'n, recovering his breath, had condensed his feelings into two epithets so elastic and comprehensive that, while they were an exact description of the able-bodied seaman, they applied equally well to Lord Tilbury. Indeed, it seemed to

Sam that they might have been invented expressly for Lord Tilbury's benefit.

A moment before, he had been deploring the inadequacy of mere words. But these were not mere words. They were verbal dynamite.

"You so-and-so!" said Sam. "You such-and-such!"

Sailors are toughened by early training and long usage to hear themselves phlegmatically beneath abuse. Lord Tilbury had had no such advantages. He sprang backward as if he had been scalded by a sudden jet of boiling water.

"You pernicious little bounder!" said Sam. He strode to the door and flung it open. "Get out!"

If ever there was an occasion on which a man might excusably have said "Sir!" this was it; and no doubt, had he been able to speak, this was the word which Lord Tilbury would have used. Nearly a quarter of a century had passed since he had been addressed in this fashion to his face, and the thing staggered him.

"Get out!" repeated Sam. "What the devil," he inquired peevishly, "are you doing here, poisoning the air?"

Lord Tilbury felt no inclination to embark upon a battle of words in which he appeared to be in opposition to an expert. Dazedly, he flapped out into the hall, the grey flannel trousers swirling about his feet. At the front door, however, it suddenly occurred to him that he had not yet fired the most important shell in his ammunition waggon. He turned at bay.

"Wait!" he cried. "I may add——"

"No, you mayn't," said Sam.

"I wish to add——"

"Keep moving!"

"I insist on informing you," shouted Lord Tilbury plucking at the trousers with a nautical twitch, "of this one thing: Your uncle said in his cable that you were to take the next boat back to America."

It had not been Sam's intention to permit anything to shake the stern steeliness of his attitude, but this information did it. He stopped midway in an offensive sniff designed to afford a picturesque illustration of his view on the other's air-poisoning qualities and gazed at him blankly.

"Did he say that?"

"Yes, he did." Sam scratched his chin thoughtfully. Lord Tilbury began to feel a little better. "And," he continued, "as I should imagine that a young man of your intellectual attainments has little scope for making a living except by sponging on his rich relatives, I presume that you will accede to his wishes. In case you may still suppose that you are a member of the staff of Tilbury House, I will disabuse you of that view. You are not."

Sam remained silent; and Lord Tilbury, expanding and beginning to realise that there is nothing unpleasant about a battle of words provided that the battling is done in the right quarter, proceeded.

"I only engaged you as a favour to your uncle. On your merits you could not have entered Tilbury House as an office boy. I say," he repeated in a louder voice, "that, had there been no question of obliging Mr. Pynsent, I would not have engaged you as an office boy."

Sam came out of his trance.

"Are you still here?" he said, annoyed.

"Yes, I am still here. And let me tell you——"

"Listen!" said Sam. "If you aren't out of this house in two seconds, I'll take those trousers back."

Every Achilles has his heel. Of all the possible threats that Sam could have used, this was probably the only one to which Lord Tilbury, in his dangerously elevated and hostile frame of mind, would have paid heed. For one moment he stood swelling like a toy balloon, then he slid out and the door banged behind him.

A dark shape loomed up before Lord Tilbury as he stood upon the gravel outside the portal of Mon Repos. Beside this shape there frolicked another and a darker one.

"'Evening, sir."

Lord Tilbury perceived through the gloom that he was being addressed by a member of the force. He made no reply. He was not in the mood for conversation with policemen.

"Bringing your dog back," said the officer genially. "Found 'er roaming about at the top of the street."

"It is not my dog," said Lord Tilbury between set teeth, repelling Amy as she endeavoured in her affable way to climb on to his neck.

"Not a member of the 'ousehold, sir? Just a neighbour making a friendly call? I see. Now I wonder," said the policeman, "if any of my mates 'ave approached you on the matter of this concert in aid of a charitubul-organisation which is not only most deserving in itself but is connected with a body of men to 'oom you as a nouse-'older will——"

"G-r-r-h!" said Lord Tilbury.

He bounded out of the gate. Dimly, as he waddled down Burberry Road, the grey flannel trousers brushing the pavement with a musical swishing sound, there came to him, faint but pursuing, the voice of the indefatigable policeman:

"This charitubulorganisationtowhichIallude——"

Out of the night, sent from heaven, there came a crawling taxicab. Lord Tilbury poured himself in and sank back on the seat, a spent force.

CHAPTER XXVI

SAM HEARS GOOD NEWS

KAY came out into the garden of San Rafael. Darkness had fallen now, and the world was full of the sweet, wet scents of an autumn night. She stood still for a moment, sniffing, and a little pang of home-sickness shot through her. The garden smelled just like Midways. This was how she always remembered Midways most vividly, with the shadows cloaking the flower beds, the trees dripping and the good earth sending up its incense to a starlit sky.

When she shut her eyes she could almost imagine that she was back there. Then somebody began to whistle in the road and a train clanked into the station and the vision faded.

A faint odour of burning tobacco came to her, and on the lawn next door she saw the glow of a pipe.

"Sam!" she called.

His footsteps crunched on the gravel and he joined her at the fence.

"You're a nice sort of person, aren't you?" said Kay. "Why didn't you come back?"

"I had one or two things to think about."

"Willoughby dashed in for a minute and told me an incoherent story. So the man got away?"

"Yes."

"Poor Lord Tilbury!" said Kay, with a sudden silvery little bubble of laughter.

Sam said nothing.

"What did he want, by the way?"

"He came to tell me that he had had a cable from my uncle saying that I was to go back at once."

"Oh!" said Kay with a little gasp, and there was silence. "Go back—to America?"

"Yes."

"At once?"

"Wednesday's boat, I suppose."

"Not this very next Wednesday?"

"Yes."

There was another silence. The night was as still as if the clock had slipped back and Valley Fields had become the remote country spot of two hundred years ago.

"Are you going?"

"I suppose so."

From far away, out in the darkness, came the faint grunting of a train as it climbed the steep gradient of Sydenham Hill. An odd forlorn feeling swept over Kay.

"Yes, I suppose you must," she said. "You can't afford to offend your uncle, can you?"

Sam moved restlessly, and there was a tiny rasping sound as his hand scraped along the fence.

"It isn't that," he said.

"But your uncle's very rich, isn't he?"

"What does that matter?" Sam's voice shook. "Lord Tilbury was good enough to inform me that my only way of making a living was to sponge on my uncle, but I'm not going to have you thinking it."

"But—well, why are you going then?"

Sam choked.

"I'll tell you why I'm going. Simply because I might as well be in New York as anywhere. If there was the slightest hope that by staying on here I could get you to —to marry me——" His hand rasped on the fence again. "Of course, I know there isn't. I know you don't take me seriously. I haven't any illusions about myself. I know

259

just what I amount to in your eyes. I'm the fellow who blunders about and trips over himself and is rather amusing when you're in the mood. But I don't count. I don't amount to anything." Kay stirred in the darkness, but she did not speak. "You think I'm kidding all the time. Well, I just want you to know this—that I'm not kidding about the way I feel about you. I used to dream over that photograph before I'd ever met you. And when I met you I knew one thing for certain, and that was there wasn't going to be anyone except you ever. I know you don't care about me and never will. Why should you? What on earth is there about me that could make you? I'm just a———"

A little ripple of laughter came from the shadows.

"Poor old Sam!" said Kay.

"Yes! There you are—in a nutshell! Poor old Sam!"

"I'm sorry I laughed. But it was so funny to hear you denouncing yourself in that grand way."

"Exactly! Funny!"

"Well, what's wrong with being funny? I like funny people. I'd no notion you had such hidden depths, Sam. Though, of course, the palmist said you had, didn't she?"

The train had climbed the hill and was now rumbling off into the distance. A smell of burning leaves came floating over the gardens.

"I don't blame you for laughing," said Sam. "Pray laugh if you wish to."

Kay availed herself of the permission.

"Oh, Sam, you are a pompous old ass, aren't you? 'Pray laugh if you wish to'! . . . Sam!"

"Well?"

"Do you really mean that you would stay on in England if I promised to marry you?"

"Yes."

"And offend your rich uncle for life and get cut off with a dollar or whatever they cut nephews off with in America?"

"Yes."

Kay reached up at Sam's head and gave his hair a little proprietorial tug.

"Well, why don't you, Sambo?" she said softly.

It seemed to Sam that in some strange way his powers of breathing had become temporarily suspended. A curious dry feeling had invaded his throat. He could hear his heart thumping.

"What?" he croaked huskily.

"I said why—do—you—not, Samivel?" whispered Kay, punctuating the words with little tugs.

Sam found himself on the other side of the fence. How he had got there he did not know. Presumably he had scrambled over. A much abraded shin bone was to show him later that this theory was the correct one, but at the moment bruised shins had no meaning for him. He stood churning the mould of the flower bed on which he had alighted, staring at the indistinct whiteness which was Kay.

"But look here," said Sam thickly. "But look here——"
A bird stirred sleepily in the tree.

"But look here——"

And then somehow—things were happening mysteriously to-night, and apparently of their own volition—he found that Kay was in his arms. It seemed to him also, though his faculties were greatly clouded, that he was kissing Kay.

"But look here——" he said thickly. They were now, in some peculiar manner, walking together up the gravel

path, and he, unless his senses deceived him, was holding
her hand tucked very tightly under his arm.   At least,
somebody, at whom he seemed to be looking from a long
distance, was doing this. This individual, who appeared
to be in a confused frame of mind, was holding that hand
with a sort of frenzied determination, as if he were afraid
she might get away from him. "But look here, this isn't
possible!"

"What isn't possible?"

"All this. A girl like you—a wonderful, splendid,
marvellous girl like you can't possibly love"—the word
seemed to hold all the magic of all the magicians, and he
repeated it dazedly—"love—love—can't possibly love a
fellow like me." He paused, finding the wonder of the thing
oppressive. "It—it doesn't make sense."

"Why not?"

"Well, a fellow—a man—a fellow—oh, I don't know."

Kay chuckled. It came upon Sam with an overwhelming sense of personal loss that she was smiling, and that
he could not see that smile. Other, future smiles he would
see, but not that particular one, and it seemed to him that
he would never be able to make up for having missed it.

"Would you like to know something, Sam?"

"What?"

"Well, if you'll listen, I'll explain exactly how I feel.
Have you ever had a very exciting book taken away from
you just when you were in the middle of it?"

"No, I don't think so."

"Well, I have. It was at Midways, when I was nine.
I had borrowed it from the page boy, who was a great
friend of mine, and it was about a man called Cincinnati
Kit, who went round most of the time in a mask, with lots
of revolvers. I had just got half-way in it when my gover-

ness caught me and I was sent to bed and the book was burned. So I never found out what happened in the little room with the steel walls behind the bar at the Blue Gulch Saloon. I didn't get over the disappointment for years. Well, when you told me you were going away, I suddenly realised that this awful thing was on the point of happening to me again, and this time I would never get over it. It suddenly flashed upon me that there was absolutely nothing worth while in life except to be with you and watch you and wonder what perfectly mad thing you would be up to next. Would Aunt Ysobel say that that was love?"

"She would," said Sam with conviction.

"Well, it's my form of it, anyhow. I just want to be with you for years and years and years, wondering what you're going to do next."

"I'll tell you what I'm going to do at this moment," said Sam. "I'm going to kiss you."

Time passed.

"Kay," said Sam.

"Yes?"

"Do you know——No, you'll laugh."

"I promise I won't. What were you going to say?"

"That photograph of you—the one I found in the fishing hut."

"What about it?"

"I kissed it once."

"Only once?"

"No," said Sam stoutly. "If you really want the truth, every day; every blessed single day, and several times a day. Now laugh!"

"No; I'm going to laugh at you all the rest of my life, but not to-night. You're a darling, and I suppose," said Kay thoughtfully, "I'd better go and tell uncle so, hadn't I, if he has got back?"

"Tell your uncle?"

"Well, he likes to know what's going on around him in the home."

"But that means that you'll have to go in," said Sam, appalled.

"Only for a minute. I shall just pop my head in at the door and say 'Oh, uncle, talking of Sam, I love him.'"

"Look here," said Sam earnestly, "if you will swear on your word of honour—your sacred word of honour—not to be gone more than thirty seconds——"

"As if I could keep away from you longer than that!" said Kay.

Left alone in a bleak world, Sam found his thoughts taking for a while a sombre turn. In the exhilaration of the recent miracle which had altered the whole face of the planet, he had tended somewhat to overlook the fact that for a man about to enter upon the sacred state of matrimony he was a little ill-equipped with the means of supporting a home. His weekly salary was in his pocket and a small sum stood to his credit in a Lombard Street bank; but he could not, he realised, be considered an exceptionally good match for the least exacting of girls. Indeed, at the moment, like the gentleman in the song, all he was in a position to offer his bride was a happy disposition and a wild desire to succeed.

These are damping reflections for a young man to whom the keys of heaven have just been given, and they made Sam pensive. But his natural ebullience was not long in coming to the rescue. One turn up and down the garden and he was happy again in the possession of lavish rewards bestowed upon him by beaming bank managers, rejoicing in their hearty City fashion as they saw those missing bonds restored to them after many years. He refused absolutely to consider the possibility of failure to unearth the treasure. It must be somewhere in Mon Repos, and if it was in Mon Repos he would find it—even if, in direct contravention of the terms of Clause 8 in his lease, he had to tear the house to pieces.

He strode, full of a great purpose, to the window of the kitchen. A light shone there, and he could hear the rumbling voice of his faithful henchman. He tapped upon the window, and presently the blind shot up and Hash's face appeared. In the background Claire, a little flushed, was smoothing her hair. The window opened.

"Who's there?" said Hash gruffly.

"Only me, Hash. I want a word with you."

"Ur?"

"Listen, Hash. Tear yourself away shortly, and come back to Mon Repos. There is man's work to do there."

"Eh?"

"We've got to search that house from top to bottom. I've just found out that it's full of bonds."

"You don't say!"

"I do say."

"Nasty things," said Hash reflectively. "Go off in your 'ands as likely as not."

At this moment the quiet night was rent by a strident voice:

"Sam! Hi, Sam! Come quick!"

It was the voice of Willoughby Braddock, and it appeared to proceed from one of the upper rooms of Mon Repos.

CHAPTER XXVII

SPIRITED BEHAVIOUR OF MR. BRADDOCK

WHEN Willoughby Braddock, some ten minutes earlier, had parted from Kay and come out on to the gravel walk in front of San Rafael, he was in a condition of mind which it is seldom given to man to achieve until well through the second quart of champagne. So stirred was his soul, so churned up by a whirlwind of powerful emotions, that he could have stepped straight into any hospital as a fever patient and no questions asked.

For the world had become of a sudden amazingly vivid to Willoughby. After a quarter of a century in which absolutely nothing had occurred to ruffle the placid surface of his existence, strange and exhilarating things had begun to happen to him with a startling abruptness.

When he reflected that he had actually stood chatting face to face with a member of the criminal classes, interrupting him in the very act of burgling a house, and on top of that had found Lord Tilbury, a man who was on the committee of his club, violently transformed into a sans-culotte, it seemed to him that life in the true meaning of the word had at last begun.

But it was something that Kay had said that had set the seal on the thrills of this great day. Quite casually she had mentioned that Mrs. Lippett proposed, as soon as her daughter Claire was married to Hash Todhunter, to go and live with the young couple. It was as if somebody, strolling with stout Cortez, had jerked his thumb at a sheet of water shining through the trees and observed nonchalantly, "By the way, there's the Pacific." It was this, even more than the other events of the afternoon, that

Sam the Sudden   18

had induced in Mr. Braddock the strange, yeasty feeling of unreality which was causing him now to stand gulping on the gravel. For years he had felt that only a miracle could rid him of Mrs. Lippett's limpet-like devotion, and now that miracle had happened.

He removed his hat and allowed the cool night air to soothe his flaming forehead. He regretted that he had pledged himself to dinner that night at the house of his Aunt Julia. Aunt Julia was no bad sort, as aunts go, but dinner at her house was scarcely likely to provide him with melodrama, and it was melodrama that Mr. Braddock's drugged soul now craved, and nothing but melodrama. It irked him to be compelled to leave this suburban maelstrom of swift events and return to a London which could not but seem mild and tame by comparison.

However, he had so pledged himself, and the word of a Braddock was his bond. Moreover, if he were late, Aunt Julia would be shirty to a degree. Reluctantly he started to move toward the two-seater, and had nearly reached it when he congealed again into a motionless statue. For, even as he prepared to open the gate of San Rafael, he beheld slinking in at the gate of Mon Repos a furtive figure.

In his present uplifted frame of mind a figure required to possess only the minimum of furtiveness to excite Willoughby Braddock's suspicions, and this one was well up in what might be called the Class A of furtiveness. It wavered and it crept. It hesitated and it slunk. And as the rays from the street lamp shone momentarily upon its face, Mr. Braddock perceived that it was a drawn and anxious face, the face of one who nerves himself to desperate deeds.

And, indeed, the other was feeling nervous. He walked warily, like some not too courageous explorer picking his way through a jungle in which he suspects the presence of unpleasant wild beasts. Drawn by the lure of gain to revisit Mon Repos, Chimp Twist was wondering pallidly if each moment might not bring Hash ravening out at him from the shadows.

He passed round the angle of the house, and Willoughby Braddock, reckless of whether or no this postponement of his return to London would make him late for dinner at Aunt Julia's and so cause him to be properly ticked off by that punctuality-loving lady, flitted silently after him and was in time to see him peer through the kitchen window. A moment later, his peering seeming to have had a reassuring effect, he had opened the back door and was inside the house.

Willoughby Braddock did not hesitate. The idea of being alone in a small semi-detached house with a desperate criminal who was probably armed to the gills meant nothing to him now. In fact, he rather preferred it. He slid silently through the back door in the fellow's wake; and having removed his shoes, climbed the kitchen stairs. A noise from above told him that he was on the right track. Whatever it was that the furtive bloke was doing, he was doing it upstairs.

As for Chimp Twist, he was now going nicely. The operations which he was conducting were swift and simple. Once he had ascertained by a survey through the kitchen window that his enemy, Hash, was not on the premises, all his nervousness had vanished. Possessing himself of the chisel which he had placed in the drawer of the kitchen table in readiness for just such an emergency, he went briskly upstairs. The light was burning in the hall and also in the drawing-room; but the absence of sounds encouraged him to believe that Sam, like Hash, was out.

18*

This proved to be the case, and he went on his way completely reassured. All he wanted was five minutes alone and undisturbed, for the directions contained in Mr. Finglass' letter had been specific; and once he had broken through the door of the top back bedroom, he anticipated no difficulty in unearthing the buried treasure. It was, Mr. Finglass had definitely stated, a mere matter of lifting a board. Chimp Twist did not sing as he climbed the stairs, for he was a prudent man, but he felt like singing.

A sharp cracking noise came to Willoughby Braddock's ears as he halted snakily on the first landing. It sounded like the breaking open of a door.

And so it was. Chimp, had the conditions been favourable, would have preferred to insinuate himself into Hash's boudoir in a manner involving less noise; but in this enterprise of his, time was of the essence and he had no leisure for niggling at locks with a chisel. Arriving on the threshold, he raised his boot and drove it like a battering-ram.

The doors of suburban villas are not constructed to stand rough treatment. If they fit within an inch or two and do not fall down when the cat rubs against them, the architect, builder and surveyor shake hands and congratulate themselves on a good bit of work. And Chimp, though a small man, had a large foot. The lock yielded before him and the door swung open. He went in and lit the gas. Then he took a rapid survey of his surroundings.

Half-way up the second flight of stairs, Willoughby Braddock stood listening. His face was pink and determined. As far as he was concerned, Aunt Julia might go and boil herself. Dinner or no dinner, he meant to see this thing through.

Chimp wasted no time.

"The stuff," his friend, the late Edward Finglass, had

written, "is in the top back bedroom. You've only to lift the third board from the window and put your hand in, Chimpie, and there it is." And after this had come a lot of foolish stuff about sharing with Soapy Molloy. A trifle maudlin old Finky had become on his deathbed, it seemed to Chimp.

And, hurried though he was, Chimp Twist had time to indulge in a brief smile as he thought of Soapy Molloy. He also managed to fit in a brief moment of complacent meditation, the trend of which was that when it comes to a show-down brains will tell. He, Chimp Twist, was the guy with the brains, and the result was that in about another half-minute he would be in possession of American-bearer securities to the value of two million dollars. Whereas poor old Soapy, who had just about enough intelligence to open his mouth when he wished to eat, would go through life eking out a precarious existence, selling fictitious oil stock to members of the public who were one degree more cloth-headed than himself. There was a moral to be drawn from this, felt Chimp, but his time was too valuable to permit him to stand there drawing it. He gripped his chisel and got to work.

Mr. Braddock, peering in at the door with the caution of a red Indian stalking a relative by marriage with a tomahawk, saw that the intruder had lifted a board and was groping in the cavity. His heart beat like a motor-bicycle. It gave him some little surprise that the fellow did not hear it.

Presumably the fellow was too occupied. Certainly he seemed like a man whose mind was on his job. Having groped for some moments, he now uttered a sound that was half an oath and half a groan, and, as if seized with a frenzy, began tearing up other boards, first one, then

270

another, after that a third. It was as though this business
of digging up boards had begun to grip him like some
drug. Starting in a modest way with a single board, he
had been unable to check the craving, and it now appeared
to be his intention to excavate the entire floor.

But he was not allowed to proceed with this work un-
interrupted. Possibly this wholesale demolition of bedrooms
jarred upon Mr. Braddock's sensibilities as a householder.
At any rate, he chose this moment to intervene.

"I say, look here!" he said.

It had been his intention, for he was an enthusiastic
reader of sensational fiction and knew the formulæ as
well as anyone, to say "Hands up!" But the words had
slipped from him without his volition. He hastily corrected
himself.

"I mean, Hands up!" he said.

Then backing to the window, he flung it open and
shouted into the night:

"Sam! Hi, Sam! Come quick!"

CHAPTER XXVIII
THE MISSING MILLIONS

THOSE captious critics who are always on the alert to
catch the historian napping and expose in his relation of
events some damaging flaw will no doubt have seized avidly
on what appears to be a blunder in the incident just re-
corded. Where, they will ask, did Willoughby Braddock
get the revolver, without which a man may say "Hands
up!" till he is hoarse and achieve no result? For of all
the indispensable articles of costume which the well-dressed
man must wear if he wishes to go about saying "Hands

271

up!" to burglars, a revolver is the one which can least
easily be omitted.

We have no secrets from posterity. Willoughby Braddock possessed no revolver. But he had four fingers on
his right hand, and two of these he was now thrusting
earnestly against the inside of his coat pocket. Wax to
receive and marble to retain, Willoughby Braddock had not
forgotten the ingenious subterfuge by means of which Soapy
Molloy had been enabled to intimidate Lord Tilbury, and
he employed it now upon Chimp Twist.

"You low blister!" said Mr. Braddock.

Whether this simple device would have been effective
with a person of ferocious and hard-boiled temperament,
one cannot say; but fortunately Chimp was not of this description. His strength was rather of the head than of the
heart. He was a man who shrank timidly from even the
appearance of violence; and though he may have had doubts
as to the genuineness of Mr. Braddock's pistol, he had none
concerning the latter's physique. Willoughby Braddock was
no Hercules, but he was some four inches taller and some
sixty pounds heavier than Chimp, and it was not in Mr.
Twist's character to embark upon a rough-and-tumble with
such odds against him.

Indeed, Chimp would not lightly have embarked on a
rough-and-tumble with anyone who was not an infant in
arms or a member of the personnel of Singer's Troupe of
Midgets.

He tottered against the wall and stood there blinking.
The sudden materialisation of Willoughby Braddock, apparently out of thin air, had given him a violent shock,
from which he had not even begun to recover.

"You man of wrath!" said Mr. Braddock.

The footsteps of one leaping from stair to stair made themselves heard. Sam charged in.

"What's up?"

Mr. Braddock, with pardonable unction, directed his notice to the captive.

"Another of the gang," he said. "I caught him."

Sam gazed at Chimp and looked away disappointed.

"You poor idiot," he said peevishly. "That's my odd-job man."

"What?"

"My odd-job man."

Willoughby Braddock felt for an instant damped. Then his spirits rose again. He knew little of the duties of odd-job men; but whatever they were, this one, he felt, had surely exceeded them.

"Well, why was he digging up the floor?"

And Sam, glancing down, saw that this was what his eccentric employee had, indeed, been doing; and suspicion blazed up within him.

"What's the game?" he demanded, eyeing Chimp.

"Exactly," said Mr. Braddock. "The game—what is it?"

Chimp's nerves had recovered a little of their tone. His agile brain was stirring once more.

"You can't do anything," he said. "It wasn't breaking and entering. I live here. I know the law."

"Never mind about that. What were you up to?"

"Looking for something," said Chimp sullenly. "And it wasn't there."

"Did you know Finglass?" asked Sam keenly.

Chimp gave a short laugh of intense bitterness.

"I thought I did. But I didn't know he was so fond of a joke."

"Bradder," said Sam urgently, "a crook named Finglass used to live in this house, and he buried a lot of his swag somewhere in it."

"Good gosh!" exclaimed Mr. Braddock. "You don't say so!"

"Did this fellow take anything from under the floor?"

"You bet your sweet life I didn't," said Chimp with feeling. "It wasn't there. You seem to know all about it, so I don't mind telling you that Finky wrote me that the stuff was under the third board from the window in this room. Whether he was off his head or was just stringing me, I don't know. But I do know it isn't there. And now I'm going."

"Oh, no, you aren't, by Jove!" said Mr. Braddock.

"Oh, let him go," said Sam wearily. "What's the use of keeping him hanging round?" He turned to Chimp. His own disappointment was so keen that he could almost sympathise with him. "So you think Finglass really got away with the stuff, after all?"

"Looks like it."

"Then why on earth did he write to you?"

Chimp shrugged his shoulders.

"Off his nut, I guess. He always was a loony sort of bird, outside of business."

"You don't think the other chap found the stuff, Sam?" suggested Mr. Braddock.

Sam shook his head.

"I doubt it. It's much more likely it was never here at all. We had a friend of yours here this evening," he said to Chimp. "At least, I suppose he was a friend of yours. Thomas G. Gunn he called himself."

"I know who you mean—that poor dumb brick, Soapy. He wouldn't have found anything. If it isn't here it isn't anywhere. And now I'm going."

274

Mr. Braddock eyed him a little wistfully as he slouched
through the doorway. It was galling to see the only burglar
he had ever caught walking out as if he had finished pay-
ing a friendly call. However, he supposed there was nothing to be done about it. Sam had gone to the window
and was leaning out, looking into the night.

"I must go and see Kay," he said at length, turning.

"I must get up to town," said Mr. Braddock. "By Jove,
I shall be most frightfully late if I don't rush. I'm dining
with my Aunt Julia."

"This is going to be bad news for her."

"Oh, no, she'll be most awfully interested. She's a very
sporting old party."

"What the devil are you talking about?"

"My Aunt Julia."

"Oh? Well, good-bye."

Sam left the room, and Willoughby Braddock, following
him at some little distance, for his old friend seemed dis-
inclined for company and conversation, heard the front
door bang. He sat down on the stairs and began to put
on his shoes, which he had cached on the first landing.
While he was engaged in this task, the front door-bell rang.
He went down to open it, one shoe off and one shoe on,
and found on the steps an aged gentleman with a white
beard.

"Is Mr. Shotter here?" asked the aged gentleman.

"Just gone round next door. Mr. Cornelius, isn't it?
I expect you've forgotten me—Willoughby Braddock. I
met you for a minute or two when I was staying with Mr.
Wrenn."

"Ah, yes. And how is the world using you, Mr. Braddock?"

Willoughby was only too glad to tell him. A confidant

was precisely what in his exalted frame of mind he most
desired.

"Everything's absolutely topping, thanks. What with
burglars floating in every two minutes and Lord Tilbury
getting de-bagged and all that, life's just about right. And
my housekeeper is leaving me."

"I am sorry to hear that."

"I wasn't. What it means is that now I shall at last be
able to buzz off and see life. Have all sorts of adventures,
you know. I'm frightfully keen on adventure."

"You should come and live in Valley Fields, Mr. Braddock. There is always some excitement going on here."

"Yes, you're not far wrong. Still what I meant was
more the biffing off on the out-trail stuff. I'm going to see
the world. I'm going to be one of those fellows Kipling
writes about. I was talking to a chap of that sort at the
club the other day. He said he could remember Uganda
when there wasn't a white man there."

"I can remember Valley Fields when it had not a single
cinema house."

"This fellow was once treed by a rhinoceros for six hours."

"A similar thing happened to a Mr. Walkinshaw, who
lived at Balmoral, in Acacia Road. He came back from
London one Saturday afternoon in a new tweed suit, and
his dog, failing to recognise him, chased him on to the roof
of the summer house. . . . Well, I must be getting along,
Mr. Braddock. I promised to read extracts from my history
of Valley Fields to Mr. Shotter. Perhaps you would care
to hear them too."

"I should love it, but I've got to dash off and dine with
Aunt Julia."

"Some other time perhaps?"

"Absolutely. . . . By the way, that man I was telling

you about. He was as near as a toucher bitten by a shark once."

"Nothing to what happens in Valley Fields," said Mr. Cornelius patriotically. "The occupant of the Firs at the corner of Buller Street and Myrtle Avenue—a Mr. Phillimore—perhaps you have heard of him?"

"No."

"Mr. Edwin Phillimore. Connected with the firm of Birkett, Birkett, Birkett, Son, Podmarsh, Podmarsh & Birkett, the solicitors."

"What about him?"

"Last summer," said Mr. Cornelius, "he was bitten by a guinea-pig."

CHAPTER XXIX

MR. CORNELIUS READS HIS HISTORY

§ 1

IT is a curious fact, and one frequently noted by philosophers, that every woman in this world cherishes within herself a deep-rooted belief, from which nothing can shake her, that the particular man to whom she has plighted her love is to be held personally blameworthy for practically all of the untoward happenings of life. The vapid and unreflective would call these things accidents, but she knows better. If she arrives at a station at five minutes past nine to catch a train which has already left at nine minutes past five, she knows that it is her Henry who is responsible, just as he was responsible the day before for a shower of rain coming on when she was wearing her new hat.

But there was sterling stuff in Kay Derrick. Although

no doubt she felt in her secret heart that the omission of the late Mr. Edward Finglass to deposit his illgotten gains beneath the floor of the top back bedroom of Mon Repos could somehow have been avoided if Sam had shown a little enterprise and common sense, she uttered no word of reproach. Her reception of the bad news, indeed, when, coming out into the garden, he saw her waiting for him on the lawn of San Rafael and climbed the fence to deliver it, was such as to confirm once and for all his enthusiastic view of her splendid qualities. Where others would have blamed, she sympathised. And not content with mere sympathy, she went on to minimise the disaster with soothing argument.

"What does it matter?" she said. "We have each other."

The mind of man, no less than that of woman, works strangely. When, a few days before, Sam had read that identical sentiment, couched in almost exactly the same words, as part of the speech addressed by Leslie Mordyke to the girl of his choice in the third galley of Cordelia Blair's gripping serial, "Hearts Aflame," he had actually gone so far as to write in the margin the words, "Silly fool!" Now he felt that he had never heard anything not merely so beautiful but so thoroughly sensible, practical and inspired.

"That's right!" he cried.

If he had been standing by a table he would have banged it with his fist. Situated as he was, in the middle of a garden, all he could do was to kiss Kay. This he did.

"Of course," he said, when the first paroxysm of enthusiasm had passed, "there's just this one point to be taken into consideration. I've lost my job, and I don't know how I'm to get another."

"Of course you'll get another!"

"Why, so I will!" said Sam, astounded by the clearness of her reasoning. The idea that the female intelligence was inferior to the male seemed to him a gross fallacy. How few men could have thought a thing all out in a flash like that.

"It may not be a big job, but that will be all the more fun."

"So it will."

"I always think that people who marry on practically nothing have a wonderful time."

"Terrific!"

"So exciting."

"Yes."

"I can cook a bit."

"I can wash dishes."

"If you're poor, you enjoy occasional treats. If you're rich, you just get bored with pleasure."

"Bored stiff."

"And probably drift apart."

Sam could not follow her here. Loth as he was to disagree with her lightest word, this was going too far.

"No," he said firmly, "if I had a million I wouldn't drift apart from you."

"You might."

"No, I wouldn't."

"I'm only saying you might."

"But I shouldn't."

"Well, anyhow," said Kay, yielding the point, "all I'm saying is that it will be much more fun being awfully hard up and watching the pennies and going out to the Palais de Dance at Hammersmith on Saturday nights, or if it was my birthday or something, and cooking our own dinner and making my own clothes, than—than——"

"—living in a gilded cage, watching love stifle," said Sam, remembering Leslie Mordyke's remarks on the subject.

"Yes. So, honestly, I'm very glad it was all a fairy story about that money being in Mon Repos."

"So am I. Darned glad."

"I'd have hated to have it."

"So would I."

"And I think it's jolly, your uncle disinheriting you."

"Absolutely corking."

"It would have spoiled everything, having a big allowance from him."

"Everything."

"I mean, we should have missed all the fun we're going to have, and we shouldn't have felt so close together and——"

"Exactly. Do you know, I knew a wretched devil in America who came into about twenty million dollars when his father died, and he went and married a girl with about double that in her own right."

"What became of him?" asked Kay, shocked.

"I don't know. We lost touch. But just imagine that marriage!"

"Awful!"

"What possible fun could they have had?"

"None. What was his name?"

"Blenkiron," said Sam in a hushed voice. "And hers was Poskitt."

For some moments, deeply affected by the tragedy of these two poor bits of human wreckage, they stood in silence. Sam felt near to tears, and he thought Kay was bearing up only with some difficulty.

The door leading into the garden opened. Light from the house flashed upon them.

"Somebody's coming out," said Kay, giving a little start as though she had been awakened from a dream.

"Curse them!" said Sam. "Or, rather, no," he corrected himself. "I think it's your uncle."

Even at such a moment as this, he could harbour no harsh thought toward any relative of hers.

It was Mr. Wrenn. He stood on the steps, peering out.

"Kay!" he called.

"Yes?"

"Oh, you're there. Is Shotter with you?"

"Yes."

"Could you both come in for a minute?" inquired Mr. Wrenn, his voice—for he was a man of feeling—conveying a touch of apology. "Cornelius is here. He wants to read you that chapter from his history of Valley Fields."

Sam groaned in spirit. On such a night as this young Troilus had climbed the walls of Troy and stood gazing at the Grecian tents where lay his Cressida, and he himself had got to go into a stuffy house and listen to a bore with a white beard drooling on about the mouldy past of a London suburb.

"Well, yes, I know; but——" he began doubtfully.

Kay laid a hand upon his arm.

"We can't disappoint the poor old man," she whispered. "He would take it to heart so."

"Yes, but I mean——"

"No."

"Just as you say," said Sam.

He was going to make a good husband.

Mr. Cornelius was in the drawing-room. From under his thick white brows he peered at them, as they entered, with the welcoming eyes of a man who, loving the sound of his own voice, sees a docile audience assembling. He took from the floor a large brown paper parcel and, having carefully unfastened the string which tied it, revealed a second and lighter wrapping of brown paper. Removing this, he disclosed a layer of newspaper, then another, and finally a formidable typescript bound about with lilac ribbon.

"The matter having to do with the man Finglass occurs in Chapter Seven of my book," he said.

"Just one chapter?" said Sam, with a touch of hope.

"That chapter describes the man's first visit to my office, my early impressions of him, his words as nearly as I can remember them, and a few other preliminary details. In Chapter Nine——"

"Chapter Nine!" echoed Sam, aghast. "You know, as a matter of fact, there really isn't any need to read all that, because it turns out that Finglass never——"

"In Chapter Nine," proceeded Mr. Cornelius, adjusting a large pair of horn-rimmed spectacles, "I show him accepted perfectly unsuspiciously by the residents of the suburb, and I have described at some length, because it is important as indicating how completely his outward respectability deceived those with whom he came in contact, a garden party given by Mrs. Bellamy-North, of Beau Rivage, in Burberry Road, at which he appeared and spoke a few words on the subject of the forthcoming election for the district council."

"We shall love to hear that," said Kay brightly. Her eye, wandering aside, met Sam's. Sam, who had opened his mouth, closed it again.

"I remember that day very distinctly," said Mr. Cornelius. "It was a beautiful afternoon in June, and the garden of Beau Rivage was looking extraordinarily attractive. It was larger, of course, in those days. The house which I call Beau Rivage in my history has since been converted

Sam the Sudden 19

into two semi-detached houses, known as Beau Rivage and
Sans Souci. That is a change which has taken place in a
great number of cases in this neighbourhood. Five years
ago Burberry Road was a more fashionable quarter, and
the majority of the houses were detached. This house
where we are now sitting, for example, and its neighbour,
Mon Repos, were a single residence when Edward Finglass
came to Valley Fields. Its name was then Mon Repos, and
it was only some eighteen months later that San Rafael
came into existence as a separate——"

He broke off; and breaking off, bit his tongue, for that
had occurred which had startled him considerably. One
unit in his audience, until that moment apparently as quiet
and well-behaved as the other units, had suddenly, to all
appearances, gone off his head.

The young man Shotter, uttering a piercing cry, had
leaped to his feet and was exhibiting strange emotion.

"What's that?" cried Sam. "What did you say?"

Mr. Cornelius regarded him through a mist of tears.
His tongue was giving him considerable pain.

"Did you say," demanded Sam, "that in Finglass's
time San Rafael was part of Mon Repos?"

"Yeh," said Mr. Cornelius, rubbing the wound tenderly
against the roof of his mouth.

"Give me a chisel!" bellowed Sam. "Where's a chisel?
I want a chisel!"

§ 2

"Bleck my soul!" said Mr. Cornelius. He spoke a little
thickly, for his tongue was still painful. But its anguish
was forgotten under the spell of a stronger emotion. Five
minutes had passed since Sam's remarkable outburst in
the drawing-room; and now, with Mr. Wrenn and Kay, he

was standing in the top back bedroom of San Rafael, watching the young man as he drew up from the chasm in which he had been groping a very yellowed, very dusty package which crackled in his fingers.

"Bleck my soul!" said Mr. Cornelius.

"Good heavens!" said Mr. Wrenn.

"Sam!" cried Kay.

Sam did not hear their voices. With the look of a mother bending over her sleeping babe, he was staring at the parcel.

"Two million!" said Sam, choking. "Two million—count 'em—two million!"

A light of pure avarice shone in his eyes. He looked like a man who had never heard of the unhappy fate of Dwight Blenkiron, of Chicago, Illinois, and Genevieve, his bride, *née* Poskitt; or who, having heard, did not give a whoop.

"What's ten per cent on two million?" asked Sam.

§ 3

Valley Fields lay asleep. Clocks had been wound, cats put out of back doors, front doors bolted and chained. In a thousand homes a thousand good householders were restoring their tissues against the labours of another day. The silver-voiced clock on the big tower over the college struck the hour of two.

But though most of its inhabitants were prudently getting their eight hours and ensuring that schoolgirl complexion, footsteps still made themselves heard in the silence of Burberry Road. They were those of Sam Shotter of Mon Repos, pacing up and down outside the gate of San Rafael. Long since had Mr. Wrenn, who slept in the front of that

19*

house, begun to wish Sam Shotter in bed or dead; but he was a mild and kindly man, loath to shout winged words out of windows. So Sam paced, unrebuked, until presently other footsteps joined in chorus with his and he perceived that he was no longer alone.

A lantern shone upon him.

"Out late, sir," said the sleepless guardian of the peace behind it.

"Late?" said Sam. Trifles like time meant nothing to him. "Is it late?"

"Just gone two, sir."

"Oh? Then perhaps I had better be going to bed."

"Suit yourself, sir. Resident here, sir?"

"Yes."

"Then I wonder," said the constable, "if I can interest you in a concert which is shortly to take place in aid of a charitubulorganisation connected with a body of men to 'oom you as a nouse'older will——"

"Do you believe in palmists?"

"No, sir——be the first to admit that you owe the safety of your person and the tranquility of your 'ome— the police."

"Well, let me tell you this," said Sam warmly. "Some time ago a palmist told me that I was shortly about to be married, and I am shortly about to be married."

"Wish you luck, sir. Then perhaps I can 'ave the pleasure of selling you and your good lady to be a couple of tickets for this concert in aid of the Policemen's Orphanage. Tickets, which may be 'ad in any quantity, consist of the five-shilling ticket——"

"Are you married?"

"Yes, sir—the three-shilling ticket, the half-crown ticket, the shilling ticket, and the sixpenny ticket."

"It's the only life, isn't it?" said Sam.

"That of the policeman, sir, or the orphan?"

"Married life."

The constable ruminated.

"Well, sir," he replied judicially, "it's like most things —'as its advantages and its disadvantages."

"Of course," said Sam, "I can see that if two people married without having any money, it might lead to a lot of unhappiness. But if you've plenty of money, nothing can possibly go wrong."

" Have you plenty of money, sir?"

"Pots of it."

"In that case, sir, I recommend the five-shilling tickets. Say, one for yourself, one for your good lady to be and— to make up the round sovereign—a couple for any gentlemen friends you may meet at the club 'oo may desire to be present at what you can take it from me will be a slap-up entertainment, high-class from start to finish. Constable Purvis will render 'Asleep on the Deep'——"

"Look here," said Sam, suddenly becoming aware that the man was babbling about something, "what on earth are you talking about?"

"Tickets, sir."

"But you don't need tickets to get married."

"You need tickets to be present at the annual concert in aid of the Policemen's Orphanage, and I strongly advocate the purchase of 'alf a dozen of the five-shilling."

"How much are the five-shilling?"

"Five shillings, sir."

"But I've only got a ten-pound note on me."

"Bring you change to your 'ome to-morrow."

Sam became aware with a shudder of self-loathing that

286

he was allowing this night of nights to be marred by sordid huckstering.

"Never mind the change," he said.

"Sir?"

"Keep it all. I'm going to be married," he added in explanation.

"Keep the 'ole ten pounds, sir?" quavered the stupefied officer.

"Certainly. What's ten pounds?"

There was a silence.

"If everybody was like you, sir," said the constable at length, in a deep, throaty voice, "the world would be a better place."

"The world couldn't be a better place," said Sam. "Good night."

"Good night, sir," said the constable reverently.

THE END

Printed in Great Britain
by Amazon

33573750R00159